Coming for What's Mine

Joseph and Journey's Tale

Edwina Fort

Copyright

Publisher's Note: This is a work of fiction. Names, characters, places, and incidents are a product of the author's imagination. Locales and public names are sometimes used for atmospheric purposes. Any resemblance to actual people, living or dead, or to businesses, companies, events, institutions, or locales is completely coincidental.

Coming for What's Mine/Edwina Fort. – 1st edition
ISBN 978-0-578-4295-26

Acknowledgements

I'd like to first thank The Heavenly Father who chose me as a vessel and allowed me to use my pen as a weapon. I'd like to thank my husband who continues to support me and hold me up when my knees give out. I'd like to thank my children who do the very best they can to make only a little noise so mama can write...(LOL) I'd like to thank My sista, GilaYah Joy Beck-Hendrix, you have proven to be an asset I can't be without. Without hesitation you joined me on the battlefield to help me carry this load, you give of yourself without expectancy of return favor. But today sista, I'd like to take the time and honor you. The world needs more Joys, but since we only have one, I thank The Most-High that I have you on my team.

I'd like to thank my editor Bernadette (Kizzy) Johnson. I know I'm not the easiest to work with, but somehow you've managed to weather the storm, when all the smoke and the dust cleared, you were still standing, and for that sis I am eternally grateful.

Finally, I'd like to thank my friends, family, and especially my fans, who took the time out to leave comments on my book and encourage me to continue writing. You guys have no idea how important your feedback is; it does wonders to defeat that voice of doubt. Thank you everybody!

Never forget in these dark days, you're worth more than you can imagine, smarter than you know, and more beautiful than they'll ever show...Smile because you are loved!

--Edwina Fort

I have something that the rich will never have...enough

- Joseph Heller

Table of Contents

Chapter One

And The Father Is...

Journey

I was just trying to better myself. I wanted to make my mama proud, so that she could say at least one of her kids graduated high school and even went to college.

"What we gon' do?" My mother asked looking back at me with desperate eyes before turning to look through the peep hole again. The pounding on the door came again but this time louder. I should have just gone to a local college. The University of Illinois had an excellent botany program. Why didn't I just go there? Why did I have to go to Georgetown? Why did I listen to my roommate and take that secretary job at the senator's office? Why...dear God why did I have to catch the eye of the senator's only son, who was so very brutal and also the youngest Senior Special Agent with the Federal Bureau of Investigation? Who would probably one day, if his father had anything to do with it, become president of the United States.

"Open up, Ms. Reevers!" I closed my eyes as that deep voice washed down my spine. He wasn't supposed to be here. This wasn't supposed to be happening. How had it come to this?

"Journey! What we gon' do?" Tears were running down my mother's beautiful face. I looked back towards my younger brother

Rob's bedroom. He and my older brother whose apartment is upstairs were frantically trying to flush their product down the toilet, but because they were going so fast pills were everywhere.

Rome, my older brother and the head of our family ran back into Rob's room before coming back out with three pistols. He looked around trying to decide what to do with them before going to the window, opening it and tossing them out. We lived on the third floor; please God don't let any children be down there to get a hold of one of them.

This was all my fault. That night should have never happened. I should have never slept with him. I knew how vicious he was. I had heard the stories. Putting my hand on my face I tried to stifle my screams when the pounding came louder. He hit the door so hard it caused it to shake on its foundation.

I should have never run from him!

"Get back away from the door!" Joseph yelled.

My mother stumbled back just in time to avoid being hit by it as it crashed in busting the lock.

"Freeze FBI!" The two officers with the man that has haunted my dreams for the last nine months yelled as they hurried in behind him pointing their guns at us. Rome and Rob threw what drugs they had left in their hands and ran out the back door.

"Where you going boys?!" Jo yelled after them with a huge grin on his handsome face. Although he smiled, it didn't reach his eyes. I knew him, he was pissed! My heart as well as my legs was frozen in fear. This was a nightmare! He wasn't supposed to be here! Why was he here?

"What's up, Journey? You look like you see a ghost!" He stared at me with that intense angry gaze of his. He had a way of looking at me that made me feel as if he didn't see anybody else in the room, only me. But I couldn't help but be confused, why was he so angry?

And yes, I did feel as if I was looking at a ghost. A dangerously handsome ghost! A powerful ghost that was well out of my league! He was the son of a senator! And as Alice his mother told me the day she came to pay me to disappear, destined to become the second black president of this great nation. Why was he here?

My mother wrapped her arms around me trying to pull me out the way as several more agents came in through the back door. She and I both cried out when we saw that they had both of my brothers in handcuffs. One of the officers carried the three guns Rome had tossed out the window with him. They forced them down to their knees on the kitchen floor.

Seeing my brother Romeo, who was something of a legend around these parts forced down to his knees was a bit of a shock to me. My heart was beating so loudly in my chest that it was causing my vision to vibrate with its force. Heavenly Father, please let Ayana stay asleep. There was a good chance he still didn't know about her.

"Search the place, bring me my baby!"

"No!" I cried breaking away from my mother to run to my bedroom. But I never made it, Joseph moved then, so suddenly he startled my mother. He grabbed me around my waist lifting me off the ground. Complete chaos erupted! Both of my brothers shot to their feet when they saw him grab me.

"Hey man, get yo' hands off my sista!" Rome yelled charging at us, but two of the agents tackled him, wrestling him back to the ground. Another agent took down Rob, both of my brothers continued to fight trying to dislodge them.

I went wild in Joseph's arms, but it was no use, he was so strong. If my memory served correctly, underneath that custom made suit was a plethora of chocolate covered muscles that he kept toned up every morning in his home gym.

"Let me go! Don't touch my baby!" I yelled towards the room where the agent had disappeared.

"Calm down, Journey!" He hissed in my ear. A shiver raced down my spine as tears came to my eyes. My body had begun to betray me already. I don't know if it was because I gave this man my virginity or if he was just that skilled of a lover, but he had a way of manipulating my body and mind to get me to do anything he wanted me to do.

I was trying to talk, trying to ask him why he was here and what he wanted with my baby. But my emotions were such a wreck; I couldn't even form a sentence around my crying. My gaze went back to Rome, who was now being choked on the ground by the agent.

"Stop resisting!" He hissed at my brother as he continued to choke him.

"You choking him!" I managed to get through my sobs. "Joseph! They choking him! Please tell them to stop!" Visions of all the recent deaths of black men by law enforcement raced through my head.

"Please!" I cried out. Rome was the rock of our family; he was what held us all together. If something happened to him I will never forgive myself.

"Let him go!" Rob yelled as he tried to get to the officer that was choking Rome. "You cowards take them handcuffs off him and let him defend himself!" Rome's eyes rolled to the back of his head.

"Please God!" My mother cried collapsing to her knees. She had her hands together and was praying through her tears.

This was all my fault!

"Joseph!" I cried, pleading for mercy to a man that it was no secret had none.

"Calm down and I'll tell him to stop!" I did, instantly. He threw me on the couch and then signaled for the man to let Rome go. When he did my brother began to gasp, greedily sucking air into his lungs. I shot off the couch to go to him, but Joseph grabbed me around my waist, throwing me back on the couch.

"Don't move!" He yelled.

He was so angry! I had never seen him like this.

The agent came out the room holding Ayana, he had taken the time to wrap her in her blanket. Instinctively, I stood to take my baby from the strange hands, but Joseph's angry gaze shot back to me and I eased back down on the couch. I was such an emotional wreck, I was shaking. On one hand, the life of my brother, who was the pillar of our family was at stake and on the other hand, strangers were handling my three-month-old baby. I wanted to scream, never in my life feeling this trapped.

Another agent came through the front door carrying a silver case in her hand. She sat it on the table before opening it. Inside the case was what looked like a mini-lab. Quickly she put on a pair of latex gloves before removing two big cotton swabs. When she walked towards Ayana with them, Rome shot off the floor again, but was soon tackled back to the ground.

"Don't touch my niece!" He hissed. My gaze shot up to Joseph.

"What are they doing to her?" I asked clutching the couch on the side of my legs so hard my knuckles turned white. It was taking everything in me to stay seated. Joseph didn't answer, he just looked down at me as if I was the dirt underneath his expensive Italian leather boot.

The woman gently ran the swab just inside Ayana mouth, who instantly begin to make the sucking sound causing my milk to come down. When the woman removed the swab, my baby started to fuss, now ready to eat. To my surprise, the agent that was holding her handed her to Joseph, who gently began to rock her, causing her to drift back to sleep.

When he looked down at her, that anger and hate that he looked at me with disappeared. He looked at her with a mix between curiosity and wonder. Something in my very being revolted at seeing him cradling her. He paid to get rid of her; he wanted me to have an abortion. Why was he now holding her as if she was the rarest thing on earth?

The female agent gently put the swab in a little canister that had blue jelly like liquid in it before she walked to Joseph.

"Open up, Boss." Without looking away from his daughter Joseph opened his mouth. After she took the sample from it, she put the swab in another canister of blue jelly. Then she went back to her make-shift lab and put both the samples in some kind of device that began to shake them so rapidly they could no longer be seen by the eye. Moments later her hands were flying across the keyboard.

Everybody sat and watched her. Even my brothers and mother had calmed down once they realized what was happening. The anger on Rome's face let me know that I was in big trouble, but his anger paled in the presence of Joseph's, who was older than my brother and more powerful. I wanted the floor to open and swallow me. I already knew what the results were.

Joseph was the only man I had ever slept with and it had only been for one night, after going out drinking with Michelle, my roommate from school. I shook my head. I blamed *her* for all of this. She was the one that told me about the secretary position at the senator's office. She said it would be perfect if I took it, because she was interning there.

I was at Georgetown on a scholarship for their botany program. And although Rome was sending me money on a regular, I'd figured getting a job on my own would be the grown-up thing to do. I was spreading my wings after all. It was the first time in my life I had been from under my brother's protective covering. And it felt good to be making decisions on my own.

I had been working in the office for two weeks before I saw Senator Warren for the first time. He was a very busy man and a big deal in D.C. Michelle told me that his family was one of the richest black families in the world. I felt like a fish out of water working there. I was the only one that didn't come from a prestigious family. The only one from the ghetto. The only one in the office with locs and the only one that wore colors. Everybody else dressed in black and white, and every now and again dark blue. Everything I owned was warm oranges, bright yellows, and vivid reds.

So, you can imagine my surprise when one day while I was filing away some things in the file cabinet, I looked up to see Senator Warren's only son that up until that day I had only heard about, who was an even bigger deal than his father standing there watching me as if I was the most beautiful thing he had ever seen.

Because he scared the hell out of me, being too big, too old, and way too handsome, I turned away as if I didn't even notice. And

I did an excellent job at avoiding him for a while, but Michelle called me all kinds of fools.

"*Girl, are you nuts? There ain't a woman in all of Washington that wouldn't give their left breast to have that man sending them flowers and candy.*" *She ran her hand through her long hair that she spent hours each morning flat ironing.*

"*I've been trying to get him to notice me for the last two years. Nothing! I can't even get him to glance my way. One time I bumped into him determined to get him to look at me, that joker didn't even look away from his phone, just muttered excuse me and kept on walking.*"

I stood there holding the beautiful bouquet of flowers that had just been delivered to the office in my arms, more flattered than I had ever been and more afraid.

"*I don't know Michelle, he's a bit much don't you think?*" *She waved that a way.*

"*So what he's older than you? What difference do a few years make?*" *I looked at her as if she had gone loco.*

"*A few years? The man is thirty-two, I just turned nineteen!*"

"*Pst! That just mean you'll have an experienced lover for your first time. Do you know how many of us wish a man with experience could've been the one to take our virginity? Mine was taken by a thirteen-year-old that had no clue of which hole he should have been aiming for.*" *My mouth dropped.*

"*Thirteen? Oh, my goodness, how old were you?*" *She waved that question away.*

"*Once again my sweet eclectic friend, you're missing the point completely.*" *I chuckled. Michelle was a crazy gal, she was attending Georgetown to become a lawyer, which was why she was interning with Senator Warren, who had been a judge before taking office.*

"Oh sorry, I wasn't aware that you were trying to make a point." She narrowed her eyes.

"Well open your ears 'cause I am. The point I'm trying to make is, aren't you at all curious as to what it would be like, to be with that type of man? He's so powerful and dangerous. Wouldn't you like to see what sex would be like with a guy that could make you and your whole family disappear like that?" She snapped her fingers.

I frowned trying to see what the appeal was in that. She waved my look away.

"Plus, he so fine. Oh, my goodness he looks just like that guy..." she snapped her fingers as she thought about it.

"What's that guy's name...?" She continued to snap her fingers. "You know the one that use to be a real estate agent but then he became a model..." she continued to snap her fingers.

"The one that looks like he could be related to Idris Elba..." Snap...Snap... "Oh goodness, what is his name? It's on the tip of my tongue." Right when I motioned for her to get to the point her eyes brightened with recognition.

"Donnell Blaylock, Jr.!"

I shook my head. "Never heard of him."

"Girl... he is a tall, fine, piece of chocolate sin on legs." As she spoke she frowned up her face as if it hurt her mouth to even speak on it. "Just like Joseph. If I were you I would get over that

shyness, stop avoiding his phone calls and accept his invitation to take you out to dinner." I exhaled.

"Michelle you know a man like that will never take somebody like me seriously." She looked at me as if I had grown a lump out of my head.

"What do you mean by that?"

"I'm from the westside of Chicago. My family don't have a name. We don't have a lot of money. He's not looking for a commitment he's looking for a little young play thing, and I'm not in the market for that."

"Why not?!" She yelled causing the people that were waiting to meet with Senator Warren to look up. I smiled at them before hissing for her to control her vocal levels.

"Because," I said very quietly hoping it would encourage Michelle to follow suit. "I have a lot going on right now. I need to focus on my studies—" she cut me off before I could even finish speaking.

"Aww Journey, give me a break! You study plants. Boring plants! I'm sure a little rendezvous with the Senator's boy ain't gon' come in the way of all that excitement. Besides, don't you think it's time you gave up your V-card? I swear you're the oldest virgin in the world right now." She slid that in before she turned and sashayed away. I chuckled at her as I put the flowers in a vase.

That had been the fifth time he's sent me flowers. I didn't tell Michelle the truth as to why I was avoiding Jo. The truth was he scared me to death; he was just too much. Because of Rome I had come up fairly sheltered. None of the guys on the block would dare try to step to me. In my neighborhood, Rome was the boss and everybody knew how overprotective of his family he was.

And Rob, only being a year older than me was no better. He kept the guys from approaching me at school. I mean sure, there were a few boys that tried to sneak and have a relationship with me, but it only got so far before their fear of one of my brothers finding out would eventually become a turn off. So, as you can see, it was safe to say that Rome and Rob were the reason I was still the proud owner of my V-card.

Anyway, that being my first time from under their protection, it felt as if Joseph was a raging storm. I had never encountered a man like him. I was used to the guys that I had grown up with. Like I said, Rome is the boss in the hood, but Joseph expanded further than the hood and my understanding. He was well-traveled and just felt more advanced that what I could handle.

I couldn't help but feel that if he ever got me, he would devour me and leave me lost and turned out somewhere. It wasn't that I didn't think I was good enough for him; being the only girl and the baby, I had come up the princess in my household. Between Rome and my mother, I was quite spoiled. It wasn't much that I wanted that Rome didn't make sure I got.

No, that wasn't the issue.

Joseph was just too…too…

Aggressive!

I'll tell you what I mean. *I was in the office cafeteria making myself a cup of tea one morning. It was early and I thought I was in the office alone. I heard the front door open, but I just assumed it was Michelle, so I didn't turn around when I heard the cafeteria door open and then close.*

"Good morning, Beautiful." The deep voice scared the hell out of me, I whipped around with my hand on my chest to see him

11

standing there looking exactly as Michelle described him, a piece of chocolate sin on legs.

"You scared me," I said trying to laugh it off. But the truth is the way he was looking at me was causing my girly parts to come to life.

"Did you get any of my messages?" I turned back to my tea facing the cabinet. I knew it was a cowardly thing to do, but this man was breaking me down.

"Mmmhhmm…" I said taking a sip of my hot lemony beverage.

"So why didn't you return my call?" I nearly jumped out of my burgundy boots. Somehow he had silently crossed the floor and was standing right behind me. I whipped around again and my breath fled my body before slamming back in. He was standing really close, so close that I could smell his expensive cologne. And he was very tall too. I had on heels and the top of my head barely reached his shoulder.

"Ummm…" Oh God, I was having a major break down. I had never had a man invade my space before. "Ummm…I…umm!"

He grinned and I had to bite my lip to keep from moaning out loud! Somebody call the law, because it had to be illegal in several states.

"Ummm, what? Cat got your tongue?" As if under a spell, the only thing I could do was nod.

"Lucky cat," although he spoke in a low tone, his deep voice seeped into my being causing serious havoc in my belly. "I'd give all I own to trade places with him." He continued.

Wow!

So caught under his spell I was, I didn't notice that he had been stepping closer to me, until I felt both of his hands on the counter on each side of me, and realized that I was now in the circle of his strong arms.

"Why won't you return my calls, Journey?" I swear I was drowning in his deep dark gaze. The way he said my name almost made me moan again. I'm pretty sure when my mother named me Journey, she never meant for it to be said in such a way.

"I-um…" My voice came out a little choppy, so I cleared my throat. His face was so close and was slowly coming closer. My eyes as if they had a will of their own were drawn to his lips that were lined perfectly by his low-cut beard and mustache. He licked them.

Oh, Dear God!

"I didn't call you back, because--" I searched my mind for a legit reason for my coward-ness. When it came to me I smiled. "I have a boyfriend." Beautifully done, Journey. I was so busy patting myself on the back, I didn't notice when his gaze changed. He looked down for a minute and chuckled dryly to himself. When his eyes raised back to mine I saw it then, that ruthlessness that I'd heard so much about.

"I don't like being lied to." He muttered. "Just admit that you're afraid of me." I opened my mouth to deny it, but then snapped it back shut. Hell, he was right, why lie? I held up my fingers.

"Just a little bit!" I admitted, using my fingers to show him how little.

"Why, baby? I'm not going to hurt you." I chuckled then, shaking my head a bit.

"You don't believe me?" When my gaze came back to his, for the second time that day my breath was stolen. His eyes were serious. The smile disappeared off my face.

"No, I don't believe you." I admitted.

"Hmmm, that's a shame." As he spoke he stared at my mouth. "I guess I'll have to show you." Slowly his head lowered to mine. I was screaming to myself that you cannot let this man who for all intents and purposes was a stranger kiss you. I told myself that it was my boss's son and this would be extremely unprofessional. I told myself...

Nothing... after his lips touched mine I was lost. At first his kiss was so gentle, it didn't take long for it to draw a response from me. But as soon as I started returning his caress, he artfully swept me away in a lust filled typhoon.

I moaned as he deepened the kiss. Standing on my toes so that I could receive more of it I wrapped my arms around his strong neck. The few times I had been kissed were nothing like this, a few innocent pecks from the braver boys at school or a smooch stolen between the bleachers had all in a way just been the innocent unsure caresses of youth.

However, there was nothing innocent about what Jo was doing to my mouth right now. His lips were very sure. His dominating kiss made me want to delve into the erotic. At some point, he wrapped his hands around my waist and lifted me so that I was sitting on the counter, bringing me up higher so that he could have better access to my mouth.

This position pushed my burgundy skirt up farther around my hips as he spread my legs with his torso. For just a moment I was startled when I felt him ball his hands up in my waist length locs, controlling my head so that my mouth was in the perfect position for his ravishment. I learned something new about myself, that really turned me on.

All reasonable thought fled my mind. He had taken me to a place where the only thing I could do was feel. At the same time he devoured my mouth, he pressed his hardness against my softness in a way that had me panting.

I had no idea what was happening to me. I had no idea where we started and where we would have ended up had Michelle not walked in on us. I was so embarrassed that I ran out of there and into the bathroom and didn't come out until Michelle assured me he was gone.

That whole day I had been distraught. I could not believe I let him do that to me in the cafeteria of my job! The senator could have walked in. Oh my goodness! The man had turned me into a savage! After work, Michelle talked me into going out for drinks with her and a few friends to help calm my nerves.

After the fourth shot of tequila, my nerves were good and calm, so calm that when I looked up and saw Joseph walking through the dancing bodies towards us I didn't even bat an eye. He held my gaze as if I was under hypnosis. Michelle leaned towards me.

"I hope you don't mind that I invited him. Maybe tonight's the night you'll unclench that V-card." She purred.

I smiled like the cat that had found a bowl of cream. Maybe she was right. I was tired of being the oldest virgin. My brothers weren't here, so why not have a little fun? I can't lie and say I haven't been curious to know what it feels like. And if Jo's love making was anything like that kiss he had given me earlier, I was in for a treat. What harm could one night be? It was time for me to become a woman.

Yeah!

When he came to the table I smiled warmly at him. That night we laughed, we danced...and we drank. He whispered in my ear that he would love to take me back to his place and prepare a late-night dinner for me.

Alarm bells were going off in my head, telling me that if I went behind closed doors with this man I was good and consumed. For a second, I got cold feet. But then my eyes crossed the table to Michelle, and she gave me the go ahead look. She even mouthed.

"Don't be a punk!"

I bit my lip as I thought about it. As if he could sense the battle I was going through, he picked up my hand and kissed the back of it.

"We don't have to do this if you're afraid." I turned back to look at this fine chocolate specimen, smiling through my nervousness. I was tired of being afraid.

"No, I want to."

True to his word, he prepared us a tasty meal of spaghetti. As we ate we drank more wine. That's when I admitted to him that I was a virgin and would love for him to teach me how to make love. Right at that moment, a look came over his face that could be described as nothing less than that of a predator. But thanks to the liquid courage I continued, although my good senses were telling me not to.

Had I known all the drama that night was going to lead to I would have stopped him. Hell, had it not been for the tequila making me feel braver than I was and Michelle making me feel like a freak for still being a virgin, I would've never been there in the first place.

But I guess fate was determined to see this through, because I was there willing and ready.

He made love to me, taking my virginity gently and lovingly. When he broke through my barrier and I cried out, he stopped and planted sweet kisses on my face, telling me that was the last of the pain. I don't think I will ever forget the look in his eyes in that moment. He kissed my lips and began to slowly move again.

At first, I was a little stiff as he continued to fill me, waiting for the pain I was feeling to get worse. But true to his word, the pain didn't get worse. In fact, the pain began to subside, although I felt as if I couldn't take all of him. He was gentle with me until I got accustomed to him. He made the pain fade completely and an intense pleasure that I never imagined I could feel took its place. And with no barrier between my most secret place and his, his loving became aggressive and relentless, like the kiss he had given me earlier. And just like earlier, it turned me savage.

That's when I learned that Jo had no mercy. Sounds that I didn't even know I could make came from between my lips. I used my nails in ways I'd never thought I would. Goodness! I didn't recognize myself. It wasn't till morning that I realized my tragic mistake. Not once did he use a condom. No...not once.

Chapter Two

Paying What You Owe

Joseph

"99.99." Karen's words seemed to echo throughout the room, sealing Journey's fate with a scorched iron.

She was mine!

I nearly smiled when the room erupted in chaos again. My gaze went down to the exotic beauty who sat on the couch biting her sexy bottom lip with her eyes closed as her brothers and mother began to yell at her. She ran from me because she knew that as soon as she conceived with my seed I owned her.

She was mine!

I exhaled feeling a year's worth of rage dissolving from my shoulders. There was somebody up there looking out for me, because today he'd delivered both my daughter and her mother into my hands. When my mother came to me crying, admitting to me that Journey came to her for money for an abortion and she had given it to her, I nearly gave into the anger that always seemed to be simmering just underneath the surface of my skin.

I went to her apartment and damn near tore it apart with my bare hands. The whole time her roommate cried assuring me that she didn't know where Journey had gone. I waited outside of her apartment for days. When she never showed up, I became a madman, searching the records of every abortion clinic in America, determined to utterly destroy the one that had killed my child.

When that still came up fruitless, I traveled to Chicago, putting a tail on every member of her family. It was then I realized that my little innocent beauty wasn't all that damn innocent; she had managed to disappear to a place where I couldn't find her. I called myself all kinds of fools, because still I wanted her. I still wanted her deceptive sneaky lying ass.

My family wanted me to give up and stop searching, assuring me that the abortion happened and maybe Journey had just gone somewhere to lick her wounds, because a procedure like that could be emotionally draining on a woman.

But I refused. I kept searching until one day like a burst of wind, she showed up at her family's apartment with a little bundle in her arms. When the pictures made it to my office in D.C., I dropped everything and called for my family's helicopter to meet me on the roof of my office building.

She was mine! And she was going to pay what she owed...

The noise caused my baby to start fussing. I rocked her like I had done before, but she was sucking on her fingers loudly and was not calming. She opened her little eyes and began to investigate me. It was like she knew that I was her daddy. She sucked at her fist taking me in just like I did her. I smiled bringing up my finger so that she could wrap her little hand around it.

Although she looked like a miniature version of her mother, she didn't have Journey's toffee colored skin. She had taken after me.

"No, Little one." I cooed when she tried to put my finger in her mouth. For the first time in a long time, the inner rage in me quieted. My heart began to swell in a feeling that was foreign to me, a feeling I had never felt before.

Love

How was it possible for one's heart to be instantly wrapped around a being so small?

"A fed Journey?!" Her older brother yelled at her, causing the familiar rage that I had lived with forever to lift its head again.

"You went and had a baby by a damn fed?!"

He was going to be a problem. My first instincts, an instinct that I found myself fighting every day of my life was to rip his damn throat out for daring to try and come between me and mine. But like I had been trained to do at an early age, I quieted that voice and put on my mask.

"Listen! I need everybody to calm down," I turned to face Journey who sat there still biting her lip, obviously this was something she did when she was nervous or unsure. I felt myself begin to stiffen. Her mouth was so damn sexy, and when she bit her lip like that it made me think of the other things that I was going to take great pleasure in teaching her to do with those plush lips of hers.

That's if of course she was still green behind the ears as she was when I first made love to her. If her innocent abandonment as I loved her body had not been proof of her virginity, then the blood she left on my sheets and my rod surely did the trick. That was one thing she had not lied about.

I bit down on my teeth trying to control the rage that rolled through me at the thought of some other man touching her, tasting her…teaching her what only I should.

"Our baby need your attention." I told her not being able to keep the anger out my voice. "Why don't we go in the room to have a little chat while you see to her?"

"Naw bruh, why don't you stay out *here* and have that chat. Anything you got to say to my little sister you can say in front of me." I smiled to hide the fact that I wanted to kill. Slowly I walked towards the *big brother*. He was right. He and I *did* need to have a little chat.

"Listen, Rome." I spoke low so that his mother and sister could not overhear our conversation.

"Your IQ has not escaped the notice of the United States Government. We are quite aware of how intelligent you are." I smiled down at him stepping a little closer, I needed for him to understand that Journey was mine and I will destroy anybody that tried to stand in the way of that.

"I took the liberty of doing a little independent study on you, *bruh*. I know more about you than you can imagine. You see I work with a group of fellas that are inclined to believe the very worst about a young black man. So when you fed them your cover, they accepted it, closed case." I leaned in closer to his ear.

"Not me, I know what we are capable of. I also know that you're far too intelligent to keep drugs and guns in the place where you lay your head. The clumsy hands that spilled out all the pills as you hurried to flush them down the toilet. You'd gladly take those three years, six months with good behavior, huh?" I shook my head.

"The Kansas City Shuffle won't work with me. You see when I start looking, I'm going to step over all those beautifully colored pills you decorated the floor with. And I don't know, maybe I'll start with that fancy computer equipment you keep upstairs. I wonder what kind of goodies I can find there. I bet a lot. What kind of criminal uses selling drugs as a decoy?" For just a moment his mask slipped, but he quickly got it back in place.

Rome was smart. Very! But I had come for the prize and nobody was going to stand in my way.

Nobody.

"Listen to me, *bruh*," I continued. "Because this has become your new reality, your little princess is mine. Now, if you'll excuse me, I have to go talk with my new Mistress." Anger washed over his face, but wisely he kept his mouth shut.

"After you." I told Journey gesturing toward the room Ted had carried my baby from. Her mother clutched her arm as if she was afraid to let her be alone with me. I almost laughed, it was far too late for that.

****

Journey

I had heard rumors about how ruthless Joseph and his father could be and tales of people disappearing who attempted to stand in the way of their rise to the top. Michelle had told me about a man who had tried to run against Senator Warren when he was going up for re-election for his second term. She said the senator had ruined the man so badly that he ended up committing suicide to escape the scandals his name was involved in.

But the man's wife cried foul. She said her husband did not commit suicide and was in fact murdered. A few weeks later, she was being admitted to the mental hospital where she remains today. After that, their family went quiet and stopped sounding the alarm about their father's death. Of course the senator denies having any knowledge about the situation. According to Michelle, the things that went on in these ghetto streets paled in comparison to the political world. The prize went to the biggest, baddest, and meanest gangstas to play the game.

Which brings me to the other reason I had tried so hard not to get involved with Joseph; he was following in his father's footsteps. In fact, he was being set up to bypass his father completely and sit in the seat of the commander in chief, which meant Jo had a lot of blood on his hands. And if that wasn't bad enough, he was a fed.

Neither my mother nor I agreed with how Rome made money to keep us all comfortable. And although we've expressed it to him a thousand times, my mother to the point of tears, he had his mind made up on how he was going to do things.

However, this meant that us and them Law Boys had to remain separated. Tonight, my brother looked at me as if I had betrayed him and I guess in a way I had. I didn't just get involved with a police officer. No, that would have been too simple; I had to go get involved with an FBI agent. I felt so bad. I felt as if I was the ruination of my family.

And now I stood in front of this man, who not only held my child in his hands, but my fate as well. I was so confused. I didn't know why he was here. His mother said that he no longer wanted me or our child. She had come to give me money for an abortion at his request. Was he angry because I decided to keep the baby? Did he think that I was going to later try and extort him for money or something? It felt like a weight lifted off my chest.

That was it!

He thought I was going to try and use Ayana to milk him of his money. I turned to face him, eager to assure him I wasn't. But my words stalled in my throat. Not only had he followed me in my room that looked small with him in it, he had shut the door and was standing so close to me that I literally had to take a step back.

"I think she's hungry."

He looked at me with eyes so ravenous at first, I thought he said he was the one hungry. And his voice…His deep voice was having a chaotic effect on my nervous system. I nodded reaching for her with hands that shook. I was so nervous and unsure right now, I couldn't help the sigh of relief that came from me when I had Ayana back in my arms. Without looking up at him I sat in my nursing chair and waited for him to step out.

I mean he did just see me take a seat to feed her.

He didn't, instead he sat on my full-size bed facing me and since my room was not that big, I was practically sitting between his spread legs. He even leaned forward resting his elbows on his knees, bringing him that much closer.

"Ummm, I nurse." I hated the fact that my voice quivered in fear. He chuckled dryly.

"If you're saying that because you want me to leave the room, you can forget it. Those days are over." Ayana was now getting good and worked up. She was using her little fist to push at my chest while aggressively rubbing her face against me.

I began to rock her trying to calm her while my mind raced for a response. Surely he didn't think I was going to do this in front of him. I know we've been intimate, but that was over a year ago. He was practically a stranger. Heck, I didn't know him all that well a year ago.

"Please Joseph, can you just give me a minute? I'm uncomfortable doing it with you in the room." His eyes turned hard.

"There was a time I would have given you the world. Now, your comfort means nothing to me. Feed my child, she's getting aggravated."

Tears came to my eyes as I lowered my head. Thankfully my locs were so long that they formed a curtain around me. With trembling hands, I unbuttoned my shirt. My heart was beating so fast and loud that I believe it was causing Ayana to be more aggravated. I peeked up at him from under my lids to see if he still looked and nearly cried out from his intense gaze.

When I finished unbuttoning my shirt I lowered one side. My hand shook as I lifted it to unclasp my nursing bra. Joseph was so close to me that I heard his intake of breath when my breast spilled out. Ayana latched on and began to greedily pull from me.

At this point I was blushing so badly that I couldn't look up. My hair fell around us like a cocoon. For just a moment I pretended like she and I were safe from the big bad wolf on the other side of our little world. But then I felt him gently move my locs out of the way, placing them behind my back. I still didn't look up. My whole breast was exposed to him.

"I have never seen anything more beautiful than watching my child nurse at your breast." I looked up at him then, surprised by his words. He was staring at us as if we were in fact a wonder to him.

"What's her name?"

"Ayana Indigo Reevers."

"Indigo?"

I nodded. "Yeah, it's one of my favorite flowers."

He slowly shook his head as he continued to watch. "I can't believe you tried to deny me this." I frowned. What was he talking about? I tried to deny him?

"What do you mean I tried to deny you? I left because you wanted me to have an abortion!" The look on his face said he clearly didn't believe me. And yeah, well, I didn't believe him either. He was never serious about me, and now he was here because he thought that I was going to try and use Ayana to take his money.

"Jo, you don't have to do this. I was going to raise Ayana alone. I don't need your help. Rome-"

His nostrils flared as fire came into his eyes. The look of anger that crossed his face was so fierce my words stalled.

"Are you serious?" He growled. "You dare sit here and tell me that my child don't need her daddy in her life?" Fervently, I shook my head.

"No- no I didn't mean—"

"You mentioned your brother," He said cutting me off. "So, your plan was to raise her with drug money, is that it?" I bit my lip. Now it felt like I was talking to an FBI agent. I shook my head no. Rome always told my little brother Rob that if he ever got picked up by cops not to speak and just wait on him, or for him to send a lawyer.

The look in Joseph's eyes let me know that I had already incriminated myself.

"This is how it's going to happen. I have four contracts with me, one for each member of your family. You are going to all sign them and do what they say."

"I—I don't know what you mean." My voice shook so badly because of the lump in my throat, my words were barely recognizable.

"It's simple Journey. I'm in need of a mistress, my last one's time expired. Your contract is a binding agreement for you to fill the position for the next year. You will be exclusively mine. I don't like sharing. We will not live together. I will provide a home for you and Ayana and cover your bills, as well as provide a twenty-thousand dollar a month stipend for whatever else you may need. And will continue to do so after our contract has expired. In which time we can work something out as far as custody of Ayana. I'm sure we can come up with something that will be agreeable to the both of us."

His words were so cold they chilled my soul. He spoke as if he hated me and my mind was having a hard time processing what he was saying. All I could do was stare at him as if he had gone mad. I still hadn't gotten past the mistress part.

"Wait, you want me to be your *mistress*?" Genuinely confused, I had to ask. If he hated me so much, why was he asking me to be his mistress?

"Yes."

I shook my head. "As in your *whore*?" He smiled then, reminding me that he was a politician and knew how to cover his true feelings with that *million-dollar smile*. I hated it.

"No, not like a whore, that's way too cheap. I'll be paying a lot of money to have exclusive rights to you. I would think of it as more like a courtesan." My mouth dropped, he couldn't have slapped me and insulted me more.

I shook my head. "Naw, you can keep your money. I'm not interested. Like I told you before, I don't need your help. My brother got my back." His eyes turned hard again, and for the first time, I was seeing the man that Michelle had told me about; the man that was the biggest, baddest, and meanest gangsta playing the game.

"Oh yeah, your brother got your back?" He gently pushed my locs back away from my face so that he could see me clearly and I could see him.

"How can he have your back if he's sitting in federal prison?" My eyes shot up to his.

"You wouldn't!" The politician smile appeared on his face.

"Oh sweetheart, I would. Please don't doubt it."

Tears of frustration came to my eyes as I gently took Ayana off my breast to change her to the other. In frustration, she began to fuss, wanting to continue her meal. I in frustration forgot to be inconspicuous and cover my empty breast before releasing the other. And it wasn't until I got her feeding again and looked up to see the hungry look in his eyes as he stared down at them that I realized what I did.

Quickly I lifted that side of my shirt back on my shoulder covering my breast.

He licked his lips. "Please don't doubt it!" He repeated in just above a whisper.

My mind raced for a way out of this. There was no way I was going to be this man's whore. Why was he doing this? *Maybe it's his way of getting back at you for not getting the abortion?* It was clear he hated me. Why would a man want to sleep with a woman he hated?

I eyed the handsome man sitting in front of me. Could that be it? Was he playing some sick twisted game where he was pretending not to know about the abortion request? So later on, if the media ever got wind of it, he could deny it while proving he did the right thing as soon as he found out about the baby?

I'd seen him on TV before, seen the way he handled the media. Like his father, he was a master at dealing with them and successfully hid his true nature from the cameras. In front of the camera, he had the charisma of Barack Obama. Behind the cameras, he had the charisma of a cold-hearted killer. It's why one should never trust what they see on TV.

I don't think I'd ever seen him genuinely smile. He put me in the mind of a professional hitman, all well-dressed, smooth lined, and violent.

"Jo, this is blackmail." I said gently, hoping I could appeal to whatever light he had in him. I found that dealing with human beings is a lot like dealing with plants. Sometimes all they needed was gentleness.

He didn't respond at first, he just let his eyes roam over me in a way that caused my skin to feel as if it was burned with fire. Lifting his hand, he gently pushed my hair back behind my ear.

"When I first saw you, I thought you were the prettiest woman I had ever seen." His gaze swept over my face not missing a detail. "Flawlessly smooth skin, the color of sun-kissed honey. Beautiful long locs that are soft to the touch. Big exotic innocent eyes that allured helpless men to become your prey. And your lips…" His heated gaze fell on my mouth.

"Do you know that your lips nearly got me killed?" Slowly I shook my head as I tried to remind myself that he was a politician.

"You see, I was thinking about them when I should have been focused on the suspect I was chasing at the time." His fingers lightly skated down the side of my face to my neck. The caress was so light it was barely there.

"I thought to myself, I need to see what she tastes like. Could she taste as good as she looked?" As he spoke he licked his lips and I'm telling yall he was masterfully spinning the web around me, bringing back to mind just how dangerous he was.

"And then you gave me my taste." He smiled as if remembering a good memory, as suddenly as it came, it disappeared. "I thought that I would be satisfied with it, but it only whetted my appetite. I tried to call you the next morning, do you remember that?" I nodded.

He did try to call me after that, but I was ashamed of my actions. So I went back to avoiding his calls. When I saw him coming through the front door of the office, I eased out the back. He even came by my apartment a couple times, but I refused to see him.

"You had become my elusive little butterfly that no matter how hard I tried, I could not catch." His words were low as he gently rubbed his finger over Ayana's little fat cheeks.

"But you are elusive no more." His gaze rose back to mine and the look in his eyes was so intense it caused me to gasp.

"I want your body, Journey." His words were low. Shaking his head he chuckled a bit. "I want it real bad."

He sat back holding his hands out to the side of him. That politician smile appearing on his face. "Don't look at it as blackmail, my sweet. Look at it as you, paying what you owe."

Chapter Three

A New Boss in Town

Journey

I carefully laid a sleeping Ayana in her crib. When I turned back to face Joseph my steps stalled, his beautiful, dark masculinity caught me off guard for just a moment. Having this powerful man sitting in my bedroom felt surreal. Next to him on the bed was the contract. My heart dropped.

Rome and my mom were going to kill me for this.

First, I showed up out of the clear blue with a baby after being MIA for months, now this. I rubbed my hand through my locs as the pressure began to build in my head. How did it come to this? This is not the way I imagined my life would be. I had visions of one day discovering the cure for soil erosion or proving GMO seeds were killing off the bees and other beneficial insects.

I had so many dreams, goals, and aspirations, none of them being a wealthy man's whore. I wanted to pick Ayana up and run as far away as I could. But alas! I knew the time for running was over. My mistake had caught up with me and he was sitting on my bed, all six-foot-plus of pure muscle, dripping-fine chocolate inch of him.

"J, you look real stressed. Come here, baby." He said sounding like he really cared. It was the first kind words he'd said to me this whole time. He even held up his big hand towards me. I guess the old saying was true, you get more bees with honey than vinegar. Because against my better judgment, I took it and let him pull me back to sit in my chair in front of him. Only this time, there was no baby in my arms to serve as a barrier between us.

I chewed on my bottom lip as my heart accelerated from being this close to him. He brought up his hand and gently touched my lip, pulling it from between my teeth. I nearly moaned when he softly rubbed his thumb over it, soothing my flesh. *Oh boy, here we go! He had turned on his politician and was getting ready to work his voodoo on me.*

All of you out there reading my tale, pay close attention to his next words and see why the DNC all felt that he would be the best candidate to replace his father's Senate seat.

"Listen, this won't be so bad. I found you a very nice place in Georgetown, walking distance from your school. You can pick back up on your classes if you want." His deep voice had gentled. "I know you want to go back to school, you love studying plants way too much."

"How do you know that? You don't even know me." One side of his sexy mouth lifted in a grin.

"Why would you assume I don't?" I shrugged.

"We were only together one time. Outside of that we barely talked to each other." He chuckled.

"You forget I had been trying to get with you for over a year. In all that time a man picks up on a few things. Like," his intense gaze looked away from me to go to my window for a moment before his eyes came back to hold mine captive.

"You're always surrounded by plants. There were plants on your desk at my father's office. Plants in your bedroom at your old apartment that you shared with your roommate. Plants in your living room here. And you even have plants surrounding you in this room. It's safe to say you love plants."

Wow! I didn't expect him to know that much about me, although if one was looking, it wouldn't be that hard to figure out. I did have a lot of plants and my major was in botany.

He picked the contract up off the bed. "Don't let this little piece of paper intimidate you. I just want to go into this arrangement with all parties knowing what is expected of them."

I took the contract out of his hand and began to read it. It stated that I will agree to move where he wanted me to, go to the appointment he made for me with a doctor of his choosing to get a medical exam, and get on the pill. And most importantly, be sexually available for him whenever or wherever he required.

My brother was never going to go for this. I'm afraid if I signed this, he was going to end up in jail anyway because I was more than positive he was going to try and kill Joseph. And from what I learned about Joseph and his family, I was more than positive they had the power to make my whole family disappear. I began to chew on my lip again.

"Come on now," he said in a soothing voice, reaching up to gently take my lip from between my teeth. "What did you read in there that have you so stressed out? Surely the thought of letting me make love to you again isn't that frightening. If my memory serves correct you enjoyed my touch."

His memory was correct. The night he and I shared haunted my dreams. How many times had I woke up hot and drenched, remembering his hands on me or his mouth, remembering how it felt to have him inside of me? However, I was not going to ever admit that to him.

"It's my brother. He's not going to go for this." He chuckled as he reached inside his jacket pocket for a pen.

"You let me worry about your brother. You just sign on the dotted line and I will handle the rest." My bottom lip fell prey to my teeth again.

His handling the rest was what I was worried about. Rome could be thick-headed. To protect his family, he would put his own life on the line. He would not see this as a sweet deal, me agreeing to be Joseph's mistress in exchange for him staying out of prison. He would see this as an insult. He's going to feel as if Joseph is coming at him.

My brother is a lion, who was used to being the alpha male of his pack. But what had I gone out and done? I attracted *another* lion that was quite obviously very used to being the alpha male of his pack, an older lion. This would not end well. Two alphas cannot co-exist. One always ended up destroying the other.

"See? I told you to let me do the worrying, but instead you've decided to try and destroy your pretty lip again." As he spoke he brought his big hand up and palmed my neck. His gaze had fallen on my mouth with a look so hungry that I was momentarily paralyzed.

"Why are you being so rough with your sexy mouth?" he whispered as he gently pulled my head closer to his. When his tongue gently lapped at my lip teasing it, a shiver went through my body that felt like electricity. I gasped and he took advantage deepening the kiss.

The spasm that shot through my center was almost painful.

"I've been waiting a long time to taste your sweetness again. Your flavor stayed on my tongue taunting me." As he spoke his hand tightened on my neck just a bit, turning my head in a way that exposed my throat completely to him. I squeezed my eyes shut when I felt him scandalously lick up my neck with his tongue.

"So sweet," he whispered before his mouth became aggressive. I squeezed my eyes and my legs shut tighter.

Oh man! He was breaking me down, awakening a hunger in me that I wasn't aware I could feel without a few shots of tequila in my system.

"Now, baby. I'm going to need you to be a good girl and sign this contract okay?" I nodded. Hell, what else could I do? The man had me thinking with the primal parts of my body. With hands that shook, I took the pen from him and signed next to the X.

The smile that came upon his face had to be the same one the devil wore when he got somebody to sign away their soul.

"Perfect!" He whispered before he was kissing me again. At some point he pulled me out of my chair and into his lap. I wrapped my arms around his neck drawing him closer. One thing I can say about Joseph…He is a damned good kisser.

A loud crash came from in the living room, followed by several more crashes. It sounded like a brawl had broken out.

"Rome! No!" My mother yelled.

Joseph moved so fast it took me a minute to realize he had stood, set me on my feet, and was out the room. After checking to make sure the noise didn't wake Ayana, I hurried behind him. What I saw nearly made my knees collapse from under me.

One of the agents who had been holding Rome was knocked out cold on the kitchen floor. Another one of the agents sat against the wall with blood running down his nose looking dazed. Rome, still in handcuffs had his legs wrapped around another one's neck and was using them to strangle the man. The agent who had gone in my room earlier to get Ayana was on the floor grappling with Rob, who had somehow slipped out his handcuffs. The female agent stood pointing her gun between Rob and Rome yelling for them to stop before she was forced to shoot. My mother stood next to her weeping, begging her not to shoot her babies.

But what was absolutely terrifying was the look on Joseph's face as he walked towards Rome while reaching into his shoulder holster to pull out his gun.

"Release my agent before I put a bullet in your head." He growled as he brought the gun to rest against Rome's temple. My brother, biting down on his teeth applied more pressure to the agent's neck.

"I will break this mutha f****s neck!" He snarled back at him.

"And I will shoot you dead. Don't try me!"

"Rome, please let him go." I cried falling to my knees next to him. Seeing Joseph holding that gun to his head was tearing me apart on the inside. Rome looked up at me.

"Are you alright?" I nodded as tears began to run down my face.

"Please, let him go. Rome, please!" He looked up at Joseph and their rage filled gazes clashed before he released the agent, who instantly started gasping for breath. It was the same agent who had choked him earlier.

Joseph straightened, returning his pistol to its holster.

"Move back, Journey!" He growled before he reached down and snatched Rome up off the ground. I frowned as I stepped back, watching as he took my brother's handcuffs off.

"You sure you want to do that, pretty boy?" Rome asked as a look of savage anticipation settled over his face. Joseph didn't say a word. I could see he was pissed by the look of rage on his face. When he had the handcuffs off, he took a few steps back giving Rome some space as he took off his jacket and carefully hung it on the pantry doorknob.

Amazingly as if it was some hidden code that only the men understood, the agents and even Rob began to clear the furniture out of the dining room kitchen area. Each of them had the look of anticipation on their faces as they prepared to see a good fight.

This was unreal. If I wasn't standing here witnessing it with my own eyes I would have never believed this was happening. This was disgusting. The look on my face was reflected on the face of my mother and the female agent who still looked a little shaken by how fast things had gotten out of hand.

Rome began to rotate his big shoulders, "I don't think you want to do this, *old man*." Jo chuckled.

"I figure we might as well get this over with. Whether you like it or not, *young blood*, I'm here to stay. And there can only be one chief in this tribe. So, let's find out today who that's going to be." A look of pure satisfaction came over Rome's face.

Oh wow! This was not good. Remember I told y'all earlier that it was impossible for two male lions to co-exist? Well, the showdown had come a lot sooner than I had imagined. I didn't know much about Joseph's fighting skills, but Rome was a seventh-degree black belt in Judi Shu and Taekwondo. He was also skilled in Capoeira.

"You two need to stop this right now!" My mother cried.

"Step back, Mrs. Reevers, try not to worry. After today, we will never have to do this again." Joseph said as he took off his watch sliding it in his pocket. I gently pulled my mother back out of the kitchen. At this point even the female agent had stepped back.

This thing was getting ready to happen.

Rome moved first, it looked as if he was going to charge Joseph only to dip down in a sweep at the last minute. Joseph jumped in the air avoiding the sweep coming down with a kick that Rome barely avoided. He rolled out of the way coming to his feet and I could tell in his eyes that he just realized Joseph was no lightweight.

"What's the matter, little brother? Just realized the game has gotten realer than your little black belt?" Joseph asked him before he swiftly charged Rome, doing some kind of maneuver with his body that sent my brother flying over his head to land hard on the ground. Rome jumped up steaming mad.

Jo smiled as he undid his tie, sliding it off. Then just as calmly, he unbuttoned the top two buttons on his shirt, revealing the pair of dog tags I remembered from the night we made love. And as if they were just playing a friendly game of basketball, he rolled up his sleeves. I tilted my head seeing Jo in a new light.

He had always come across as the distinguished gentlemen to me. But now, with his tie off and the buttons opened on his shirt showing his dog tags, a shoulder holster that hugged his massive shoulders and sleeves rolled up over well-muscled forearms... Wow! He came across as something of a brute.

He even had a tattoo on his left forearm that I didn't remember seeing that night.

"Yo, I think that's a Navy Seal tattoo." Rob whispered elbowing me in the side.

"What does that mean?" I asked him as Rome held up his fists.

Oh, did I fail to mention that my brother also held a heavyweight belt for underground boxing here in Chicago? I've heard him and Rob talking about it being his strong suit. However, the look on Rob's face left me feeling uneasy.

"It means they put a suit on a goon...your brother is about to get his ass handed to him." The female agent supplied without looking away from the fight that had just gotten real.

It looked like the men had settled on boxing. After about five minutes, it became clear that Jo was toying with Rome. At first, it looked like they were going blow for blow. But then Jo's phone rang, and he did quick work at ending the fight. Rome swung at him with a hay maker. Jo ducked, delivering a crushing blow to Rome's ribs.

We all flinched. There was going to be damage. He came right back with a jab that seemed to stun my brother before coming up with an uppercut that took Rome off his feet. The fight was over.

"Sorry, buddy." Jo spoke, looking down at him as he rolled down his sleeves. "I've run out of play time. Listen, we're going to have to wrap this up. I need to get back to D.C." He took his coat off the doorknob and put it back on over his massive shoulders.

"Karen has three contracts for you guys. I need you all to carefully read them over and sign them." He looked at my mother and his voice gentled. "Of course, Mrs. Reevers, your contract is different from your sons'. Yours is mostly a confidentiality agreement."

"Man, we ain't signing sh*t." Rome said from where he still lay on the floor clutching his ribs that I was pretty sure were broken. Rob, my mother, and I helped him to sit up. For a moment, Jo's eyes fell on me and it looked as if he was angry at me for helping my brother.

"Journey sweetheart, you need to go pack whatever you can carry of yours and Ayana's belongings. We need to go. I'll send someone to get the rest of your things later." His voice was mild, but I could hear his anger in the undertone. Rome, Rob, and my mother stiffened as they turned to look at me. My face got heated as my emotions began to scramble like my thoughts. I was such an emotional wreck, the lump increased in my throat.

"What is he talking about?" Rome growled. I opened my mouth to answer him, but Jo cut me off.

"Journey, now!" I stood, the authority in his voice brooked no argument.

"I'll explain everything to you guys later." I told them with a shaky voice as I turned to head into my room.

"Do something, Romeo." I heard my mother say before Rome called after me.

"Journey, stop!" I stopped because all my life my brother has been the boss. It was in my very DNA to obey him. But my DNA was changing. It appeared as if there was a new boss in town. I turned to face them, but the look on Jo's face got my feet moving again.

Tears came to my eyes. "I'm so sorry y'all, please forgive me for this. I'll explain everything to you later." My heart was broken. For the first time in my life, I felt as if I was being torn away from my family.

"You think I'm going to let you get away with this?" I heard my brother hiss at Jo as I stood in the middle of my room with my hand over my mouth, holding in my cry. The knot in my throat was so big that I was having a hard time breathing around it.

"You will do exactly what this contract states." Jo returned speaking to him in that calm tone that made him appear civil, when the truth was he was a goon in a suit just like the female agent said.

"To deviate either to the left or right will find you serving hard time. That little touch up you did on your boy Milo's record alone will get you sent away for life. There ain't nothing the United States Government hates more than some little punk hacker who thinks he's smarter than he really is."

What? With hands that shook I hurriedly packed Ayana's main essentials in her diaper bag. What the world was Jo talking about? Rome was a drug dealer, he was no hacker.

"Now do your family a favor, read and sign the damn contract."

"I won't let you get away with this." I heard Rome mumble. "You got a problem on your hands. That's my word. You got a real problem on your hands."

A few minutes later, my mother came into the room with tears in her eyes and quietly shut the door behind her. Without saying a word, she pulled out my suitcase and began to help me pack.

My limbs felt weak with grief. I silently wept as I stuffed as many diapers as I could in the bag.

"Baby." My mama cried before she wrapped her arms around me. I collapsed against her and let go.

"Shh!" She said as she rubbed my head. "It's going to be okay. We're going to get through this. Shh!"

"I'm scared, mama." Lowering my head, I couldn't even look her in the eye. I hated being the reason my mother was crying. She shook her head drying her eyes.

"No, don't be, you going to be alright. God gon' make a way for us. But right now, you have to do what you have to do. We all do. I don't know what Romeo is into. But it's not what we thought it was. Baby, he into some serious stuff. Whatever it is he be doing on those computers upstairs is what brought this down on us. If not for that, that man would have no leverage on us." She pushed my locs behind my ears.

"But don't worry, you know your brother. He's going to fix this. Sit tight baby, he's going to fix this." I nodded as I dried my tears. She was right, Rome will fix this.

Chapter Four

Welcome Home

Journey

Hugging my mother goodbye was the hardest thing I had to do in a long time. I tried to imagine it was like the time I left for school, but the truth was, it wasn't. I hugged Rob and then threw myself into Rome's arms. He flinched.

"Sorry," I mumbled forgetting about his ribs. Tears came to my eyes.

"Naw, don't worry about it, I'm alright. I promise, I'm going to take care of this. Okay?" I nodded. Poor Rome. He's had the weight of the family on his shoulders since our dad died when I was five and he twelve.

"We have to go." Jo's deep voice came from where he stood at my door with Ayana in his arms. The other agents had already left with my bags. Rome's gaze was full of hate when he looked up at Jo.

"Don't do this, man. This my baby sista." He tried to reason with him, but because he spoke the words through clinched teeth, it sounded more like the threat it really was.

"Yeah, she's your baby sister. But she's also the mother of my child, which now makes her *my* responsibility." I nearly jumped when he reached down and took my hand pulling me away from my brother to stand next to him. With his fist balled, Rome walked right up to him and got in his face. I squeezed Jo's hand, not wanting them to start fighting again.

He didn't even bat an eye. It was like he was daring Rome to open that can again.

"Mine!" He growled, just in case the younger man didn't understand him the first time.

"Come on Romeo, now ain't the time." My mother said putting her hand on my brother's chest trying to push him back. At first, he didn't move. In his gaze was a promise of retribution.

"Like I said earlier, *Romeo*." Jo said his name with a slight smirk on his face, intentionally riling him up. The muscle in my brother's cheek twitched. He hated that name, always have, which was why he told people to call him Rome.

"Get used to me. I'm not going anywhere." Jo continued quietly before he turned to look at my mother bowing his head slightly. "Have a good evening, Ms. Reevers. I regret we had to meet this way." He looked at Rob.

"Keep your hands clean, kid." And then with my hand firmly in his, he turned and walked out the door.

I looked back at my family through a blur of tears. My mother put her hand that slightly shook to her lips and blew me a kiss.

Joseph

If I was a decent man, I would not rip her out of her family's arms like this. It was clear they were a close unit, with young *Romeo* being at the very center, the glue that held them all together. Maybe if I knew what family love felt like, I would have some compassion, but then again, maybe not. Journey was mine and I had zero tolerance for anybody that saw it differently. She tried to take her hand from me once we reached the bottom of the stairs in her building, but I didn't let her. In fact, I pulled her closer.

Baker and Michaels both waited for us downstairs at the truck. As soon as they saw me they held their heads down. They should be ashamed. They'd let a little punk kid civilian get the best of them.

"Boss, about what happened upstairs—" Baker began, but I raised my hand cutting him off.

"We'll discuss it later. I assume you were able to assemble the car seat correctly. I mean it didn't get the best of you, did it?"

"No sir, the car seat is assembled." Michaels muttered.

"Good," I let Journey's hand go to secure my daughter in the seat. I was pleased that they put it in by the right-side passenger door, which meant Journey was going to have to ride next to me in the middle. When she got in she scooted over as close to Ayana as she could get. I slid in the seat next to her as Baker and Michaels climbed in the front.

As soon as we pulled off she leaned her head against the car seat where she silently wept. I looked down at her and for the life of me, I couldn't strum up an ounce of guilt for what I'd just done. She was so beautiful. Her royal essence called out to me like nothing else ever did. It had since the first day I walked into my father's office and saw her standing there next to the file cabinet dressed to kill in a pair of burgundy high-heel boots and an African print wrap skirt.

Her long, soft locs fell down her back to kiss the top of a nice, round behind that gave me an instant erection. To me in that moment, she embodied the exclusive beauty that only a black woman can carry. Everything about her said she was proud of who she was and how she had been born to look. And it was something about that pride, that confidence…about the way she wore her uniqueness that called out to me.

That was the first time since I was boy that a woman had ever caused my mouth to water. She became my obsession. The more she ran from me, the more I wanted her, until I found myself thinking about her all the time. She was a yellow dot in a sea of grey.

It took everything within me to be civil around her, to be a damn gentleman and not pull her into one of the empty rooms in my father's office and ravish her. I knew she was squeamish and innocent, but that made me want her all the more. That morning when I had gone by my father's office to pick up some papers he had left for me on his desk, I found her there alone.

I could not control myself. I had to find out what she tasted like. I told myself to go easy, so that I didn't scare her. But my little kitty once coerced, turned into a tigress. Had her irritating friend not come in and interrupted, I would have been able to taste my tigress a little more deeply.

But then her friend had redeemed herself when she told me about the bar they were going to and invited me to come along. Of course I didn't have time for that, I had two meetings and a dinner date with my father and one of the heads of Macon Corporation, a company that was the major founding behind my father's campaign and would more than likely be the major founding behind mine, *if I decided to run.*

However, the thought of Journey loosened up with a couple of drinks had me picking up my phone postponing my meetings. And when I walked into that bar packed full of hormonally charged youths to see her sitting at the table smiling at me in a way that let me know she too was hormonally charged, I knew it had all been worth it.

I should have felt guilty for taking advantage of one so young, but like I said, it was something about her that called to me and it transcended age and time. And then she told me she was a virgin. I told myself to stop there, to not go any further. A virgin? That could get messy. She could get attached and become clingy.

But then she opened her plush lips and said she would love for me to teach her how to make love. Every nasty dirty thing I imagined doing to her flashed in my mind and my sound reasoning fled, coupled with the massive amount of liquor I consumed that night.

I couldn't get enough of her. I had planned on just making love to her once and then taking her home, but I had not counted on her feeling and tasting so good. I had not counted on her being the best I ever had. I took her again and again even when she told me she was sore and couldn't take any more. I simply soothed her with my tongue and brought her to peek, until she was begging me for relief.

When I woke up that morning reaching to make love to her one more time only to find her gone, I was pissed. And then I realized I had done something that I've never, ever did, which was to have unprotected sex. A man in my position could never afford to make such a mistake.

I wasn't worried about disease, because I had been so busy of late; I had not been with a woman since my last medical exam. I had pulled Journey's records months ago and knew all there was to know about her, so it was safe to say she hadn't been with anyone since her last medical exam. But I knew there was a possibility that she could be pregnant.

However, it didn't frighten me as much as I thought it would. Even after that night we shared, I wanted more of her. I felt like only the edge of my hunger for her had been assuaged. I went by the office to see her the next day and ask her why she slipped out of my bed like a thief in the night, but she wasn't there.

I tried calling her, she wouldn't answer my calls. I got very busy with some things from work and my father's campaign that I was only able to try and seek her out a couple times a month, but each time, she slipped through my fingers. My evasive butterfly she became until she disappeared altogether.

Yes, I wanted her back to punish her for killing my child, for being a deceitful little witch in sheep's clothing. But I also wanted her back because I needed— I needed to have her body again. I needed to have her repeatedly until I got her out of my system, until she was no longer my obsession.

I put my arm around her waist and pulled her towards me. Maybe I've lost my mind. I didn't recognize the man I've become. I find myself jealous of the strangest things. First, the love and dependency she had for her older brother and now the damn car seat she leaned her head against for comfort. I felt that it was *my* job to comfort her. It was *me* she needed to learn to lean on.

"It's alright, sweetheart." I whispered so that only she could hear me. "I know you're afraid. The unknown is a frightening entity. But you don't have anything to worry about, I will take care of you and Ayana, I promise."

Journey

There was something wrong with me. I closed my eyes and told myself it was impossible to feel this safe in the arms of the man who had just brutally tore my family apart. He squeezed me tighter and his strength seemed to seep into my bones and envelope me, wrapping me in a protective area where no one could get to me.

By the time we made it to his helicopter, I had nearly fallen asleep in his embrace. And of course, like she always did whenever I feel asleep, Ayana woke up, ready to be fed. Jo told the other agents to wait for us in the helicopter, leaving us alone in the SUV. I'd hoped he would leave too, but wasn't surprised when he didn't.

I looked down as I unbuttoned my shirt. He put his arm on the seat behind my head and used his other hand to gently move my locs behind my back. I guess I was going have to get used to him watching me feed her. I could tell in his eyes he really did think it was beautiful. It was strange, I didn't understand his attitude at all. How could he go from wanting me to have an abortion to all of sudden being so deeply in love with his child?

Unless—

"Thank you for not killing my seed." He said quietly, looking down at us as he gently rubbed Ayana's cheek.

Something was wrong here. I looked up at him, but his gaze was so intense that I quickly looked away. With jerky movements I nodded.

"You're welcome." I whispered and like a bucket of cold water, a realization hit me.

His mother had lied.

I played back over that day in my head. *I had just found out I was pregnant. Silly me had been living with the symptoms for months, but had thought my period was acting up, which it sometimes did. Sometimes I wouldn't get it for months, although I would still have the blotting, cramping, and cravings. I always felt fat during that time because I ate like a pig. So my appetite increase and the little weight gain I had didn't raise any major red flags.*

It wasn't until after six months without having a period and worse than usual blotting that I got a little worried and went to the doctor. I sat there in shock as he told me that I was pregnant and even showed me my baby on a sonogram. A plethora of emotions raced through me. Excitement and fear. I wondered what Jo was going to say when I told him or what my family was going to say.

The doctor told me I was six months and that felt overwhelming because that meant in three months I was going to give birth. I felt like I didn't have enough time to prepare mentally for that. I called off work that day and kind of just roamed the city lost in thought. It was while I was sitting in a little coffee shop drinking a cup of tea that I looked up and surprisingly saw Alice, Joseph's mom sailing in.

She was so regal and beautiful. I could remember thinking that she didn't fit in this small coffee shop for college students. Two men dressed in black suits and dark glasses came in with her and stood by the door. When I saw that she was heading towards me I nearly choked on my tea. I had seen her a few times at the office, but she never spoke to me. She was like a queen and I just a secretary.

"Can I join you?" She asked. I straightened in my seat feeling extremely underdressed in my Proud to Be a Nerd t-shirt and jean skirt. She stood before me in an expensive cream suit with what I believed was a dead cream fox wrapped around her neck. Whiffs of her expensive perfume that was a blend of vanilla and power

floated to me to overshadow the smell of the Lavender Chamomile tea I was drinking.

"Please," I told her removing my bag and jacket from the chair opposite mine. She pulled out the chair and eased down into the seat.

"Can I get you anything, ma'am?" The barista asked coming from behind the register to take her order. I had never seen them come from behind the register to take an order, which meant Alice Warren's regal presence was enough for the manager to send one of his employees to her. She looked up as if startled.

"Oh! No! I'm perfectly fine, thanks for asking." And then her sharp gaze came back to mine, the young barista forgotten. Feeling a need to try and impress the woman, seeing as I had just found out I was pregnant with her grandchild, I asked her if she was sure she didn't want anything.

"This will be a quick visit, dear. I have a meeting with the Duchess of Langbural in ten minutes." I nodded looking down at my tea. One thing I had learned about the wealthy, they were notorious name droppers.

"It has come to my family's attention that you are pregnant with my son's child." I did spit my tea out then.

"Oh, I'm so sorry!" I said reaching for a napkin. How in the world did she know that? I had just found out.

"But, how do you know that? I've only just found out myself." She chuckled.

"Aren't you adorably naïve. There are no such things as secrets from a man like my son. He is a very powerful force here in Washington. As you know, he will soon be running for his father's seat in the Senate and then shortly after president of these great

United States." She spoke her passion filled words as if she was standing in front of a room full of press. I began to get a bad feeling in the pit of my stomach.

"Yes ma'am, I am aware of your son's impressive future." My words were soft because my heart was breaking. Before she'd come in, I'd been sitting here fantasizing about the possibilities of what could be. The look in her eyes brought all those thoughts to a savage death.

"So, you can understand why he sent me to have this talk with you?" Now she wore a look of pity that only served to twist the knife in my heart. As if she could see my hurt, her eyes softened.

"I'm so sorry to have to be the one to break this news to you. He was so angry, that's why he didn't come himself. You can imagine a man of his position has a lot of women set out to try and trap him this way."

"Trap him!" I looked around embarrassed, I didn't mean to yell that. She placed her hand on mine and I was astonished at how cold it was.

"I just had this talk with another young lady around your age just a month ago. For the life of my husband and I, we can't quite understand why he likes them so young."

"Why are you here?" I asked her so ready for her to be gone. The sadness in her gaze deepened.

"Joseph sent me here to clean up his mess, as usual. He wants you to get an abortion, dear." My mouth dropped as rage flooded my system.

"No!" I closed my lips and took several deep cleansing breaths. When I spoke again I had more control over my vocal levels.

"No. You tell him neither I or this baby need anything from him. He can just go on with his illustrious career and just pretend like we don't exist." She chuckled again.

"I wish it were that simple. You can understand why he can't afford to leave loose ends. If the press got wind of this, it could be the end of his illustrious career. Hell, it could be the ruin of our family. I know my son, he will never let something like that happen." She touched my hand again and I wanted to snatch it away from her frigidness.

"Journey, you're so fresh and innocent, I can understand what attracted him to you. But this can be a dangerous place for a girl holding such a thing as an illegitimate child over the head of a man like Joseph."

"But that's just it. I'm not holding my child over his head. He can continue on with his life as if he never met me." She inhaled before she reached in her bag and pulled out a manila envelope.

"Listen, I want to help you. In this envelope is a credit card my son cannot trace, it's enough money on it for you to live comfortably for the next six months." Her eyes fell to my Proud to Be a Nerd shirt. "Somehow, I knew you would be against his wishes and you're such a sweet girl, so I took the liberty of making a way for you to escape him. You must leave today. I will have a driver waiting on you to take you to the address in this envelope. Go back to your apartment and pack as little as possible. If Jo gets wind that you refused the abortion—" she paused as if she couldn't bear to say the words.

She didn't have to. Michelle had already told me how dangerous the political world was. Folks committed suicide left and right in these parts. Fear washed over me imagining what the ten second slot on the news would say.

"Journey Reevers, a botany student at Georgetown University was found dead in her apartment. Cause of death, suicide. Investigators believe she took her own life because GMO seeds were ruining the planet and there was nothing she could do about it. In other news, BINGO, the singing dog sang the Star-Spangled Banner Friday night at the Washington Nationals game.

Clearing her throat, Alice continued. "This is an undisclosed address. Jo won't be able to find you here, but you can't stay. Just lay low till you have your baby and then wait three months before returning to your family. And Journey, whatever you do, never come back to Washington again." I looked at her confused.

"Why can't I just go back to my family now?"

"You need to give Joseph some time to forget about you. If he finds you now, he will force you to abort your child." She looked at the crushed look on my face and reached out and touched my hand again.

"I'm so sorry this happened to you, darling." Then she stood and as grandly as she came, she left.

As I looked up to the handsome man next to me, I wondered why she lied. There was love in his eyes as he looked down at his child. Suddenly it felt like I could breathe again. I mean yeah, it was horrible he was forcing me to be his mistress, but it was a great relief to realize he didn't want our daughter dead. I smiled and he sucked in his breath.

"What is it, beautiful?" He whispered, curious at the sudden lift of my spirits. I bit my lip as I shook my head. The game had changed slightly; I no longer felt that I and my child's life were in danger in Joseph's hands. Maybe that was premature thinking of me, but I didn't.

"Nothing, just wondering if you know it's inappropriate to watch me breast feed." He chuckled as he gently rubbed his thumb along my bottom lip.

"Not when it's my child you're feeding."

****

"Oh Jo! It's beautiful!" I cried as he brought his black Aston Martin to a stop in front of a small Victorian-style farmhouse that sat back a good distance from the street. While I was attending school here in Georgetown, I would often walk in this neighborhood to clear my head. I loved this neighborhood with its old-world style homes, but none so much as this one. It reminded me of a country cottage.

I used to just stop here and stare at it, imagining what it looked like on the inside. I turned to look at him amazed as he sat back watching me, once again looking like the distinguished gentleman behind the wheel of his expensive sleek luxury car.

"How did you know?"

He chuckled. "How did I know what?"

"How did you know that I loved this house?" He looked over at the little house.

"How do you know that's the house I bought for you? Maybe I bought *this* one." He pointed to the house across the street. My face burned with embarrassment. I had not considered that.

"Oh! I guess I don't know." He put the car in reverse backing up to the gate in front of the house I loved.

"Open the gate." He said to no one in particular. My hand flew to my chest when his dashboard that already made the car feel like a spaceship began to talk to him.

"Welcome back, Mr. Warren." A female voice purred over the speakers before the gate started to open. My heart raced with anticipation and amazement as we seemed to glide up the long drive that was lined on both side with old Sakura trees.

A sound of pleasure escaped my lips when suddenly the wind blew, causing a shower of blush pink petals to rain down on the car. Quickly I opened the window not wanting this opportunity to pass and turned in the seat so that I could stick my head out the window and look up at them as they rained down on us. I closed my eyes feeling their gentle caress against my face as the wind blew through my locs.

"Amazing!" I cried feeling like this moment was a gift from God. One should never let such a moment pass and not take advantage of it. When I slid back in the car, Joseph was looking at me in awe and hunger.

"You have flowers in your hair." He reached over to pull one out.

"Aren't they pretty?" I said sliding back down in my seat. He shook his head.

"Not as pretty as you." He whispered. I bit my bottom lip trying not to blush from his words, but I knew I was failing miserably. When he finally brought the car to a stop in front of the house, I had to force myself not to jump out of it like a kid. But I could barely keep still from the anticipation that was strumming through my veins. I rubbed one of the leaves of a flower vine that was growing up the side of the house just needing to do something with my hands.

With a grin on his face Jo took his time taking Ayana's car seat out the car. He knew what he was doing.

"Do you want me to get your bags now or—" I didn't let him finish, he was torturing me.

"Later, let's go in!" I cried losing control. He chuckled as he walked past me taking a pair of keys out his pocket.

"You shouldn't tease me like that."

"Why not? You look so sexy when you beg." I bit my bottom lip again. Why did he keep saying stuff to make me blush?

"And you look a whole lot sexier when you blush." I turned my head to hide the smile. Jo could be quite charming when he puts his mind to it.

However, all thoughts fled when he finally opened the door and we stepped in. I had dreamed of looking inside this house, wondering what I would find.

"I had some renovations done on it," he said as he watched me walk in falling under the house's spell.

"It's beautiful…"

"Not much has been done to it since the original owners had it."

"It's beautiful…" The living room was small, but cozy. There was a white old-world brick fireplace that sat opposite the big bay window. I smiled when I walked into the kitchen, it was perfect. Just the kind of kitchen I always dreamed of one day having. It was surrounded by windows, so it let in a lot of light. The window over the sink looked out at a huge backyard that was filled with ancient Sakuras. Whoever had first owned this home must have been in love with the trees.

There was a small intimate deck on the other side of a pair of vintage glass doors that would be perfect for sitting on while watching the sun set. Feeling a burst of excitement, I ran up the small flight of stairs past Jo, who was watching me, to see if the upstairs was as beautiful as the downstairs. I loved how cozy the house was.

There were three bedrooms on the second level. I walked into the first one.

"Oh Jo! It's a nursery!"

"I took the liberty of arranging for you to have a few pieces of furniture. Essentials you would need to be comfortable here on your first night. A bed for you, a crib for Ayana. I figured you would want to handle the rest.

"It's perfect." I told him touched at his thoughtfulness. The nursery had been painted a pastel lavender that blended in perfectly with the top of the Sakura trees outside her window. Next to this room was an adjoining room that looked like it was made for a nanny. I walked down the short hall to a pair of white wooden double doors that had that distressed look, adding to the vintage appeal of the house.

I threw open the door to the main bedroom and all the air whooshed out of my lungs. It was by far the biggest room in the house. A beautiful white four poster bed sat upon a raised platform in front of a row of big square windows. Off to the side was a little cubbyhole of windows that had a softly padded bench seat in it. Surrounding the outside of the windows were the weeping branches of the tallest Sakura tree I'd ever seen…

"It's rumored that Douglas MacArthur had this home built for his Filipina mistress that was also an actress. He put her bed up on a pedestal because he said it was there that she truly shined. The story goes that once word got out about his affair, he stopped seeing her. And every night she would sit in that very spot wondering if it was the night he would return to her, but he never did." I turned and looked at the cubbyhole of windows and I imagined that I could feel her sadness.

Scrunching up my nose I shook my head a bit. "That's not a true story, is it?"

He shrugged. "Rumors…"

Off in the corner of the room was a small set of steps that led up to another glass door. I was half way up them when I realized what it was. I turned stunned eyes to look at Jo, who wore a smile on his face as if he knew a secret.

Opening the door, I walked into the space and tears came to my eyes.

"It's a greenhouse!" I gushed putting my shaking hand over my mouth as I turned and looked around. It was a greenhouse that was the whole length of the top of the house. The windows were stained with age, only adding to the charm. Outside of them, the top of the Sakuras looked like clouds. The flowering vine that grew up the house covered some section of the window where it met in the back of the house. It was amazing, truly and utterly amazing.

I knew there was a reason this house called to me. And it wasn't because it was possibly built for the foreign mistress of one of America's Founding Fathers. It was because I had always dreamed of having my very own house and greenhouse. Most girls dreamt of flashy cars, expensive clothes, and maybe diamond rings.

Not me, when I closed my eyes, I fantasized for the very thing in front of me. I whipped around to face Joseph, to face this man who had just hours ago looked like a monster. This man who got me to sign a contract to be his paid whore to keep my brother out of prison.

This man who had somehow given me the home of my dreams.

"How did you know?"

Chapter Five

Pause Moment

Journey

After I'd finished looking around my new home, Jo helped me bring my bags in and then showed me what keys went to what doors and how to get in and out of the front gate. He had a device connected to his car that opened the gate, but because I didn't have a car, he had the device on the key chain of keys he'd given me. There was also an intercom inside the house that had a little screen over it. Whenever someone called at the gate, their face would show up on the screen.

He went into grave detail telling me that under no circumstances was I to open that gate unless I recognized whoever it was on the other side. It was clear that Joseph was big on security and had spared no expense on making sure the house was safe. There were several brand-new state-of-the-art cameras around the property. When I asked him where the footage went, he chuckled and told me in safe hands.

Okay, I guess I had to take him at his word on that.

Anyhow, after his hour-long speech about security protocol, he took Ayana and I to the grocery store to grab a few items. On the way back, I had gotten extremely nervous, wondering if he would be expecting me to start fulfilling my end of the contract tonight. However, I needn't have worried. After he helped me put away my groceries, he got called away.

"Listen, I'm going to be out of town for a few days." He told me as he watched me lay Ayana down in her new crib. I nodded trying not to let my relief show. Once I got the baby settled in, he took my hand and gently led me out of the house to his car. He reached into his glove compartment and came out with a beautiful rose gold phone.

I stared down at it as he handed it to me. Rose gold was my favorite color. I looked up at him, wondering how he knew. "This is my favorite color."

He nodded. "Yes, I know."

"I already have a cell phone. Rome got it for me before I went away to school." Just the mention of my brother caused his nose to flare.

"Now you have a new one."

Instead of arguing with him, telling him I didn't need a new one, I just nodded. If he insisted on paying my phone bill, fine. I'll just tell Rome he didn't have to anymore.

"I've arranged for you to have a driver while I'm gone. His number is already programmed in your phone. Just press three. His name is Albert and he's been working for me for many years, I trust him." He leaned against his car and put his hands on my waist, pulling me so that I was standing between his spread legs. I bit my lip, nervous at being so close to him.

"If you want a car, we can look at some when I get back." He said bringing his finger up to pull my lip from between my teeth. As if he could not resist it, he leaned in and gently touched his lips to mine.

"Every time you torture you lip like that, you make me want to come to its rescue." He whispered before he leaned in and scandalously ran his tongue over my bottom lip. And then he was kissing me again, but this time, there was nothing gentle about the kiss. His lips took possession of mine, causing a moan to escape my throat. Jo kissed like a conqueror. He dominated, manipulated, and left me devastated.

I know just minutes ago I was sweating bullets at the thought of having sex with him again, but for the life of me at this moment, I didn't know why. That night when he made love to my body, he had swept me up in an ocean of pleasure, the pleasure that he was awakening in me right now. I stood on my toes, wrapping my arms around his neck to pull him closer.

He wrapped his arms around my waist, pulling me as close as he and I could possibly get. The feel of their strength encasing me and his lips devouring mine was a mind-numbing aphrodisiac. I wanted to—

His phone rang, sounding loud in the night. I drew back, looking down at it where it vibrated on his waist between us. His hungry gaze was still on my lips, it looked as if he was going to come for them again, but the loud shrill of his phone killed that.

Frowning, he took one of his arms from around me and snatched his phone off his waist.

"Yeah!" He said bringing it to his ear. He exhaled as he listened to whoever it was speaking to him while looking down at my slightly swollen lips that still glistened from our kiss.

"I'm aware of that. I'm scheduled for the next flight out." He told them before he hung up.

"As much as I hate to leave you, duty calls." He reached into his pocket and pulled out a black credit card handing it to me.

"Use this and get whatever you need. My number is programmed in your phone also. Just push one. If you or the baby need anything, call me, I don't care what time it is. You remember what I went over with you about the panic button?"

I quickly nodded my head, not wanting to get him started on his safety speech again.

He grinned at me as if he knew my thoughts. "Okay then, you be good till I get back."

He pulled me in his arms and kissed me again before he turned and got into his car. I stood and watched him go, wondering when I was going to see him again. Amazed that I actually wanted to continue what we almost got started. Exhaling I turned and went back into my new home, I couldn't help but feel a little giddy.

I loved it!

I couldn't wait to decorate it. I was going to keep with the rustic look of the house when making my choices. After taking another tour, mentally formulating a loose plan, I checked on Ayana one more time before settling on my big bed and using my cell phone that Rome had gotten me to call my mom.

"Hey, baby." She said in the phone sounding like home, instantly causing my soul to feel warm.

"Hey, ma."

"How is everything going? Is he being nice to you?" I lay back in the bed with a huge smile on my face.

"He bought me a house."

"Oh, ain't that wonderful? It must be a nice one, I can hear the smile in your voice."

"It is…It's my dream house. I don't know how he knew about it, but he got it for me. It's amazing. More beautiful on the inside than I'd imagined."

"Halleluyah! I was praying for you, baby. You know my spirit tell me about folks before they mouth do. And as soon as Jo came through my door, I knew he was bringing change with him." I grinned.

My mother was very spiritual. She carried her Bible with her all the time and she swore angels talked to her and guided her through life. I don't know if that's true or not, but she was a good call on people's character.

"Did you call your brother yet?"

I exhaled. "Naw, I wanted to call you first to see how mad he is."

"His pride hurt. He ain't never been beat in a fight before."

I chuckled. "Yeah, I know. Ma, tell Rome I'm okay and I'm going to call him tomorrow. It's been a long day and I need to get some rest before Ayana wake up." I knew I was being a coward, siccing my mom on Rome, but I wasn't lying. I have barely gotten any sleep over the last three months since Ayana's birth. And after the night I had, I had no more energy left to deal with Rome.

"You go ahead and get some rest, I'll handle your brother."

"Thanks, Mommy. Love you."

"Love you too, baby."

After I hung up with my mother, I closed my eyes for just a second before I drifted to sleep. But no sooner had I begun to dream, Ayana's little cry filtered through it. Groggily I came awake.

This had to be the worst part of being a new mommy. No sleep!

The next day, I got started bright and early. I didn't bother calling Jo's driver. I knew the city pretty well and didn't have a problem getting around on the bus. My first stop was my school. I wanted to touch bases with my botany professor, Mrs. Paxton and let her know I was back in town. She was the one who'd gotten me the scholarship to Georgetown in the first place.

She'd heard me reading my thesis on the effects drilling and fracking was having on the soil for Earth Day at Harold Washington Library back home when I was a junior in high school. When she'd approached me and asked me if I would like to attend Georgetown University, I had initially thought she was joking, thinking that surely she could not be interested in a ghetto youth like myself.

But she was, she contacted me the next month, telling me she'd used my thesis to get me a scholarship for their botany program. Mrs. Paxton was the first person to make me feel like I was on to something in my theory on what was happening to the nutrients in the soil.

"Journey, is that you?" That familiar voice pulled me out of my thoughts. I turned around and smiled at Kyle, a really cool brother that was also here for the botany program.

"Hey, Kyle." I told him waving to him, but in typical Kyle fashion, he bypassed my wave and wrapped his strong arms around me, pulling me into a hug.

For just a moment, I took the time to observe how his strong arms did not have the same effect on me that Jo's did. Kyle's arms didn't make me feel safe. They didn't make my insides dance or make me want to close my eyes and just inhale him. His strong arms made me impatient to get out of them.

Hmmm...that's interesting.

"Where you been? You just disappeared on us. I went by your place looking for you, but your roommate said you'd moved back home." Right then, his eyes fell on the stroller and a look of understanding came on his face.

"Ahh, so that's what happened." He squatted down to look in the stroller. I pulled the blanket back so that he could see Ayana's little face.

"She's beautiful." He whispered.

"Thank you."

Kyle was a nice-looking brother. Like me, he had long locs and he was physically fit. I think he told me he practiced some kind of martial art. Before Jo so ruthlessly inserted himself into the picture, Kyle and I were doing some light flirting with each other. Out of everyone here, I'd imagined it would have been *him* who I'd eventually start dating.

But that was before Jo came along. Where Kyle was nice and gentle, Jo was aggressive and thorough. Kyle had allowed me to put him in the friend zone and maybe it was because he wasn't the type to wrap his fist in my locs, holding my head so that he could ravish me with his lips. Kyle was the type of man that would take you out on a date and then give you a gentle peck at the door. Kyle was the type of man that would wait till your body said it was ready for him. Whereas Jo was the type of man that *made* your body ready for him--

No...He made your body *crave* him. He made your body shake all over, anticipating his next touch. He made your body once, depleted, feel as if it could go for another round. He made you clamp your teeth down on the pillow to keep from screaming so loud the neighbors came running. Made you—

Kyle stood looking at me as if something was wrong with me. It was then I realized while I was standing here fantasizing about Jo's lovemaking, he had asked me a question. I blushed with embarrassment.

"Hmmm?" I asked feeling ashamed of myself. Jo was turning me into a sex crazed lunatic.

"Why did you leave without telling me you were going? I tried calling you...nothing. I was worried."

"I—um... I just wanted to be with my family after finding out I was pregnant." I didn't know why I was lying to him. It wasn't like I had anything to be ashamed of.

Yet...

I felt ashamed. The father of my child had come back in my life, not with a marriage proposal. Nope, he'd come back into my life with a *mistress* proposal. Hell yeah, I was ashamed.

"And the dad, where is he?" I gave him a little frown. It kind of irritated me that he said it like that. *The dad*, as if my daughter was an *it*.

"It's complicated, Kyle."

His gaze became serious. "It shouldn't be. Not with a girl like you. Anybody fool enough to let things become complicated don't deserve you."

"Umm, you know what? You may be right. Hey, let me talk to you a little later, I need to go and see Mrs. Paxton before her classes get started for the day." I didn't wait around to hear his response. Like the coward I was, I fled instead of facing the truth.

My run in with Kyle had put a damper on my day. It brought a few things back into perspective.

Yeah, it was true, Jo had given me my dream home and now that he'd found us, had stepped up in a major way to accept his responsibilities. But the fact remained that his mother told a vicious lie to separate us and he'd believed her to the point where he'd come back and offered me a contract to be his whore.

He said it was only for the year. Like my mom said, at this point, I had to do what I had to do. I would be his mistress for the next year, then I was free. I wasn't going to continue to take his money afterwards either. Whatever he did for his daughter he did, but that's as much as I will accept.

Although the thought of leaving that beautiful house saddened me, it was exactly what I was going to do. After my year with him was up, I was going back home to lick my wounds. My mom raised us to thank the Heavenly Father when we had plenty and to thank him when we didn't. I would enjoy my home now, enjoy each day of it, but when it was time to go, I would walk away without looking back.

After meeting with Mrs. Paxton, my spirits lifted a little. She was always so kind. Born and raised in Italy, she said hospitality is in her blood. I sat and talked with her for nearly an hour. We caught each other up on the things we've researched since last we met. We even talked about me starting classes back in the fall, which would be perfect, because it allowed me enough time to find proper child care for Ayana as well as wean her off my breast.

However, I assured her that now that I had access to a greenhouse, I would be continuing with my research. This excited her and she encouraged me to carry on, saying that the earth needed all the warriors it could get to fight for it. That's why I loved Mrs. Paxton, she shared my passion for helping to restore the health to this planet.

When I left her class, it was to see Kyle waiting for me at the end of the hall. Instead of going that way, I went back into Mrs. Paxton's room and left out through her greenhouse. I didn't want to see Kyle. I didn't need him telling me how stupid I was for settling for Jo, I already knew.

Needing a serious rush of feel good, I found myself at Nola's Gardens, the best nursery in all of D.C. There is nothing that made me feel better than going through inspecting the plants, the stems, the roots, and the soil. Nola's Gardens was so big one could get lost. I even sat Ayana's stroller up so that she could look as well.

I'm telling yall, I know this is my child, because the whole time we were there she did not fuss or cry once. She didn't even go to sleep. She stared wide-eyed at all the plants.

By the time we left, I had spent a great sum of money, so much money that Nola had sent a three-man team with their company truck to my house with all the plants and supplies I ordered for my greenhouse and research.

I had days' worth of work ahead of me. My spirits had past lifted, they were now vibrating with anticipation. I ordered tables, garden boxes, bags and bags of soil, compost, and peat moss. I had over fifty plants that I couldn't do without. I even ordered a sprinkler system for the ceiling that will water the plants in a rain simulation.

Over the next few days, I buried myself in the work of getting my babies secured in their new home. I got so involved with the greenhouse I had completely forgotten about furniture for the rest of the house. I didn't remember till Jo called to check on me and tell me his trip was going to take longer than he'd expected.

"How is furniture shopping coming?" his deep voice seeped out the phone.

"Furniture?"

He chuckled. "Furniture, you know, couches and tables, dressers, that kind of thing."

"Well, about that. I've been a little busy with the greenhouse. Kind of forgot about furniture." I chewed on my bottom lip, thinking I may have a bit of an addiction when it came to plants.

"Stop chewing on your lip."

I laughed. "How did you know?"

"I know you."

"Well, if you knew me that well, you might have thought twice before giving me a credit card and a greenhouse."

"I could think of worse addiction than plants. However, you have to buy furniture, so please call Albert and let him take you shopping."

I exhaled, not wanting to leave the house. With so much stuff still yet to do in the greenhouse, the thought of spending hours shopping for furniture sounded like torture.

"Okay." I told him reluctantly.

"And Journey, no more plant stores until you get the things you need to have a functioning house."

"Bossy much?"

He chuckled. "I've heard it said a time or two."

After I hung up with him, I called Albert and set a time for him to come and pick up Ayana and I in the morning. Albert was a breath of fresh air. He was the grandfather everybody dreamed of having. As soon as I walked out the house with Ayana in her car seat, he hurried to help me.

"Allow me, my dear. And how are you today?"

I smiled at him. "I'm good, how are you?"

"Excited! You called and got this old man out of the house. There is nothing I like more than furniture shopping."

I would find out that there is nothing Albert like doing more than anything he was doing at the time. Midday when we stopped for a break, he said:

"There is nothing I like doing more than stopping for a cool glass of lemonade on a warm sunny day."

And when we went curtain shopping:

"There is nothing I like doing more than shopping for curtains."

We ended the day at Best Buy, where I purchased a flat screen television. Albert was in his element here.

"There is nothing I like doing more than shopping for new toys." Indeed, he spoke the truth. I was just going to get a little 22inch because I barely watched television. If I did at all, it was either early morning news or late-night news. However, Albert would have none of that.

"Don't deny yourself the pleasure of a 72inch. You haven't lived unless you've experienced the theater effect on your very own couch." I frowned.

"I don't know, Albert, that's pretty big." He waved that away.

"Nonsense…72inches is tiny compared to what I have at home."

"What do you have at home?" He looked at me with a devious look.

"105 inches!"

My mouth dropped. "Oh, my goodness! That's ridiculous." He looked up surprised.

"What?" I asked.

"How did you know? Ridiculous is my middle name."

Albert had me laughing from the time he picked me up till the time he dropped me off. He told me he was Joseph's driver when he was a boy, then he went on to tell me all the crazy things Jo used to do. He said once when Jo was twelve, he tricked old Albert into eating a ghost pepper, and then proceeded to tell his parents Albert was having a heart attack and that he had to rush him to the hospital so that he could get out of school.

I was crying laughing when Albert told me that story. He said the whole time he was trying to tell Jo's parents that he wasn't having a heart attack and that the little bastard had tricked him into eating a ghost pepper, but his mouth was on fire and the only thing he could do was wheeze while calling on the Most High for help. He said the whole time, Jo was pushing him out the driver seat and into the passenger seat, while telling his parents, who were busy suggesting he call the ambulance that it was no time, because Albert was dying.

Once he got his parents off the phone, he gave poor Albert a carton of milk, apologizing for using him like that. He said however, they had an amazing day after that. They drove around the city and got into all they could.

It sounded like Albert and Jo were pretty close. He spoke of him like one would do his son. He was proud of the younger man's accomplishments, including Ayana, who he gushed over the whole time. When he dropped us back off at the house, I invited him in for dinner.

"Oh no, I can't take advantage of your kindness like that. I will just go on home and see what kind of canned goods I can rustle up." I couldn't help but laugh at him. He spoke of Jo being a character when he was younger, watching this old man perform, I knew where he got it from.

"Please, Albert. I insist. I'm not making anything fancy, just grilled chicken salad. But that's a lot better than canned goods. Plus, I'm going to need help setting up that *ridiculously* big television you talked me into buying."

His head popped up. "You know, you may be right. Well, if you insist."

As I prepared dinner, Albert worked on getting the television all set up in the living room. The stand I'd purchased for it was going to be delivered with the rest of my furniture on Wednesday. So, he set it up on the floor and insisted we eat our salads in front of it.

However, I nearly choked on my first bite when he turned on the tube and Jo's face appeared on the screen.

"Oh my God, that's Jo!" I nearly yelled. Chuckling, Albert turned it up.

It looked like the footage was from earlier in the day. Jo and his father were being interviewed by a bunch of reporters at what looked like a campaign rally.

"So, what's it going to be, Mr. Warren? By your father being the first African American to hold the senator seat for Florida and a 10-year incumbent, it's safe to say the Sunshine State loves and trusts your family. Some say you'll have the Senate seat in the bag should you choose to run." A very attractive news reporter said clearly flirting with him. She looked at him with very inviting eyes.

He smiled down at her before he waved a *no no* finger at her, as if to say, he sees what she's up to.

"Right now, I just want to focus on my retirement from the Bureau, it's going to be tough walking away from people I've come to look at as family." Jo's mother was right, he displayed a natural charm that made people feel safe. Both of his parents stood next to him looking at him with all the pride they felt. In both of their eyes was the assurance of the continuation of their legacy in Joseph.

"And what are your plans after retirement? Can we expect your announcement then?" The reporter was diligent. Jo wasn't ruffled a bit, he chuckled.

"We can expect for me to continue to serve my father and the people of this great nation. Thank you very much." And then with his hand on his mother's back, he moved on. A representative from their office told the many reporters that they were accepting no more questions.

Albert turned the television back down.

"Wow..." was all I could say.

Albert sighed. "He doesn't want to do it." Shocked, I turned to look at him.

"What do you mean? His mother said he's been born and bred to become the next president."

"And he has been. But it doesn't mean it's something he wants to do."

"Can you explain?"

He rested his back against the wall, we sat on two big pillows we had picked up from Target today.

"Jo was a war hero. The boy had too many metals for his uniform. He and his team did the missions nobody else would do. You know, the real nasty stuff. And he loved it. He thrived in it." He shook his head. "I know that sounds bad, but you have some folks that's born warriors. That's Jo. The Navy hated to see him go. But the powers that be decided it was time for him to move on in his path to the White House. He hates all the refinement. Always has. But his parents have forced it on him since he was a small boy. He knows his duty and he's going to do it. But he doesn't want to."

Well that would explain why he defeated my brother so easily. Rome was feared everywhere he went. Jo didn't even break a sweat taking him down. It's like that agent told me back at my house, they had put a suit on a goon.

"What does he want to do?" I asked curious.

"He likes being an agent. He likes the danger, the thrill of the chase. But apparently that's not his destiny."

I thought about Albert's words well into the night. I couldn't imagine being forced into becoming something I didn't want to become. I loved plants, always have since I was a little girl. And my family has been nothing but supportive of me and what I love. The rich operated differently from normal folks. People think they are happier because they have so much money, but I didn't agree.

Poor Jo, he must be miserable inside.

Over the next few days, several things happened. Albert took me to my doctor's appointment and was even kind enough to sit in the waiting room with Ayana during my visit. I left there with birth control pills and literature about them. Now my only challenge would be remembering to take them every day. I was horrible with stuff like that.

The places I had gone to order furniture began delivering it. I was pleased with my selections. In keeping with the rustic feel, I had decided to go with a rustic, Afrocentric country farmhouse look and in the end, I thought it was beautiful.

Albert came over and helped me hang my curtains. Although they were in the design of the African Mud cloth, they were cream and sheer. I chose sheer because the trees that filled both the front yard and the back were just too beautiful to block out. Plus, when I opened my windows I loved the way the curtains looked blowing in the breeze.

Albert also helped the delivery men and I arrange the furniture where I wanted it to go. When everything was done, he and I sat back and enjoyed some Chinese take-out at my brand-new kitchen table. That's when he told me about his wife and for the first-time since knowing Albert, I was sad instead of deliriously happy.

"My wife died three years ago and I feel as if I've lost half of my soul. I've been sitting around the house lost with no true purpose. That's why I was so glad when Jo called me, assigning me as your driver."

"I'm sorry to hear that. If you don't mind me asking, how did she die?"

He shook his head. "Naw, I don't mind. Breast cancer. We had fought it for many years till finally it got the best of her. Jo had made sure she had the best doctors. In the end, it was in God's hands though. It doesn't matter how skilled the doctor is. When God calls, what man can tell him nay?" I reached across the table and took his hand.

"That's what my mom said when my dad died. She grieved many years, but she said she found peace when she realized that everything is in the Heavenly Father's hands and it was vain of man to assume differently."

He looked at me and nodded. "Telling God how you want to do things. Vanity at its finest."

He and I talked for a little more before he went home. Ayana and I spent the rest of the night working in the greenhouse. I had brought her a little swing that I sat her in and she was content to watch me work.

I had this little *pause moment* that I did every day either before I started my day or at the end, sometimes both, where I took a spray bottle mixed with water and my essential oil blend of Lavender, Lemongrass, and Frankincense and I sprayed it in the air, letting the mist caress my face. And for just a moment, I stopped and thanked the Most High for allowing me to be.

In that moment, all my worries fell away and I felt free, it was a time where I connected with my creator and just partook of his energy. Now, thanks to my new sprinkler system that had a mist setting, my plants could also participate in my pause moment, something I'd discovered years ago they enjoyed.

After laying Ayana down for the night, I mixed my blend and added it to the system. And then I just stood as the gentle fragrant spray caressed my face and hair. I opened my arms feeling like I could fly. In this moment, there were no worries, only the truly important thing mattered, the Heavenly Father's breath that he gifted to me.

The next day, Jo came home.

Chapter Six

I'll Never Let You Fall

Journey

Completely clueless to the fact that Jo was going to make an appearance today, I began my day like always… In my greenhouse. However, by noon I realized that I was just too tired to do any serious work. Last night, after I finally drifted off to sleep, my little buttercup's inner alarm went off and she woke me right back up.

I ended up staying up most of the night with her. By the time I got back to sleep it was morning and Ayana was back up an hour later.

Goodness, mommy hood was a sleepless endeavor.

Anyway, by the time I got her down for her nap, I decided I was going to have some well- deserved needed me time. I started by taking a long hot shower, after which I found myself standing in the mirror looking at the horror show that stared back at me.

I looked haggard. The sleepless nights were taking a toll on me. My skin looked dull and my locs needed a fresh twist like nobody's business. Even the nail polish was chipped on my nails. There were huge bags under my eyes.

"Shame on you, J. If your mama could see you now she would get on you." I told my reflection. And it was true. One thing my mother did not tolerate was neglection of one's self. If she saw me now she would nag me to death until I got it together. It was her voice I heard in my head when I began to moisturize and then re-twist my locs.

I pulled them up into a high messy bun on top of my head and then I moisturized my skin really good with cocoa butter. When I was done my skin had its natural glow back. There wasn't much I could do about the bags underneath my eyes outside of getting some sleep.

But to make myself feel a little prettier, I bypassed my nightgown for one of my long slender skirts that could also serve as a halter dress. It was my sky blue and purple skirt. I loved it because the material was very soft against my skin. When I was done I painted both my finger nails and toe nails purple to match my skirt. When next I looked at myself in the mirror I was a far better sight than before.

I was going to climb up in my bed and take a nap, but I decided against it. The weather outside was perfect. It was one of those days where it wasn't too hot or too cold, just right there in the middle. There was even a gentle breeze that caused my back yard to become a work of art as it caused thousands of Sakura petals to litter the ground.

I took a blanket out back and spread it over the petals. Then I lay on it and turned on my back so that I could stare up at the weeping branches as they blew beautifully in the wind above me. A few were so long that they caressed my skin. I closed my eyes enjoying their gentle touch. But it wasn't long before they lulled me right to sleep.

Joseph

"Open the gate." I spoke to my car feeling starved for the sunshine I knew awaited me on the other side.

"Welcome back, Mr. Warren."

It felt good to be back. The last seven days had been pure hell for me. I didn't intend to be away so long. I felt like a kid that had just gotten the toy of his dreams and before he could touch it or play with it, had been forced to put it away for a while.

The only thing I could think about was Journey. Her beautiful hair and skin. Her firm, upturned breasts. Her thick thighs and curvy butt. I found myself gazing off into space imagining how it will feel when I slide into her soft heat again.

Of course my parents and the whole damn Democratic Party were not happy at my distracted mind. They all wanted me to officially announce that I was running for my father's senate seat, but I would not. I had already announced my retirement from the Bureau, they will have to be happy with that.

Truth was, I was still undecided. I had been reared my whole life to fill this role, but it wasn't for me. Although I wore the suit, I felt suffocated in it. There was a rage inside of me that was only soothed in two ways. The first I knew well, the second had been a surprise to me.

All my life I knew that something was seriously wrong with me. By some strange freak of an occurrence, I had been born for violence. And no matter how much I told myself something was wrong with that and that I needed to change, I couldn't. It's like I didn't feel alive unless I was in the middle of conflict. I lived for the ferocity.

Much to my parents' dismay, the thought of sitting in an office and becoming this public figure made me feel ill. I thrived behind the scenes. When I left the Seals to join the Bureau, it had been tough because I didn't see nearly as much action as I saw with my brothers in arms. But luckily my Director, who was also a close friend of my family had seen this restless energy in me early and put me on the more vicious cases to soothe the need in me.

Up until I met Journey I had thought that was the only way that restless energy could be quieted. I exhaled as I brought my car to a stop in front of her door. This was not the place to think of any of that, not war and for damn sure not politics. I had already decided that I would leave all things political at her gate and not bring it in. I've come to look at my time with her as something sacred. And I refuse to let it be contaminated with the filth of politics.

After removing my bag from my trunk, I used my key to let myself in and I came up short at the sight that greeted me. A feeling of home flooded every one of my senses. At first, I stood there dumbfounded. I had never felt this feeling before. I didn't even know what to do with it. This caused the restlessness in me to not only be calm, but for the first time in my life it vanished. I didn't feel it there simmering just beneath the surface of my skin.

Walking into her home gave me the same feeling I got the first time I saw her. Everything about the décor screamed Journey. She had chosen to go light and breezy with it. A beautiful cream plush sofa that looked as if it would be heaven to sit on sat against the far wall. In front of the big bay windows was a matching love seat. On both sides of the love seat was a tall plant with huge vibrantly bright green leaves.

There was a big flat screen television mounted to the wall over the fireplace. I frowned. That didn't seem like her. Chuckling I shook my head. That had Albert written all over it.

The house was filled with a pleasant bouquet of fresh scents, fresh linen, citrus, and there was even a hint of chocolate. It made me feel as if I were walking into a country home full of fresh flowers instead of a little bungalow that's minutes from D.C. She had managed to create an oasis in the mist of chaos.

As I made my way upstairs I thought about my cold, lonely penthouse that was triple the size of this house. I don't ever remember feeling anything upon entering it.

When I got to my daughter's room all thought fled as I quietly walked in. She slept so peacefully in her crib sucking her little fingers. Gently I touched her head. She was so tiny lying here in this bed. I can't believe she came from me. She is the only perfect thing I'd ever done.

I now knew what true love felt like. I had just met her, but already I will be willing to lay down my life for her. Ayana, the perfect. I wanted to kiss her little cheek, but I didn't want to wake her, so I eased back out of the room. When I got to Journey's bedroom, I stood in the center of the room and looked around it. The fury that had just seconds ago been calmed to the point that I thought maybe I had been healed, began to simmer to life.

She had not brought any furniture for this room. The only thing here was the bed I'd gotten her. Her suitcase and bags still sat against the wall.

A big part of my training for the Bureau had been in the studying of human behavior, her action spoke volumes of her true intentions. She bought furniture for the rest of the house because I told her to. By not buying furniture for her bedroom she was trying not to get too comfortable, to make walking away as painless as possible.

My little elusive butterfly had it in her heart to flutter away from me again.

I took the stairs up to her greenhouse two at a time. The emotions she caused in me were all first. This was the first time I wanted to claim a woman, to put my seal on her and somehow mark her so all the world knew she was mine. She had become my peace, my quiet and she wanted to take that away from me.

"Wow!"

This had to be what paradise looked like. I glanced around amazed that she was able to do so much in seven days.

"Wow!"

The earthy smell in here made me feel...I don't know. It made me feel alive. There was a small metal garden table with two matching chairs that sat in the center of the room. Next to the table was a baby swing. On the table was an empty tea cup with an old tea bag in it. I could tell that my girl spent a lot of time here, more time than she spent in the rest of the house, especially her bedroom.

I chuckled dryly. We were going to change that.

"Journey." I called, careful to keep my voice low enough not to wake the baby. When I didn't get an answer, I took my phone off my hip and clicked on my security footage app. A few minutes later I was walking through the sliding doors to the back deck.

My little butterfly was fast asleep in the center of the backyard. When I approached her I just stood for a moment and took her in. She was so beautiful. The petals from the flowers had fallen to blanket her. Carefully I lifted my phone and snapped a picture. Too late realizing I didn't have it on silent.

Journey

The sound of a picture snapping woke me. Jo stood above me with his phone in his hand.

"Dang it, Jo! Did you just take a picture of me sleeping?" He chuckled nodding his head.

"Yep."

I frowned. "Why? Was I snoring or something?" He shook his head.

"You're covered with flower petals."

I lifted my head looking down at my body and was amazed to see that I was. Slowly I sat up and the petals rained down from my hair. I chuckled, shaking my head causing more to fall to the ground around me.

He took another picture. I covered my face.

"Jo, stop taking pictures, I must look—"

"Beautiful. Simply and utterly beautiful." His deep voice cut me off. Blushing I looked up at him and started to return the compliment. This man's chocolate good looks was a sight for sore eyes. He stood over me looking so very powerful in an expensive white linen suit that was made just for him. Its startling whiteness contrasted beautifully with his dark skin.

Right then the wind blew, causing the jacket to open a bit, revealing just how well his white shirt with the top three buttons undone fit against his muscled chest and stomach.

He squatted down in the grass next to me and his spicy cologne tempted my senses.

"I missed you." He said quietly as he gently picked a petal off my lap. "I brought something for you." He reached in his jacket and came out with a thin box.

I took the box with hands that shook slightly. "You didn't have to get me anything. You've already done so much." I gave a nervous chuckle.

"Naw, I wanted to, open it."

I opened it and gasped. "Oh my God! It's beautiful!"

It was a rose gold necklace with a ruby pendent that sat in the center of a rose gold flower. There were small little specks of diamonds on the flower petal that looked like drops of water. I've never seen anything more beautiful. I looked up at Jo at a loss for words. This necklace had to be very expensive.

"Here, let me help you put it on." He took the necklace out of the box and squatted down behind me. I was so nervous as his strong hands came around my neck to gently lay the ruby against my chest. When he was done clamping it I waited for him to come back in front of me, but he didn't. When I felt his warm lips touch the back of my neck I gasped as a shiver raced through me.

"Your skin is so pretty." He sniffed. "And it smells like chocolate." I bit my lip, so glad I decided to give myself that moisturizing treatment, he was smelling cocoa butter.

"Thank y—" I began, but he used his hand to gently turn my head and then he was kissing me. And I'm not talking about a *hi, nice to see you again kiss*. I'm talking about a having to squeeze your thighs together, toe curling kind of kiss.

I cried out when he suddenly put one arm under my knees and the other behind my back and swooped me up from the ground.

"Jo, you're going to drop me!" I laughed as he spun me around holding me high in the air. I wrapped my arms around his neck clinging to him. I'm not the smallest girl in the world, especially after having Ayana.

"I got you, baby. I'll never drop you." He whispered close to my ear. I moaned, 'cause when he was done he took my ear lobe in his mouth. That was one thing I remembered about my night with Jo. He did some nasty things with that mouth of his.

He carried me across the yard, up the deck and into the house. Without making a sound he carried me up the stairs past Ayana's room and into my room. Holding me up with one arm, he took his other hand and gently shut the door as not to wake up the baby.

As he carried me across the floor to the bed he looked down at me with his hungry gaze, a gaze that didn't waver as he gently laid me on the bed. My heart was pounding with fear and anticipation. The time had come.

"I've waited so long to taste you." He said so low I barely heard him. I balled my hands into fists to stop myself from doing something like pulling the covers over me. His gaze was so intense as he stood and took off his jacket letting it fall to the floor. Shortly after, his shirt followed.

I bit my lip. His muscled chest and stomach looked so good. The dog tags lay against his chest showing that Albert was right and at heart, Jo was more warrior than politician. After sliding out his shoes he put one knee on the bed and fisted the bottom of my dress. When he began to pull I panicked and put my hand on my chest stopping him.

"It's so much light—"

"I just want to see you, J. Please…let me see you." The look in his eye was that of pure want. I have never had a man look at me that way. Slowly I removed my hand and he began to pull at my dress. Because the top of it was elastic it had to stretch to pass my breasts causing them to spring free.

"Oh sh*t…" He whispered, hungrily eyeing my breasts. When I saw his head lowering toward them my first feeling was fear. I was afraid he was going to cause my milk to come down and ruin everything, but he didn't. He kissed my tips very gently, opening his mouth to taste them without causing my milk to release.

I moaned closing my eyes. I couldn't help but arch my back, offering more of myself to him. His warm mouth felt so good. However, my breasts were the only place Jo showed restraint. What seemed like minutes later, he had me screaming my release all without even removing his pants.

But my goodness, when he removed his pants…

Emm… Emm… Emm…

He reminded me of his ability to turn me into a savage, to have me begging for mercy while screaming out his name. He had the ability to cause me to lose feeling in my face and cause my legs to spasm uncontrollably. This purely primal feeling was out of this world. I bit down on my lip till it hurt, trying not to lose myself completely, but it did no good.

I was lost, panting and clawing, feeling as if I could not take anymore, yet begging for more. There were tears coming from my eyes and I didn't know why. Maybe I was dying of the pleasure he was causing me to feel.

When he finally held me tightly against him and released his warm seed in me, I thought for sure after that performance, he would be tired. I sure was.

But I was wrong.

Jo rested for only a minute with his arm around me, spooning me. I'd even began to drift off, still very tired from the lack of sleep I've gotten. Even my nap earlier had been short lived. I couldn't have been asleep that long before Jo showed up.

However, a moan escaped my lips when I felt him begin to gently kiss me on the back of my neck. I smiled sleepily, thinking that was very sweet. But then his tongue turned wicked and that sweet little gestured turned into me biting down on my pillow as not to wake Ayana as he took me from behind.

When my world shattered for the third time, so did my ability to remain awake. In fact, I think I may have passed out. I don't know if it was the orgasm that depleted me of my last remaining strength, but when I tell ya'll I slept...

I slept.

I didn't even hear Ayana cry. I remember at some point Jo bringing her to me and putting her to my breast. I helped her latch on, but that was the last thing I remembered doing. At some point I opened my eyes a bit and half sleepily watched Jo lay the baby on the bed in front of me and change her diaper. At least that's what he was attempting to do. He was talking his way through it like a military drill. I smiled sleepily at him. That was cute.

And I must have thought it was good enough 'cause I drifted on back to sleep. When finally my body had enough rest to function again, it was some time in the middle of the night, early morning. I sat straight up in the bed at first panicked that I'd slept so long. And I knew I'd slept long because I actually felt rested.

Confused, I touched the ruby that lay between my breasts as I turned to look around the room and spotted Jo dressed in a pair of black silk pajama bottoms sitting in the little nook window with Ayana lying on the cushion in front of him. He was playing with her toes. Now I realized what woke me. It was Ayana laughing, her daddy was tickling her.

He looked up at me with a huge amazed smile on his face.

"She's laughing!" He said as if he could not believe it.

I slid out of bed looking for my dress, when I couldn't find it I just wrapped the sheet around me and approached them. Sure enough, she was looking up at her daddy, starstruck and laughing as he kissed her little toes. His beard and moustache were tickling her feet.

His beard and moustache left its mark on my body as well, but not in the same way.

I put my hand on his shoulder. "Thank you for looking after her while I slept." I laughed shakily. "I was so tired." He took my hand and gently kissed it.

"Don't thank me, baby. It's my duty to be here for you guys. I hate to see you so tired. I'm sorry I haven't been here till now." I shook my head.

"Naw, it's not your fault." I wanted to tell him it's his witch of a mother's fault, but he and I was not at that place. That was not my job. I was just his mistress in a one-year contract. It wasn't my place to get involved in his family drama. After my contract was over, I would go back to my own family.

"Can you look after her while I jump in the shower?"

He looked up at me with the, *what did I just say* face. I chuckled throwing up my hand that was not holding the sheet. "Okay, okay."

But no sooner had I gotten into the shower did Ayana start to fuss. Minutes later, Jo came in rocking a now screaming baby.

"I think she must have known her mommy was there and left. As soon as you walked away the smile disappeared and this look replaced it."

I looked at him through the shower glass and held my head back and laughed at the face he was making. I'll be doggone, that's the exact look she makes when she's irritated.

I pointed at him. "Now I know which parent she gets it from."

I made quick work in the shower. However, I was barely able to dry off because Ayana was raising the roof. When I came out the bathroom with a towel wrapped around me, it was to see poor Jo with a look of extreme distress as he paced the floor trying to calm her.

"I've fought in wars less stressful than this." He muttered as I took her out of his arms. Chuckling I sat on the bed opening my towel and as soon as she latched on, Jo fell back in the bed behind us exhausted.

"Wow! How in the world can something so tiny be so loud?" He muttered. Moments later, he was out.

After I finished feeding Ayana, I laughed out loud when I went to change her diaper. Poor Jo, he did the best he could. He got an A for effort. When I slid back into bed after getting the baby down, Jo wrapped his strong arm around me pulling me back so that I was tucked into the front of his big body. And surprisingly, I had no problem falling right back to sleep.

However, hours later I came awake with a gasp and a shutter…my body was racked with pleasure so intense it was almost painful. Clutching the covers in my palm I squeezed my eyes shut. I was seconds from coming apart. Jo was using his mouth on me in a way that was driving me wild.

"Jo!" I screamed as my world shattered, making me feel detached from my body. Before I could even come back to earth he was filling me and I was lost. He made love to me in a way that branded me. It was as if his touch was imprinting my body and it would forever be his. No man would ever be able to crack his code.

When finally he and I made our way out of bed, I was a bit uncertain of what our next step would be. What defined our relationship? Was it just sex? Was he something like a boyfriend? I pondered this as I showered and went through my morning routine. I guess the best thing to do would be to let him lead the way.

I stood in front of the bathroom mirror with a towel wrapped around me putting on my cocoa butter when he knocked on the door.

"Come in."

"Can I jump in the shower?" He asked peeking around the door.

I smiled at him. "Sure." And although he and I had just made love, I still blushed when he dropped his drawers and stepped in the shower. I watched him out the corner of my eye as I rubbed the little stick of cocoa butter over my arms.

Jo is a fine specimen of a man. His muscles flexed beautifully as he lifted his arms and washed his—

"I hope you don't mind I brought few items with me to leave here so that when I'm over here and I have to go to work, I don't have to run all the way home." I grinned shaking my head slightly.

"Of course I don't mind. Technically, this is your house." He stopped washing himself and looked at me through the glass door.

"Is that why you haven't bought any bedroom furniture? Because you see this as my house?"

"Umm—" I was at a loss as to how to answer his question. He's right; I hadn't bought any bedroom furniture. I tilted my head staring at him. Now that he mentioned it, I guess I had subconsciously not bought furniture for a room I didn't really consider mine.

He chuckled. "Good thing for you, I've done something I haven't done in over twenty years."

"Oh yeah? What's that?"

He began to rinse the soap off himself. "Take a vacation. Today you and I are going shopping for bedroom furniture, my love. This is your home, the sooner you begin to see it that way, the better."

I frowned slightly as I went back to rubbing the little stick in my palm so that I could rub my legs with cocoa butter.

"I mean, I do look at it as my home, for the time being." He stepped out the shower grabbing one of the towels off the stand.

"What do you mean time being?" He walked up to stand behind me looking at me through the mirror. I looked so small in front of his big powerful body.

"For the year. After our contract is over, I'm going back home." My words upset him, but he did a great job of not showing it. However, I could tell by the hard look in his eyes and the way that little muscle began to twitch in his cheek.

"Hmm," was all he said before he lowered his head and sniffed my shoulder and neck.

"What is this stuff you're rubbing into your skin? It's smell like chocolate butter."

I laughed. "That's 'cause it's cocoa butter."

He frowned at the little stick I held in my hand. "It comes in a stick?"

I nodded. "The good kind does."

He began to kiss me on my neck and my eyes drifted shut as my already thoroughly loved center hummed in anticipation of his touch.

"I like the way this cocoa butter smells." He whispered putting his hands on my waist turning me around so that I was facing him. His head was buried in my neck and he was open mouth kissing my throat. I wrapped my arms around his neck surrendering to him, knowing what was getting ready to happen. Jo's big hands came up to the front of my towel, opening it and letting it fall to the ground. And then he was lifting me up on the sink in front of him.

When he entered me, I cried out as a shiver ripped through my body feeling like it was cutting me in half. In minutes he had me panting and biting my lip to keep from screaming. He had never made love to me like this. It was hard and aggressive. I felt like I was one stroke away from shattering into little pieces. I lost feeling in my face and once again, there were tears coming from my eyes.

"I don't want you to leave me." He whispered as he took me with a force that pressed my back up against the mirror. I wrapped my legs tighter around his waist.

"Say you won't leave me, Journey." My toes curled as I bit my lip, trying not to explode, he was going to kill me, I was pretty sure I was about to die. It felt like it was too much, like my body couldn't handle it, like I was going to lose myself to never be found.

He took my chin in his hand bringing my face to his. His kiss was savage, it robbed me of my last ability to reason.

"Say it, Journey." He continued as he drove into me relentlessly.

"I'll never leave you." I gasped, really meaning it at that moment. Jo was master of my body. He could get me to agree to anything when he was doing the things that he was doing to it.

"Say it again." He growled as he increased his tempo.

"I'll never leave you!" I screamed as my world came apart. I clung to him whimpering, feeling as if I'd been fractured.

"Shh...I got you, baby; I'll never let you fall."

He held me close, calmly and gently bringing me back to this time and place after taking me somewhere with his love making I had never been before.

Chapter Seven

Weather the Storm

Joseph

Journey has cast a spell on me. I didn't even recognize myself. The more I discovered about her, the more I wanted to own her. And yeah, I know that sounds sick as f***, but I did. She was like this rare gift that was way too good for us mortal men. But yet, I somehow ended up with her within my grasp. And the more I got to know her, the more I didn't want to lose her.

After we got Ayana dressed and made our way to the kitchen to grab some breakfast, Journey walked to the fridge and after seeing the little pink post-it taped to it, hit her hand against her head.

"What is it?" I asked coming up behind her wrapping my arms around her waist pulling her into me, needing to feel her soft curves pressed up against me. I couldn't get enough of her. I had taken her several times this morning and already I wanted her again.

She pointed at the post-it that read: *Don't forget to take your pill.*

"I am horrible at remembering to take my birth control pills. If not for this little paper, I would forget I even had them. Hold on, I'll be right back."

She turned and jogged back up the stairs. I stared at that little paper before my eyes went to Ayana who sat in her little swing looking at me. I put my finger on my lips signaling for her to keep my next action a secret. Then I reached up and snatched the paper off the fridge, balled it up and then tossed it in the garbage.

And before you guys jump on my case for what I just did, let me remind you of what I just said.

JOURNEY HAS CAST A SPELL ON ME...

She was my woman, she should bear my children. Maybe if we gave Ayana a brother, their mother won't be so quick to try and leave me all the time. I went back upstairs to grab my wallet and came up short at the sight of her standing in front of her bathroom mirror with her hand over her head spraying something in the air. Holding her head back with her eyes closed she opened her arms and just stood there as whatever it was she sprayed rained down around her.

Once again, I found myself spellbound by her beauty as I walked towards her. Whatever she sprayed smelled like citrus.

"J, what are you doing?" I asked in a low voice, not wanting to frighten her.

She took a deep breath. "Taking a moment to just be."

After standing that way for a little while longer she turned to me and smiled.

"Ready?"

I studied her before I spoke. Everything about her seemed brighter. But it was her gaze that held me captive. She had the same look in her eyes she had when she opened them after an orgasm. What the hell did she just do to give her that feeling?

"Yeah, I think I am."

****

For the first time in my life I went shopping with a woman. I actually enjoyed myself. So much so I came to the realization that Journey was the only human being in my life right now that did not cause me stress, which was crazy because a few weeks ago she was the leading cause of my stress. But now that I had her back, it seemed as if I could breathe easy.

The entire day I struggled to understand this side of me that I was just meeting. This side of me that wanted to cuff a woman up. Hell, if I was being honest with myself, I've been this way for the last year. Why else had I not let her go?

I don't know why I spent nearly a year searching for her without cease. I don't know why her taste is the sweetest to ever touch my tongue. But I did know that my thoughts of her have become a huge complication. When she was just going to be my mistress for a year, things were fine. Now…

Now, things were complex. There is no way she would be out of my system in a year's time. I can't see myself ever getting tired of the feel of her. She felt like home to me.

Damn, complicated…

After we finished shopping for bedroom furniture I took them out to lunch. It was during lunch that I received the urgent call from my father's assistant saying my dad needed to see me right away. I exhaled wondering what the hell he's gotten himself into now. It was a full-time job making sure he kept his hands clean, especially since he didn't know how to keep his dick to himself.

"Hey, I'll be back a little later. I need to run by my father's office." I told Journey as I pulled up in front of the house.

A look of concern crossed her face. "Is everything okay?" Her question surprised me.

"Yeah, why do you ask?" Carefully I took the baby's car seat out and walked to the door using my key to open it.

"I don't know, your whole mood has changed." I chuckled, my girl was observant. My mood changed anytime I had to deal with my parents. I didn't hate them, but I can't say I loved them either. And I know that sounds horrible, but my family isn't the loving type. We didn't do things like that.

"Yeah, well my parents have that effect on me." I told her. And for the second time it seemed as if there was something she wanted to tell me but changed her mind.

Before I left, I pulled her to me and tasted those lips that have tempted me all day. She moaned in my mouth submitting in that sweet way that she does. And hell… the rest was history. I took her against the front door.

I tried to tell myself to be gentle with her, seeing as to how I had already taken her three times today, she had to be a little sore. But for the life of me, it was something about the feel of her warm heat stretching to accommodate my hardness that caused me to lose my ability to tame the beast.

After making her come apart twice in my arms, I left her sleeping on her couch. I prayed Ayana stayed asleep for a little while and give her mommy a chance to nap and regain her energy. She was going to need it when I got home.

Hmmm… Home…Damn this thing was getting extremely complicated.

****

"Great, it's an ambush." I muttered when I walked through my father's office door to see him and mother waiting for me.

"Joseph dear, how are you?" My mother asked from where she stood in front of the window looking out on Capitol Hill. My mother in all her illustrious elegance had dreams of becoming the next black first lady. But thanks to the many scandals my father has gotten himself involved in, must now settle for being the mother of a president.

I don't know who was driving this harder, her or my father, who was seeking to find his redemption in the eye of the people through me.

"I'm fine, mother. Why would you assume something was the matter?" I sat down in the chair across from my father.

"Quite naturally your mother was worried once we heard that you had put in for a vacation."

I chuckled shaking my head. "Me taking a vacation caused you to worry?" I waved away their answer, I was ready to get this over with, the longer I spent here, the less time I had with Journey.

105

"Gerald told me you needed to see me and that it was an emergency. What's happened now?"

"You left the convention really fast, we didn't even get a chance to say bye." My mother said coming to sit next to me with a counterfeit wounded expression on her face. I exhaled, in no mood for her theatrics.

"My job was done, I didn't see why I had to linger."

"Son, we were hoping you would officially announce your candidacy for the Florida Senate seat in the up and coming election." I didn't even blink.

"Why would I do that, seeing as to how I'm still undecided?" My mother collapsed back in her chair, always the over dramatic that one. My father growled.

"Dammit, Joseph! How can you say that this late in the game? Everything you've done in your life has prepared you for this moment. There are a lot of people depending on you—"

"Cut the sh*t," I said interrupting him. "You forget I was raised behind the scenes of this hypocritical astonishment called politics. When you say everybody is depending on me, who do you mean? Macon Cooperation and your other deep pocket investors, are they who you speak of? Yeah, I'm sure they are depending on our family, who for a few bucks will guarantee them impunity from all the lives they destroy."

My father, who was now red with anger opened his mouth to no doubt berate me for my words, but I continued to speak, not letting him.

"You forget father, that I know who really runs the show." I chuckled. "And it ain't the people."

My mother made a sound in her throat. "Ain't Joseph? Really? Please don't be crass. What has gotten into you?"

Leave it to her to find me speaking slang the only offense. God forbid I sound ethnic in any way.

"Perhaps it's his new mistress that he's set up in a little bungalow hidden from the prying eyes of his parents." My father sneered. I lifted my head to look at him, but my mother was not done with her theatrics.

"Please tell me it's not the little girl with the dreadlocks?" My father chuckled before he reached in his drawer and withdrew pictures, tossing them on the desk in front of us. I didn't reach for them, I could see them from where I sat. It was pictures of Journey and I out today. The picture on top showed me with my arm wrapped around her neck pulling her close so that I could whisper something indecent in her ear.

My mother reached for the pictures and looked at them all as if she was looking at a murder scene. I chuckled shaking my head again...My parents.

"Jo, what are you trying to do? Ruin your whole life? She has *dreadlocks* for Christ's sake!" The last my mother yelled as she slammed the pictures back on the desk.

"When were you going to bring our grandchild by so that we can meet her? Or had you planned on keeping your little secret family stashed away forever?" My father asked. I leaned back in the chair resting my head against it and rubbed my hands down my face.

Stress...

"Joseph, do you hear your father speaking to you?"

"Yes mother, I heard him."

"Well?"

I sat up. "I don't know, eventually." Both of my parents wore an expression on their faces as if I had slapped them.

"And what about Chloe?" My mother asked.

Sh*t, I had forgot about her.

Knowing I was cornered, a grin spread across my father's face. "How do you think your fiancée is taking the news of your new mistress? As we know, there is only a matter of time before she finds out."

As if to confirm my father's words, my phone vibrated at my hip. Sure enough, the screen read Chloe.

Damn! Chloe was easily forgotten. Our marriage, like most marriages of the elite had been arranged in a boardroom when she and I were in grade school. She had been raised to be a first lady. My mother adored her and my father gushed over her, but I could barely stand the sight of her. There was nothing spectacular about her. She wasn't a yellow dot in a sea of grey. She was just the grey.

"Alice, please give me a moment to talk with my son alone." My mother didn't like being dismissed, but with the air of a queen she nodded and quietly left the office. Once she was gone, my father stood and came to lean on his desk to the side of me.

"Listen son, man has had wife and mistress since the beginning of time. But now that there is a child involved, I worry that more of your feelings will get involved than what is wise."

"Don't worry, I have my feelings under control. I know what I have to do."

"Do you?" He reached back to pick up the pictures. "Because this looks like a man in love to me."

He held up a picture that showed me chasing a laughing Journey after she'd stolen the apple I was eating, then another of me catching her and scooping her up in my arms.

"If it was this easy for me to get these pictures, how much easier would it be for the media to get wind of this? You were very messy today, son, you can't let this happen again. You know more than anybody that there are always eyes watching us."

It was crazy having him give me this talk, when it was generally *me* getting him out of a sticky situation. My father fancied himself a lady's man and didn't see anything wrong with sampling all the ladies. I had one lady… And Chloe. And here he saw fit to give me this speech.

"How about you stop spying on me." I drawled.

My dad got up from his desk chuckling as he walked back around to his chair, he reached into the golden box on his desk and took out a cigar. He looked at me as he lit it, the flame reflected in his eyes for just a moment, making him look like the damn devil.

"I'm sorry, son, I can't do that. Too much has been invested in you." For a moment, he looked sad. "If only you knew how much. This thing is bigger than both you and I. You have been chosen to fill this position, your destiny has already been mapped out for you, and there is nothing either you or I can do to change it."

Journey

A sharp pain in my stomach woke me. I balled up on the couch clutching my stomach.

"Ahhh!" My period was coming. And judging by the cramps I was having, it was going to be a bad one.

Okay, so you guys remember when I told you how crazy my period can be? Well, I may have left out a few details. Sometimes I got cramps that felt worse than child birth. And I know because I've experienced them both.

I stumbled up the stairs to my bathroom and ran me a hot bath. Heat always helps. I soaked until I heard Ayana start to fuss. I didn't want to get out the tub, but I had no other choice. By the time I fed Ayana and got her changed and back into her crib, aunt Flo had made an appearance.

Miserably I crawled back into my bed, lifting the rose gold phone to shoot Jo a text.

Me: Hey Jo I am so sorry but I'm going to have to cancel our plans for tonight, something came up.

I put the phone on the bed next to me, but no sooner had I pulled the covers up over my head did it ring.

"Hello." I mumbled into the phone trying not to sound as miserable as I felt.

"What's the matter?" I closed my eyes as his deep voice washed over me. Jo was the kind of man that fixed things. So much so that when I heard his voice it tricked my brain into releasing endorphins to numb the pain in my stomach just a little.

"I don't feel good."

"I'm on my way—"

"No!" I cut him off, not wanting him to see me like this. "You can't come over."

"Why not?"

"Because, Jo!" I didn't mean to whine those words, but I was in misery.

"Because what, Journey? Talk to me, tell me what's going on."

I exhaled, in too much pain to argue. "I got my period. I'll call you when it's over."

I hung up the phone. The p word was like the plague to men. And since I couldn't fulfill my end of the contract right now, I didn't have to worry about Jo. I drifted off to sleep, but woke up when another sharp pain shot through my womb and up my spine.

"Ahhh!" I yelled balling up clutching my stomach.

"Baby, you alright?" Jo asked coming out of nowhere.

I was in too much pain to answer. My cramps came like contractions. If I could just bite down and bear the intense pain for a moment it will eventually slacken. Jo got up from the bed and disappeared. He came back with a cool towel that he pressed on my head.

"Oh! That feels good…" I muttered before I drifted back to sleep. When next I woke, it was to see an older white man peering down in my face. I frowned looking up at him wondering if I was dreaming. Reaching up I touched his face and snatched my hand back when he giggled.

"Ahhh!" I yelled sitting up in my bed.

"J, it's okay, this is Dr. Tiler. He came at my request." I turned to look at Jo, who sat in a chair by my bed feeding Ayana a bottle. I had shown him this morning how to thaw the breast milk I had frozen for her.

"Why is he here?" My gaze went back to the doctor that was wiping his stethoscope off with an alcohol pad.

"Take a deep breath for me." He said placing his warm hand on my back and his stethoscope to my chest. I took a deep breath, but my angry gaze went to Jo, who had the nerve to smile at me encouragingly.

"Well, because you scared the hell out of me earlier and I figured we needed a second opinion."

What the hell! Second opinion on what? Rather or not I got my period?

"Second opinion? I got my period, not cancer! I told you to stay away!"

"Again." The doctor said to me. I inhaled, but I was getting good and irritated.

"Sweetheart, that's why we have the doctor here, let's wait and see what he says."

This ni---

"Jo, I don't need no doctor to confirm I got my period!" I yelled him. He had the nerve to look startled.

"Calm down, J." Then he looked at the doctor. "Is it some kind of fever or something? Could that be what's causing the pain and the aggression?"

Oh, I was going to kill him!

The doctor asked me to lay back. I didn't lay back as much as I slammed back on the bed, good and upset. He squeezed my stomach a little.

"Does that hurt?"

"Yes!" I growled folding my arms across my chest.

"When was your last menstrual cycle?" The kook asked me. I rolled my eyes, unbelievable.

"I am on my period right now."

"Oh!" He said helping me back into a sitting position.

"It appears as if you're suffering from severe Endometriosis."

Jo frowned. "What exactly is that?"

"Severe menstrual cramps." The doctor told him matter of factly as he packed up his bag. He pulled out a note pad and made a list. When he was done he handed it to Jo.

"Go get those things on the list, and…" He scribbled something on a prescription pad. "Get these from the pharmacy and our little patient will be right as rain in no time." Jo laid the baby on the bed next to me so that he could show the doctor out.

As soon as he came back into the room I laid into him.

"A doctor, Jo?!" He held up his hands.

"Hey, you can't blame a brotha for wanting to play it safe. What was I to think? You woke up clutching your stomach screaming. Is that normal? Does that always happen?"

I exhaled laying back in the bed. My anger was gone. It was kind of sweet that he came to check on me anyway, although he knew I wouldn't be able to have sex with him.

"Yeah, it happens like this a lot. Sometimes it's not that bad." I chuckled. "Sometimes I don't get it at all."

"Okay, try to get some rest. Ayana and I are going to go out and get what's on this list." I stiffened. My baby has never been away from me. He must have seen the concern in my eyes because he came and sat down on the bed next to me.

"Do you think I'm going to hurt our child?" He asked softly as he reached up and slid the loc that had fallen into my face behind my ear. I shook my head.

"It's not that. It's just that this will be the first time she will be away from me."

"Would it make you feel better if I didn't take her?" For just a split moment, I saw Jo's vulnerability for the first-time since I've known him. He will be hurt if I didn't trust him with our daughter. I took his hand and kissed his knuckles that were so scarred up. It looked like they had been busted on more than one occasion.

"No, go ahead. You guys have fun, I'm going to sleep till you get back." He chuckled and leaned down and kissed me gently on my forehead. I smiled, I loved when he did that.

"Okay, we'll be back in no time."

Oh y'all, I got to know another side of Jo over the next few days. He was so sweet. He cooked for me and he ran baths for me.

He even held the hot water bag the doctor told him to get on my belly when my cramps got really bad. He dealt with the furniture delivery men when they came with the bedroom furniture.

Not only did I stay closed up in the house, he stayed with me. I was surprised that he didn't leave to go to work, but he said he was on vacation, so everything was cool. He rode out the storm with me. The whole time I was telling myself not to read more into it than what it was in order to protect my heart, but how could I not.

Seeing this sensitive side of Jo made me feel as if maybe I was in love with him. And that scared the heck out of me, because I know I was setting myself up for heartbreak.

The morning after my period had gone, I woke up in need to feel rejuvenated. Jo was sleeping in the bed next to me, so I gently slid out and grabbed his button up shirt that lay across the chair and put it on. Carefully I walked across the floor and up the stairs to my greenhouse.

After mixing my essential oil blend into my misters I stood in the center of the room as they began to gently mist me and my plants. The sun had just begun to kiss the sky and touch me with its warm glow. The sharp fragrance of citrus opened my lungs. I held my head back and I thanked the Most High.

I thanked him for his son.

I thanked him for creating me.

I thanked him for loving me.

I thanked him for gifting me with his breath.

I thanked him for never forgetting me.

I thanked him for my mind and my hands.

I thanked him for Ayana…

It was in the middle of me silently thanking him when I felt Jo come behind me and wrap his strong arms around me pulling me into his safe embrace. And together we stood as the mist gently sprayed us both.

And finally, I thanked the Heavenly Father for Jo…

Chapter Eight

The Warning

Journey

Over the next few weeks Jo and I fell into something of a pattern. I know he said at the beginning that he and I will have separate places, but he must have changed his mind. He was always over here. If he went home, it was just for a minute to grab more of his stuff. He was firmly integrated in my home and I didn't mind at all. I liked the pattern he and I had settled in.

We woke up in the morning and the three of us had breakfast together. He'll kiss us both on his way out. We'd text each other back and forward throughout the day if something awesome happened to us. He texted me a picture the other day of a man they had been after for insider trading or something like that, who had painted himself white and stood up against his wall with his eyes closed in an attempt to blend in to the wall and hide from Jo. Under the pic it said: *I can't make this stuff up*, with crying laughing faces.

When he came home from work he'd sometimes bring me flowers or jewelry. He's now taken to bringing me rare plants. I don't know how he comes across them, but I love them more than the jewelry.

"I've never met a woman that prefers plants over diamonds." He'll say.

"That's 'cause you never met a woman with eyes to see. The real treasure is flowing through the stem of this plant."

And because he makes me feel so good, I try and return the favor. So, I've started preparing meals for him that are ready when he comes home and I've even taken to bathing him. I prepare his bath with an essential oil blend that helps him to relax after a long day. And as I bathe him I tell him about my day and the amazing things Ayana did on that day.

It was during one of these baths that he gently grabbed my arm and looked into my eyes.

"How do you do it?" He asked. I frowned slightly confused.

"Do what?"

"You make me feel like a king." I smiled, his words more precious than gold. When he got out the bath he'll then lay me in the bed and make me feel like his queen.

It felt surreal. He and I began to experience baby firsts together. Like Ayana's first word believe it or not was dada. She said it one night while the three of us lay in bed watching a movie. Well at least we were trying to watch a movie. At almost five months Ayana was on the move, she scooted all over us seeming thrilled to have both of her parents with her. It was then she pulled herself up on Jo's chest and yelled dada to his face.

His mouth opened in surprise, you would have thought somebody had named him father of the century with the way he jumped out of the bed with her in his arms. He had me dying laughing as he did a little dance no man his size should ever do while chanting that he was our baby's favorite parent. I lay there a little salty because he and I had a little wager to see which parent she was going to call on first and I was sure it was going to be me. Anyway,

I don't feel too bad, I read an article that said the d sound was a lot easier for most babies to say, which is why most of the time, their first word is dada.

We even witnessed her pull up on the furniture for the first time, eat baby cereal for the first time, and even try to hold her spoon for the first time. And I'm not going to lie, it felt good to have somebody else that love her just as much as I do to share those moments with.

I said all that to say that I was helplessly in love with Jo. And no matter how I tried to tell myself I was all kinds of fools, I kept falling deeper and deeper in love. So much so that when he showed me he was the jealous type, I just brushed it off as a mishap. I would later find out that I should have paid more attention, but I'm getting ahead of myself in my tale.

Let me tell you guys about the first time it happened.

That week had been a busy week, I'd come home from the nursery that Monday to find my mom and Rome sitting in my living room.

"Oh, my goodness! How did yall get in here? I have a high-tech security system at the gate." Rome looked at me for a moment to gage whether or not I was serious, when he saw that I was he held his head back and barked with laughter. The jerk! All this time I'd been living with a hacker and didn't even notice it.

My mom didn't answer, she just got up and took Ayana out my arms.

"How is my grandbaby doing? Granny has missed you so much." She cooed as she began to take off her little jacket.

"I'm good mom, thanks for asking." After hearing the belligerence in my tone my mother finally acknowledged me.

She smiled. "That's wonderful, baby." But then all her focus was back on Ayana. "Grandma got to change your diaper, somebody wet." And then she was gone up the stairs.

Still standing there by the door in a bit of a shock to see them inside my home, I looked at Rome and gestured after our mother.

"I see yall have made yourselves comfortable."

He chuckled, coming to his feet to hug me. "Aww, don't worry 'bout that, little sista, you know we had to come check you out and make sure everything was okay."

I took my coat off eyeballing him. That was a bunch of crap. He wasn't the visiting type, he was the calling type.

"Mmmhhhmmm, so what's the *real* reason you came?" A smile appeared on his handsome face. The light brown eyes he'd inherited from our mother brightened.

"I need you to keep ma for a while. We got her things settled into that spare bedroom next to Ayana's."

"I'm not a child, son! I don't need a baby sitter!" My mom yelled down from upstairs.

"Why?" I asked him.

"Got a little situation I need to handle back at the house and I don't need ma nosing around in my business." I frowned.

"What kind of situation?"

"Rome got a hot babysitter!" My mom yelled down before he could even answer. I lifted an eyebrow looking at my brother with a smirk on my face.

"You've got a babysitter?" I could tell by his grin he was feeling whoever this was.

"Yeah, yo' boyfriend sent her after me." Something in his tone made me worry.

"Where is she?" I whispered, knowing my brother well. He grinned wickedly.

"Chained to my bed." He whispered back. My mouth dropped.

"Oh, my goodness, Rome! Are you crazy?!" I yelled. He snatched me to him putting his hand over my mouth.

"Would you shut yo' big mouth!"

"What has he done now?" My mother called from upstairs.

"Nothing, Ma!" I looked at him shaking my head. "Have you kidnapped this woman?" I whispered.

The grin on his face grew as he nodded.

"Dammit Rome, you breaking your contract." This made the grin disappear.

"Fu—" He began, but it was me who now covered his mouth. "F*** that contract and f*** that bastard fed that got my little sista knocked up. I got somen for that mutha f***a." I bit my lip. It pained me to see that my brother still hated Jo, especially now that I loved him.

"Rome, he ain't that bad." He shook his head.

"Naw, I see you done got comfortable with dude. But you don't know the stuff I know about him. He bogus as hell."

"What do you know?"

He looked at me for a minute before he just pulled me in for a one arm hug. "Don't worry about it shorty, your big brotha gon' handle everything. And on that note, I got to ride. Ma, I'll be back to get you in a few weeks." He called upstairs.

She came down the stairs with Ayana in her arms. "Okay, baby. Be careful."

Wrapping her free arm around him she hugged him, but then she pulled back just a bit and gently palmed his handsome face.

"Ms. Bonita is a beautiful woman, not just on the outside but on the inside as well. She just don't know it. Maybe my son can show her." He held his head down for a moment before he looked back up at her.

"How?" He asked so low I could barely hear him. My mother smiled.

"Tenderness, baby. Nobody has ever been gentle with her." Rome nodded and kissed my mother on the forehead.

Tenderness?

It was a little too late for that. Rome had the poor woman chained to his bed. I shook my head as he walked out the door. I couldn't believe he'd kidnapped a woman. Rome had girls and women alike throwing themselves at him and always had. Although he's my big brother and gets on my nerves a lot, I'll admit to the fact that he is quite handsome, both of my brothers are.

We stood in the door and watched him go. As soon as his rental disappeared out of sight, I turned and looked at my mom.

"Alright, woman! Spill! Who in the world is Ms. Bonita? And how in the heck did she catch Rome?"

Joseph

For the last two weeks I have been working from my office inside of my father's senate office. I wanted to make sure I had a smooth transition from retiring from the Bureau to working full time here. I was working on closing my last few cases and after that I would be finished with that chapter of my life.

I settled back in my chair. The time was soon approaching where I was going to have to decide what it is I was going to do, whether I was going to run for my father's senate seat or not. Don't get me wrong, I would love to be able to take the job to fight for the common man and to fight for all those without a voice. Ideally that's what's been sold when you think of a politician. But the fact was I knew the truth. I knew what was really happening behind the scene.

The people haven't put a politician in office since the days of Roosevelt, and yeah, they make it sound good, flash all the right lights, and play all the right commercials. But the fact remains, every political figure in office is just a puppet and the money that put them there is the puppet master. I've watched my father jump through hoops for as long as I can remember. He's never looked like a man to me, because there was always someone else controlling him.

The African-American community of the state of Florida put him in office in hopes that he can bring *change* to their suffering. That's how he ran his campaign; he jumped on the *Change* band wagon at the right time screaming, *Yes, We Can!*

Ha! What a damn joke!

My father can't do anything that Macon Cooperation won't allow. He was there damn mouth piece and now he wanted me to trade places with him and I just wasn't feeling it. A knock on my door brought me out of my head.

"Yes," I called picking up the file on the Turner case.

"Mr. Warren, there is a Rome here to see you, sir." I stared at my secretary surprised. I couldn't help the smile that came to my face.

"Send him in."

My secretary stepped to the side as Rome dressed in designer jeans, Jordan's and a white t-shirt walked through the door. Outside of the gold watch he wore on his wrist and the diamond stud in his ear, there was nothing on him that testified to the true wealth he possessed, way more wealth than any drug dealer whose file has ever crossed my path.

This was my first clue that he was involved in something way bigger than the dope game. Well, that and the fact that he had several Swiss bank accounts that were hidden so well my tech team barely found them.

He whistled as he came through the door looking around my office.

"Wow, look at you. I see you're being a good little boy and following in your daddy's shoes just like you've been trained to do. I'm sure he's so proud."

God, I hated this kid.

I sat back in my chair raising my arms to fold my hands behind my head. The smile was still on my face.

"And I see you've finally grew a pair of balls and ventured out of your *hood*. Didn't think the *gangstas* ever did that."

He wasn't ruffled in the least as he sat down in the chair across from my desk slouching a bit. I shook my head.

"How have you been enjoying my sista, chump?"

"Just fine, thanks for asking." There was the anger... it flashed swiftly in his eyes before he got it under control.

"I got an interesting visitor the other day. Claims she's from your office. Said you sent her to keep an eye on me."

I didn't twitch a nerve. Another thing I learned about this kid is yes, he looked dumb as a bag of rocks, your everyday average hoodlum. But he wasn't, this little f***er's brain will probably end up in a museum after he dies.

"And?"

He grinned at my answer. The bastard.

"And I just come by to say thank you." My eyebrow rose.

"What are you thanking me for?" He settled back in his chair.

"Well chump, it's been a long time since another human has entertained me. And your Ms. Bonita is very entertaining. I look forward to exploring her gifts a little further."

I dropped my arms from my head and sat up straighter in my seat. If this bastard has done anything to hurt Nak I was going to kill him.

"What have you done?"

He lifted a finger in the air. "Oh! Don't you worry about your spy. She is no longer your concern. However, you have bigger issues to deal with like James Bennet Law."

I frowned. What the hell was he talking about?

"Never heard of him."

Resting his elbows on the arm of the chair he crossed his fingers in front of his month.

"Hmmm…" He said looking thoughtful. "That's interesting because he knew you

very well."

"Where did he know me from?"

He tapped his lip with his index finger. "I don't quite know yet. The picture is

slowly coming together. But what a picture it's proving to be. Ah! Well." He said coming to his feet.

"It appears as if you, my not so good friend, have a homework assignment. Let's see if those imbeciles the FBI call their tech team can figure it out." He began to walk towards the door.

"Tick-Tock, Joey boy, the race is on. You'd better find out who James Bennet Law is before I do. Once I get the information I need, I'm going to use it to destroy you and your reprobate of a father's career." He smiled. "I told you, you had a problem on your hand."

I balled up my fist as I watched him quietly shut the door behind him.

Never in my life have I wanted to kill a man more than my woman's brother.

I opened my laptop that I used when dealing with only my team and sure enough, I had a message from Nak.

Clicking on the link I settled back in my chair as her beautiful face appeared on the screen.

"Hey, boss..." She said as she tied her boot, she sounded tired. I felt horrible for pulling her from one assignment and putting her right on another without giving her a chance to rest, but I had no other choice. Rome has been digging and he hasn't been quiet about it. I need to know what information he has found so that I can do damage control before the f***er tries to go public with any of it.

"You were right about this Rome kid. He's really smart. He's not buying the baby-sitting story. The only way I'm going to be able to get your information is if I allow myself to be caught. Don't worry, he's attracted to me, so this should prove to be interesting. I'm going to be off grid for a little while. I'll send you the files when I have them." She powered off.

I smiled, his little parting threat inconsequential.

He didn't realize he's taken in the Black Widow. She was going to destroy the bastard from the inside before he knew what the hell hit him. Knowing that she was in, I was able to breathe a little easier. However, I still found myself typing James Bennet Law in my search box.

Journey

I was so nervous about what Jo was going to say when he came home and found my mother here.

"Stop chewing on you lip, Journey. He's going to be alright with having me here for a few weeks. You're worrying for nothing." My mother said as she chopped red onion for her pot on the stove.

I didn't know what he was going to say, but I was glad to have my mommy here. I had only just gotten her back before Jo showed up to take Ayana and me away. And it felt good to have a pro around to give me advice and show me how to do some mommy things that I still haven't quite grasped.

Not to mention my mom was the world's best cook. She enjoyed cooking and told me when I was younger that the kitchen was her comfort zone. And guess what? She loved my kitchen and had already made out a grocery list for all the goodies she was going to make us.

And like any sibling, I loved when I had my mother to myself.

"Wow! What smells so good?" Jo said as soon as he opened the front door. I smiled when his deep voice washed over me and just like every other day, I realized how much I missed him. I ran to him and jumped into his waiting arms. Then I gave him a kiss before telling him how much I missed my man.

I loved the way he looked at me. "Hey, beautiful."

I smiled down at him. "Hey back at you, my king. How was your day?"

He exhaled as the smile left his face. Slowly he let my feet slide to the ground. "It was great till the pain in my as—" his words stalled suddenly as he looked up toward the kitchen.

"Mrs. Reevers, how are you?"

"Jo, I pray you don't mind if my mom stays with us for a few weeks." He smiled genuinely. Not like a politician, but like a human. I exhaled in relief.

"Of course not. I was hoping she and I could start over, so that I can show her I'm not the jerk she first met."

My mother returned his smile and then surprised me by opening her arms to him.

"Come on over here and give me a hug, son."

Seeing my mom and my man hugging was the most beautiful sight. Let me tell yall, if I worried that Jo was going to have a hard time with her being here, I shouldn't have. Over the next week my mom began to spoil him in only the way a parent could and he shamelessly sucked it all up.

She cooked for him and Jo discovered he loved soul food. I couldn't believe him when he said he didn't eat it growing up. What kind of black people in America didn't eat soul food? Apparently the rich ones.

Well, my mother didn't have a problem making up for all the times he'd lost and he didn't have a problem accepting it. He began to bring us both home flowers from work. It wasn't long before my mom was singing praises to her boy Jo and of course, Rome was not happy to hear that. Whenever he talked to mom on the phone and she told him about something amazing Jo had done, Rome would balk and change the subject.

I thought now that my mother was here, Jo would stop spending the night as much, but he hadn't. Just like before, he was here every night. Now we shared the adventure of trying to keep our loving making quiet, so she won't hear.

Okay, so I told you guys I was going to tell you what happened the day I discovered Jo was the jealous type. This first incident was quite mild compared to the second, but once again I'm getting ahead of myself...Let me tell you what happened first.

My mom had been here for about a week and I needed to make a run to the nursery, so I decided it was a perfect day for me to show her around D.C. I'd called Albert to see if he wouldn't mind driving us and of course, Albert showed up in true Albert fashion.

"Wow! It's been a long time since my eyes have seen beautiful?" He stared at my mother as if she was truly the most beautiful sight he'd seen in a while. Pulling his hat off his head he held it pressed to his chest. My mom, who was coming out the kitchen at the time looked up startled because she had not heard him come in.

Albert stopped knocking weeks ago.

"Albert, this is my mom, Abigale Reevers." I said coming down the stairs with Ayana in my arms. Chuckling, I just realized how similar their names were.

He walked towards her as if in a trance, holding his hand out for her's. "With eyes like that, maybe I'll call you... Abbycat."

I rolled my eyes at his corny rhyme referencing my mom's light brown eyes. But would you know she cheesed as if she was a school girl. I tilted my head looking at old Albert. I guess he wasn't bad looking. You can see that in his day he was the Billy Dee Williams smooth type. So now, he was the retired Billy Dee Williams smooth type.

Hmmm, this was going to prove interesting.

That whole day Albert had both my mother and I in tears. He was so funny. And yes, he went out his way to impress my mom.

She was so flattered by his attention that most of the day her cheeks were flushed.

Goodness, if Rome was here to witness this, he would no doubt try to murder poor Albert.

It was when we had stopped for lunch that I ended up running into my old roommate Michelle and she was not alone. She was with none other than Kyle and his cousin Ben, who Michelle had been flirting with on and off for some time now.

"Oh My God, Journey! That is you!" She called across the restaurant, scaring me to death.

"Well, isn't she a loud one." My mother muttered to my right.

I put a smile on my face, although I must admit to not being that happy to see Michelle. Remember, I still blamed her for what had happened to me. Had I not listened to her, I would have never gotten into this mess in the first place.

And to top it off, she was with Kyle, definitely not a pressure I needed right now. I couldn't help the moan of despair that escaped my lips when I saw him and Ben start to head my way with her.

"Hey, Michelle, how are you?" I got up to hug her, trying to avoid making eye contact with Kyle. When we pulled back she had a fake pout on her face.

"Not good. My best friend has been here for almost three months and she has not come to see me once. Had it not been for Kyle I would have never known you were here at all. Not to mention the fact you had a baby and didn't tell me. That is no way for besties to act!"

Besties? Since when have we been besties? I didn't know how to respond to that, so I turned around and gestured toward my mom and Ayana, who was sitting up in a high chair watching us all with wide eyes.

"Michelle, let me introduce you to my mom and daughter. And this here," I gestured towards Albert. "Is a very dear friend of the family, Albert." I refused to call him my driver.

As they were getting acquainted, Kyle made his way to my side. I tried to scoot over as close to Michelle as I could get, but it wasn't close enough.

"Hey Journey, I haven't seen you around lately. Is everything alright?"

Fake smile back on my face, I looked up at him.

"Sure Kyle, everything is fine. Here, let me introduce you to my mom." And once again, I was granted a little reprieve as Albert took control of the conversation in only the way Albert could. However, my irritation rose once again when Michelle invited her little group to join us for lunch.

I went to shake my head, but my mother elbowed me in the side.

"Don't be rude, sweetheart." She muttered through her smile without moving her lips.

So, our party grew from four to seven. Lunch wasn't so bad. But I couldn't help but look over my shoulder remembering what Jo's mom had told me about him having eyes everywhere. Although technically, I didn't have anything to worry about seeing as to how there was nothing going on between Kyle and I.

The problem was *Kyle* didn't seem to know that and his body language screamed that there was something going on between us. To anybody looking, it seemed that the three of us were on a triple date. Albert sat next to my mom, who sat to the right of me. And Michelle slid in next to Ben, it seemed that they had taken their relationship further since I've been gone. And instead of Kyle sitting next to Ben, what did he do? You guessed it, slid on my other side, which made my mom and Albert have to reposition themselves so that I could have Ayana at one of my sides.

Okay, now if that wasn't irritating enough, he put his arm on the back of my seat and leaned into me.

Great! He would pick now to be assertive.

And yall, he was being so assertive that several times Albert and I exchanged looks. There was actual concern in Albert's eyes and even he began to look around with me, no doubt having the same thoughts I was having, that Jo was going to pop up any minute.

I breathed a sigh of relief when the waitress brought our check. So ready was I to go, I put my credit card on the tray and told everyone that lunch was my treat. Then I began to put Ayana's jacket on.

"Ben, you don't mind if we stop over at Journey's house on the way in, do you?" Michelle cooed giving Ben goo-goo eyes. "I have to see her new place for myself, it sounds amazing."

MUTHA F****!

I held my breath wondering if I had yelled that out loud or just in my head. When I didn't see anybody turn to look at me appalled, I exhaled.

I was so screwed.

Chapter Nine

The Damn Poet

Joseph

That bastard Rome hacked my damn personal computer. It was a subtle strike, barely a caress. Had it not been for Tyler, the head of my tech team who noticed the slight glitch, we would have never known he'd been there at all. Apparently when he had come to visit my office the other day, he had some kind of transmitter on him that barreled into my system.

Thus, the reason for the surprise visit. The little sh*t had stayed long enough for his little burrower to find a weak spot in my structure and connect. Tyler was amazed with the technology. He was even more astounded by the fact that it had to have been something Rome designed himself, because there was nothing like it on the market or behind the scenes.

We have been spending all week changing out codes and protecting everything. Our office has vital information that if landed in the wrong hands could make major waves for our investors. It irked me beyond means that Tyler couldn't tell me exactly what Rome had touched. If I didn't know he was as good as destroyed, I would be dispatching a different kind of team to his case, setting aside the money to buy Mrs. Reevers and Journcy those black dresses.

Needless to say, I was exhausted. So, you can imagine my aggravation when I pulled up to Journey's to see the extra vehicles parked in front. I turned my car off and sat there staring at them for a minute. Rubbing my hand frustratingly down my face, I exhaled.

The only thing I wanted to do was sit down and eat whatever delicacy Mrs. Reevers put on the table in front of me, kiss Ayana's fat cheeks till she screeched, and then pull Ayana's mama under the cover and make love to her till she screams. Was that too much to f***en ask for?

Letting myself in the front door I smiled when my presence made the conversation in the living room and the kitchen come to a halt. I recognized Journey's old roommate, but the man with her I didn't know.

"Jo my boy, how was work?" The nervous energy in Albert's voice caused me to raise an eyebrow in question. He and Mrs. Reevers both shot concerned glances towards the stairs.

Hmmm…

"Work was work old man… how is everyone doing this evening?" I addressed the room as I leaned down to kiss Mrs. Reevers' cheek.

"Wow! Journey didn't tell me you were the mystery man she was hiding over here in her little love nest." Michelle spoke up as she sashayed over to stand in front of me.

I almost shook my head. This woman was shameless, I was ecstatic her internship with my father was over. She looked up at me now with the same flirty eyes she'd had when she worked there.

"Mr. Warren—" she purred, but I interrupted her.

"Please we're not at work, call me Jo." She grinned as if I had just gifted her a million dollars.

"Jo…allow me to introduce you to a really good friend of mine, Ben."

Her really good friend hurried towards me with a huge star struck smile on his face. Damn, I was too tired for this. Shaking his hand I turned my head to look around for Journey, needing to feel her in my arms.

"Please to meet you, Ben." The smile on his face grew to the point I feared his cheeks may break; his hands shook with his nervousness.

"Wow! May I say the honor is all mine, sir." He went into his spill about he and I belonging to the same fraternity before attempting to impress me with how well he knew my resumé. But I'd already tuned him out as Albert handed me a glass of whiskey.

"Where's Journey?" I asked the room when Ben here paused for breath.

"Let me go get her!" Mrs. Reevers said jumping up from her chair. I put my hand on her shoulder stopping her.

"No, that's okay, I was heading up anyway." I told her before turning to look at the other occupants in the room.

"If you guys will excuse me."

Before I turned to leave, Albert and Mrs. Reevers shared one more concerned look with each other. I took a sip of my drink.

Hmmm…I had a strange feeling I was getting ready to be upset. After I looked in on my beautiful baby sleeping in her crib, I found out just how upset I was getting ready to be. When I didn't see Journey in the bedroom I went up to the greenhouse. And what did I find?

My girl and another man with their heads nearly touching as they stared down into the dirt of one of her plants. Now that alone is no big deal. But the fact that he stood with his arm around her shoulders was going to get him hurt.

Badly…

I turned my glass up and drained my drink. Old Albert may have just saved this man's life. My eyes narrowed when he reached his hand up and gently touched Journey's locs, bringing one up to sniff it, all without her knowing.

Then again, maybe not.

Journey

The sound of a glass being set down rather roughly caused me to jump. Kyle and I both turned toward the door to see a smiling Jo standing there looking so very handsome in his suit. Goodness, this man could have a very successful career as a model if he so chooses.

"There you are." He said opening his arms to me.

Not being able to resist his pull I went to him and hugged him, closing my eyes for just a moment to savor the feel of his strong arms wrapped around me. He smelled so good. Then he looked down at me in that way that he does when he comes from work, as if his eyes were starved to take me in, like he can't relax until he sees me. This look of his caused everything else to fade to black. In that moment, it was just he and I.

"Hey, beautiful." He whispered.

I smiled. "Hey, my King, how was work?"

"Outside having some computer issues, not too bad." I frowned slightly.

"It would be nice if you and Rome got along better. He could probably help you. He always fixed our computers when they started acting up." Jo chuckled before he gently swept my loc out of my face and behind my ear.

"You are probably right. Too bad indeed. How was your day?" The sound of Kyle clearing his throat behind us caused the room to abruptly come back into focus.

"Wow, how rude was I? I'm so sorry about that. Kyle, this is Jo—"

"I know exactly who he is." Kyle interrupted me as he shot daggers at Jo. The hostility in his voice was shocking. "But I have to admit being surprised to see him here with you." I frowned.

"What do you mean—"

"Kale, is it?" Jo asked cutting me off as he reached out his hand to Kyle.

Wait, did he just call him Kale?

"Kyle." My friend who was now clearly insulted muttered, taking Jo's hand in a not so friendly handshake. The energy in here was not right. "You don't remember me."

With that politician grin on his face, Jo blinked at Kyle as if he was insignificant.

"And why would I remember you?"

"My father owns Executive Delights Catering." Jo's eyebrows lifted in recognition of the company. "As you know we cater some of your parents' events as well as many events for Chloe Anderson's family."

Jo's eyes harden. Who in the world was Chloe Anderson?

"Who's Chloe-" I began, but Jo cut me off.

"Sweetheart, why don't you go and check on our other guests while Kale and I have a little chat?"

"Jo, his name is *Kyle*." I softly admonished. I couldn't believe he was acting like this. He smiled.

"Oh, right...Kyle."

I was not buying that he couldn't remember that. And now he wanted me to leave him and Kyle to talk alone. There was a dangerous energy about Jo right now. I eyeballed him, not sure me leaving was a good idea.

"Why don't we all go check on the others?" I asked him in a hesitant voice.

His hand caressed my hair until it got to the back of my head. He gently took my locs in his fist, guiding my head to him until he had access to my lips. He kissed me in a way that made me forget Kyle was standing there watching. I moaned balling up the front of his shirt in my fist the same way he was doing my hair. The kiss was mind numbing.

He wrapped his other arm around my waist pulling my body flush against his as he scandalously sucked on my bottom lip before his tongue was invading my mouth again. Kyle who? By the time he pulled back from me, I only had one thing on the mind, the flush in my cheeks testified of it.

At this point, I was too embarrassed to look back at Kyle.

"Go ahead, baby, we'll be down in a minute." Jo whispered as he gently touched his lips to mine again. I nodded and quickly left the room. Oh man, that was savage what he'd just done in front of Kyle, and I was savage for participating in it.

Joseph

A wise man thinks before he acts. He deliberates the consequences of his actions. He knows that the feeling of rage doesn't last and eventually the sound mind will return. Seeing this Kale guy smell Journey's hair nearly blinded me with rage. It took all my years of practicing to control it to keep from ripping his damn throat out.

And now he stood before me with his chest inflated, working up the courage to try me.

"You know when I saw her with that baby I never would have imagined in a million years that it was yours."

I bit down on my teeth. Hearing him call my beautiful baby girl that baby, like she was an it made the rage inside of me rev to life. This guy wanted Journey, but didn't want to have nothing to do with Ayana.

"Does Journey know about your fianc—"

"You say her name one more time and so help me God, I will break your neck." I didn't yell my threat, as a matter a fact, my voice was barely over a whisper. I took a step closer to him. The polished refined Joseph had melted away and what was hidden underneath stood in its place.

"If I see you anywhere near her, I will make you disappear. Do you understand me?"

He sized me up, surprised at the change in me. I could see the wheels turning in his head as he pondered whether or not Journey was worth the risk. He flexed his fists. I smiled praying he gave me the slightest excuse to let go of what was bottled up inside me.

"She's a good girl." He muttered. Some of the heat had left his voice. "She doesn't deserve the kind of life you are getting ready to put her through." Wisely he didn't say her name, but foolishly he continued. "Since you in all sense and purposes already have a wife, then that means you've made a queen…your whore." He shook his head looking down at my boots.

"Maybe that's worth going to war for. I would never make her my whore. Not ever!"

All this he said without looking up at me. I almost laughed. He was the poetic kind of brotha. He made sh*t sound good, but he didn't have the balls to keep a *queen* as he said. Journey would run circles around this guy. Have him somewhere heartbroken and crying in his bed as he hugged the teddy bear he'd won her at the carnival.

"Trust me, Kale, you and your catering family ain't ready to go to war with me. But that's exactly what's going to happen if you so much as speak a word to Journey again. She is my most valuable treasure and I will kill you and anybody else who tries to change that." I took a step closer to him, because he still had it in him to fight for what is mine.

"Trust me! Think about all you stand to lose." I shook my head, pleading with him with my eyes. I needed him to know that unlike him, I wasn't reciting poetry, I meant every word I was about to say to him.

"You don't understand. The thought of you touching her...kissing her, f*cking—" My words came to a halt as I gritted my teeth fighting the urge to kill this man where he stood.

I balled up my fist. "I will never stop hunting you. I will never stop hunting your family. I will tie you all up so that you're hugging each other, douse you in gasoline and then light a match. As your parents burn to death you can look in their eye and know that this all happened because you chose to trespass in another man's garden, and the penalty for that was death."

He blinked at me waiting for me to show the slightest hint that I was joking. But I wasn't. Every word that I said to him was true. Welcome to my mind...

"Buu—but your father is a senator?" My frown deepened.

"And his son is a killer. Check my record. I will ghost your ass and not lose any sleep. Before I put on this suit, that's what I did for a living. Guess what, Kale boy. I'm good at it."

I saw when he made the connection and realized I spoke the truth.

"Now listen closely, because this is what I want you to do. You are to walk down these stairs and get the f*** out of my house. Don't look to the left or the right. Just down the stairs and out the door. You speak to Journey again and I'm going to make your face look like ground beef. And that's my word."

Wisely he didn't turn his back on me as he stumbled out the greenhouse and down the stairs. Like a good boy he walked out the front door without looking back. F**king poet!

Journey and Michelle rushed to the living room.

"Oh my God, Jo, what did you do?" She cried going to the window to look out.

I shrugged. "Kale realized he had somewhere else to be." I pulled her away from the window wrapping my arm around her waist, I didn't even want her looking out the window at that mutha f****. She twisted around in my arms to look up in my face trying to read me. I smiled down at her, bringing my finger up to gently rub her brow.

"Stop frowning, beautiful. He and I just came to a gentlemen's agreement, that's all."

"Was that Kyle that left out the door?" Ben asked hurrying out of the kitchen. He and Michelle grabbed their coats as well as Kale's from the coat rack.

"It was really nice meeting you in person. I hope we can get together some time and have lunch." He said coming to shake my hand.

"Absolutely, just call my secretary and she'll let you know what my schedule is like." He smiled big as he hurried out the door behind the frightened poet.

Michelle, still eyeballing me gave Journey a hug. "I'll call you a little later." She told my lady before they shared a look. I chuckled. Journey wanted her to find out what happened with Kale and I.

When they were gone, I clapped my hands together turning to face my sweet little mother-in-law with a smile on my face.

"Mmmm…something smells mouthwatering?"

Journey

The three of us stared at Jo as he went to take a seat at the kitchen table. Me in horror, my mom in wonder, and Albert with a proud smirk on his face. As if to prove how he felt, he walk to Jo and patted his shoulder.

"That's my boy!" He muttered before he took a seat in the chair opposite his.

Slowly my mother's eyes came to mine. She now wore something of a smirk on her face as well, shrugging she went into the kitchen and informed the fellas dinner would be ready shortly. I still stood by the door looking like, *what the hell just happened?*

Jo looked at me from where he sat at the kitchen table. He tried to hide what he really was, but one's eyes always told the truth. A killer looked back at me through Jo's eyes. He grinned then and nodded slightly as if he could hear my thoughts.

"Come over here, baby and have a seat, you've had a long day." He said as he patted the chair next to him.

As I eased down into the chair, I kept a wary eye on him. I know that Kyle is not the toughest guy on the block, but he's not the tuck tail and run type either. So, what the world could Jo have said or done to him to make him tuck tail and run?

After dinner, Jo walked Albert out to his car while I helped my mom with the dishes. She and I quietly discussed what happened and she surprised me by saying she was glad Jo did what he did.

"Mom!" I admonished. She waved that away.

"Don't mom me. I don't like that Kale guy."

I rolled my eyes. "*Kyle*...his name is Kyle."

"I don't care what his name is. I don't like him. He doesn't like Ayana."

"How do you know that?"

"I can tell. He never looked at her. And at the restaurant, he sat on the bench between you and her. Everybody knows that you don't sit between a baby and their mother at a restaurant. Some men can't deal with other men's children and he's one of them."

Hmmm... I didn't even think about that. I played over his actions tonight and yeah, my mom was right, he'd never looked at her, touched her, or even talked to her for that matter.

Wow...

"Still, that doesn't give Joseph the right to be a caveman."

She swatted me with the dish towel. "Hush now, he was protecting his family. He has a right to do that."

Jo had a champion in my mom, I on the other hand continued to give him the side eye as he and I retired to our bedroom.

"Oh, come on now J, how long you going to give me the I-killed-your-dog look?" He said as he settled back in the bed in only his pajama bottoms looking like a yummy piece of chocolate.

I stood at the sink brushing my teeth. When I was done I slowly walked to the bed.

"Tell me what you said to Kyle." This was my fourth time asking.

He exhaled. "Okay, come here and I'll tell you what I said."

I shook my head. The grin on his face let me know that if I came to him, it would be over, he had seduction on his mind.

"How about you stay there and I stand here, and you tell me."

He chuckled shaking his head. "If you want to know what I told him, you'll have to come here, non-negotiable." He reached out his hand to me.

Against my better judgment I took it. "Okay, tell me." I said as he brought me down to lie next to him. For a while he didn't speak, he just stared down at me from where he leaned on his elbow. Very gently he moved my loc out of my face.

"I told him you are my most valuable treasure. And for you I'll do anything." I was drowning in his eyes as he whispered his words to me.

"If it's poets that you like, then for you I'll recite poetry." He made a showing of clearing his throat. I couldn't help but grin. Jo was no poet.

"Roses are red. Journey's in my bed. Why are we talking about Kale, when we can be making love instead?"

See what I mean? I cried laughing at his proud look. He was really pleased with himself, like he was amazed he actually did it.

"Will you look at that?" he said stunned. "I am a damn poet after all."

So, okay, Jo made me forget all about Kale—I mean Kyle, that night. Geesh! His bad habits are rubbing off on me. But first thing the next morning, I was on the phone with Michelle.

"Girl, I don't know what happened. When we caught up with Kyle, he was half way home. He got in the car and didn't speak to either of us. I tried to pull some info out him, nothing. He just said he didn't want to talk about it."

"Wow!" Was all I could say.

"I think Jo hurt his manly pride." Michelle purred.

Yeah, I do too.

Anyway, Jo continued to be absolutely amazing and I forgot all about what my mother and I had taken to calling the Kyle incident. My mom, who was only supposed to stay for a couple weeks ended up staying for a couple of months. Neither Jo nor I was complaining. My mom was awesome, people loved her. But I suspected she was still here because of one driver named Albert.

I think it was safe to say they were officially dating. If Albert wasn't over here, then it was because he was taking her on a drive around town. The other day, he took her out to the movies and dinner. She came in glowing and laughing. It had been a while since I saw her looking that way, well before my father passed away.

She and I both agreed that it was best that we didn't tell Rome. My brother would not take the news well. He believed it was okay for him and Rob to be with as many women as they liked, but growled whenever a man so much as looked at me or my mom. He was such a hypocrite.

Now do you guys remember when I told you I should have paid more attention to Jo's interaction with Kyle? Remember when I told you the first situation was very mild compared to the second? Okay, well, let's just say the happy bubble I was living in with Jo burst and it didn't burst neatly. There was pain and yes, blood. I would soon find out that Jo was nothing like the man that was being sold to the public. When that agent had told me way back in Chicago that they had put a suit on a goon, you guys have no idea how true that statement would prove to be.

From this point on, the rest of my story is going to be a bit of a whirlwind. So, I'm going to warn you guys now to hold on, it's getting ready to be a bumpy ride. A ride that all begun with a surprise visit from Alice Warren.

I was in my greenhouse transplanting some avocado seedlings to bigger pots when my mom called me downstairs. Using a towel to wipe some of the dirt off my hands as I came down, I came to a complete halt when I saw Jo's mom sitting on my couch.

"You have a visitor, honey." My mom said coming from the kitchen with a teacup for Alice. "Here you go, dear, I added honey instead of sugar."

Alice took the cup smiling kindly. "Thank you."

I stood there as my mind scrabbled to find a way to deal with this situation. I wanted to tell her to get the hell out of my house, but had to remember that this was Joseph's mother and although he didn't talk about her much, probably really loved her. I was so glad I had laid Ayana down for a nap.

"Why are you here?"

My mother jerked her head to stare at me surprised at my greeting. I'd never told her about my encounter with Alice. She didn't know it was her fault all that drama took place back at the house. Alice smiled at me a little nervous.

"I've come to apologize." Now it was my turn to be shocked. I sat down on the couch next to my mom and just stared at her with my mouth slightly agape.

She chuckled as she placed her cup on the table after taking a sip. "I didn't know that Joseph loved you. I thought—" her words died off as she shook her head.

"It doesn't matter what I thought. It was foolish. I've come because my husband and I want to be apart of Ayana's life. We want to be apart of yours, if you will have us?" She spoke hesitantly, as if she feared I would reject her.

I was astonished. I didn't know what to say. I turned to look at my mom, who was watching Alice, I'm sure now wondering what the woman was talking about. However, I couldn't get past the fact that she said Joseph loved me. Although he never told me that, could he have told his mom? My heart swelled so full it felt as if it was going to burst. Tears came to my eyes as I nodded my head.

"I would like that very much." I told her.

She smiled. "Oh wonderful, I was so afraid you were going to say no. Of course, it would be no more than I deserve." The relief was evident in her voice.

"We're having a casual little dinner party for Jo at the house tonight to celebrate his retirement from the Bureau, and it would be an honor if you would attend. It's just going to be a few friends, nothing fancy. So, you don't have to rush out to buy anything elaborate, I'm sure whatever you have in your closet will do just fine."

Smiling, I nodded, thrilled that Jo's mom was inviting me to their home. Jo has not even taken me back to his place. I mean, sure, he was always over here, but still, I was beginning to feel like he was hiding me or something.

"I would love to come."

"Wonderful," she said standing. "I will send my driver for you at around eight o'clock, is that alright?"

I nodded. "That will be perfect."

"It was very nice meeting you." She told my mom, who now wore a look of doubt on her face.

"I'll see you tonight, Journey."

"Can't wait." I told her, showing her to the door.

"I don't like her." My mom said as soon as it closed. I was so happy my mother's words didn't bother me none.

Jo's parents had finally accepted me and Ayana. I was so worried about what I would tell her when she finally asked about her grandparents.

"Oh, come on mama, mama…" I sang as I did a little dance around her. "You don't like Kyle, you don't like Alice…Who *do* you like?"

She frowned at me crossing her arms. "What did she do to you that she had to apologize for?"

No way was I telling her all the details. If she knew what Alice had done, she would be dead set against me going anywhere near her or her husband.

"She thought I was too young for her son and she told me so." My mother looked at me skeptically. I bit my bottom lip. I really hated lying to her.

"Why are you lying, Journey?"

I exhaled. "I'm not! Now will you help me find something to wear?"

Chapter Ten

Shattered

What happens to a dream deferred? Does it dry up like a raisin in the sun? Or fester like a sore, then run? Does it stink like rotten meat? Or crust and sugar over like a syrupy sweet? Maybe it sags like a heavy load. *Or does it explode?*

--Langston Hughes

Journey

In all my life I have never experienced pain like this. For just a moment I thought that maybe I was going to die from the feel of my heart shattering. I once read a poem by Langston Hughes that asked the question: *What happens to a dream deferred?*

I reckon that everybody's answer to that question would be different. But I can tell you what happened to me when my dreams came crashing down to taunt me for being dumb enough to believe in the impossible.

Once again, Alice had played me for a fool. She was the very essence of pure unadulterated evil. The small casual dinner party turned out to be the event of the season. At least that's how the papers described it. The few friends and family she said would be attending turned out to be dignitaries, movies stars, *the Obama's,* and even a royal or two.

She told me that I didn't have to rush out and buy anything fancy. She said she was sure that whatever I had in my closet would suffice. If I had to guess, the price tag on some of the gowns worn to this *event of the season* I would guess it to be more than what most of us would pay for a house.

Meanwhile I stood amongst this glamour in my burgundy corduroy skirt, burgundy swoop neck sweater with the matching burgundy suede ankle boots. Embarrassment burned my cheeks. I wanted to turn and run, but as soon as I came through the door of this mansion that looked more like a palace, a butler took my coat and purse, another young lady who said she was Alice's assistant took my arm.

"Journey, how are you? I'm Mrs. Warren's assistant, Dorthey. Come with me, I'll show you where everyone is." She sounded winded as if she was running around doing a lot of stuff.

"Thank you." I'd said with a smile, even though doubt was now crawling up my spine. At that point, I knew Alice had pulled a fast one, I just didn't know how bad it was. The closer we got to the golden doors that Dorthey said led to the ballroom, my suspicion was growing by leaps and bounds. The sight of two more men dressed like butlers standing at the doors waiting to open it for us only fed said suspicion.

Chuckling nervously, I turned to look at Dorthey. "That's a little formal for a casual dinner party, isn't it?"

She didn't respond, she just gave me a reassuring smile. However, when the men opened the doors to let us in, I knew I had been betrayed. The room was packed full of glamour. The sparkle from the diamonds and other jewels that were being worn was blinding. I reached up to touch the ruby that Jo had bought me, so glad I had decided to wear it. But even so, I was extremely underdressed. I pulled back on Dorthey's arm, but she didn't relent and continued forward.

"Wait, I'm underdressed. Maybe I should go home and change." She waved away my statement.

"Don't be silly, you look great. Besides, Mrs. Warren's driver won't be back until the party is over. How will you get home?"

Oh My God! Don't panic Journey…

"But I don't understand," I cried confused, looking around at the cream and golden decorated tables. "I thought this was a retirement party for Joseph."

"It is, all of these people have come out to wish him well." She spoke with a calm smile on her face as if she was not rocking my world. I looked back at the door that was getting farther away. Where was she taking me?

"Where are we going?" My desperation began to bleed through my voice.

"Mrs. Warren reserved you a special seat of honor."

Don't panic…

People were beginning to give me the side eye. A couple of women whispered about me behind their hands as they took in my outfit. There were several media stations set up where some of the famous people in attendance were being interviewed.

"Here you go, this is where you will be sitting." On the table in front of the golden place setting was a fancy place holder with Journey, spelt J-o-r-n-a-y written on it. My eyes went around to the other people sitting at the table. Like me, it seemed as if they were a bit underdressed. I felt instant relief. This would probably explain why they weren't mixing and mingling with everyone else.

I turned around to thank Dorthey, but surprisingly she was already gone making her way through the crowd.

"Hi," I muttered to the others as I eased down in the chair. Several of them returned my greeting while the others continued to look around wide eyed, no doubt this was their first time being around so many famous people as it was mine.

Right off I noticed a few things about the occupants at this table, we were all black, young, and underdressed. It was then I saw the sign on a little stand in the middle of the table. It read: *Florida's Community Project.*

Wow, Alice was in rare form. If she thought sitting me at a table with my people that was from the ghetto like me was going to insult me, she didn't know me that well. Out of all the tables in the room, there was not a one I would have rather sat at.

"Journey, is that you?" The sound of Kyle's voice caused me to look around. He was coming towards me carrying a golden tray of hors d'oeuvres.

"Kyle!" I cried, so relieved to see another body that I knew. I reached for him. "What are you doing here?"

He sat the tray on the table and squatted down next to me, taking my hands. I clung to him, in that moment he was the most beautiful thing I had ever seen. I wanted to beg him to take me away from here.

"Several caterers got the contract for this job, my father was one of them." His eyes raked over my body. "Wow! You look amazing!"

I gave him the look that said, yeah right. "Aww, Kyle you just saying that 'cause you're my friend."

He shook his head. "No, I'm serious. You the only woman here tonight that's not fake. If a fire breaks out, most of these women will melt." I chuckled.

That was the Kyle I remembered before he had decided to push the envelope and take our relationship to the next level. I liked him better as a friend. I opened my mouth to ask him if he drove, but right then another waiter approached us.

"Kyle, your father needs to see you right away." Kyle nodded.

"I'll be back." He told me as he stood with his tray.

I still clung to his hand. "Promise?"

He chuckled squatting back down. "It's going to be alright. Just because these people got money don't mean they're better than you in any way. You're the prettiest girl here Journey, by far."

"Thank You, Kyle." I muttered putting on a brave face. However, I wanted to grab his arm and tell him not to leave me. The term feeling like a fish out of water was a vast understatement to how I felt right now.

Like the other occupants at my table, I looked around wide eyed. I couldn't believe the faces I was seeing. The Obamas! Are you kidding me? The Obamas were here. I had to stop myself from completely fan girling out and pulling out my phone to get a couple of pictures to show my mom.

Who was I kidding? If that butler guy hadn't took my purse with my phone in it, that's exactly what I would be doing.

I continued to scan the crowd when my eyes landed on Alice. She was dressed to the nines in a golden creation that was simply breathtaking. Never once did her eyes fall to the table of have-nots, like we were too beneath her to even notice. I started to get up and give her a piece of my mind and demand she call her driver back to take me home, but with a huge smile on her face she linked arms with Senator Warren and headed toward the golden double doors. My eyes followed and—

"What?" I muttered coming to my feet confused. I clutched the back of the chair next to me for support.

Jo was walking through the door escorting a tall, brown beauty on his arm. Everything about her screamed *first lady*. Her long, processed hair seemed to float around her shoulders as she waved and shook hands with the people she passed. The dress she wore was a mix between Jacqueline Kennedy and Michelle Obama. She didn't wear high-stepping heels like most of the women here tonight. She wore sensible heels like a good first lady should.

I felt sick…

Everybody in the room stopped what they were doing and began to clap for them. Senator Warren and Alice joined them and together they stood and smiled, waving for the cameras.

Out of sheer self-preservation, I told myself not to jump to conclusions. This could be Jo's cousin or friend. But the way he touched her with his hand on her lower back screamed something else. Oh God, he had played me.

In that moment, something else came to mind that I never even thought of. Jo never told me about this event. He didn't invite me, his mother did. In fact, he told me he would be working late and for me not to wait up. I had been so excited about being invited that it never crossed my mind to question his statement.

I put my hand on my stomach trying to settle the queasiness. I felt like such a fool. This is why I avoided him in the beginning. I knew a man like that could never take a girl like me seriously. I was just a young ghetto plaything for him to bide his time with. With desperate eyes I looked around at the other occupants at my table. Hadn't that been the message Alice Warren wanted me to get?

By inviting me here, she reminded me where my place was, and it was not standing next to her son. No, that will never be my place. I had been so foolish.

Jo, his parents, and Mrs. Future first lady were escorted to one of the interview stations. It just so happened the station was close by my table.

I'm sure that was just a coincidence.

Because the bright lights were in his face he didn't see me, but Alice did. The wicked smile she wore made me want to kick her. I balled up my fists. What did I do to this woman to make her hate me so? I didn't ask for any of this!

The reporter began asking him questions about his future senate seat, but I didn't hear any of it, because my eyes were too busy taking in the woman who was standing with her hands on my man. The man that had just made love to me this morning and had me calling out his name. She touched his chest and straightened out his bowtie, she threw back her head and laughed at something he whispered in her ear.

Did he make love to her the same way? Did he make her feel as if she was melting in his arms? Did he--

"And can we expect an engagement announcement between you and the beautiful Ms. Chloe Anderson when you officially announce that you're running for your father's seat?"

My world darkened.

Langston asked what happens to a dream deferred. My answer is simple, golds turn to browns, and whites to greys, the sparkle of diamonds dull, as your love dies and crumbles away...

So that was Chloe Anderson. No wonder Kyle said he was surprised to see Jo there with me. I put my hand on my chest to try to ease the pain of my heart shattering into a million pieces to fall to the ground around my feet.

Lift your head, Journey! An inner strength that I didn't know I had yelled inside of me.

Although it was the hardest thing I ever had to do, I lifted my head, even though my body was wracked with pain. As if he could feel my pain, Jo suddenly looked up and his eyes connected with mine. He looked away, but then his head jerked back to me.

I willed myself not to cry in front of him. He was not worth it. I will never give him that. Yeah, I may be from the ghetto and to him and his peers, a piece of disposable trash, but to the Heavenly Father I mattered, I know I did. And it was him I called on to give me the strength to walk out of here.

"You know Journey, had I known you were a good time girl, I would have put my bid in before my son. What's he paying for your services anyway?"

My mouth dropped as I slowly turned to look at Senator Warren. With what he thought was a seductive smile he winked at me. Jo told his father he was paying me for sex!

I was going to be sick…

 I hurried across the floor towards the doors.

"Journey, are you okay?" Kyle asked as he reached for me.

"Please Kyle, get me out of here. Please!" Desperately I clutched his strong arms, any minute I felt like my knees were going to give out. I'd always dreamed that one day I'd win the Nobel Peace Prize for my work with the soil. I'd be known far and wide for my studies. But thanks to Jo, I'll now and forever be known as the silly ghetto girl who once became the mistress of a president.

"Of course. Come on, my car's out back." Kyle said.

As soon as we exited the golden doors I collapsed in his arms, a dark cloud settled over me and it was suffocating.

I was dying!

"That bastard! I hate you had to find out this way." He whispered as he lifted me in his arms. I didn't care that the few people that stood in the grand foyer stared at us. I just wanted to get out of here.

The butler disappeared for only a moment before he came out with my coat and purse. I lay my head on Kyle's shoulder, kind of hiding my face in his neck. The truth was, my head felt too heavy to lift.

"Thanks, Kyle." I muttered feeling lifeless as he set me on my feet at his car and opened the passenger side door for me. When I slid in and he closed the door, I gave into the tears that would wait no longer. As soon as Kyle opened his door to get in, the kitchen door burst open and Jo ran out.

"Go Kyle, hurry!" I cried as he slid in and turned the key. Just as Jo made it to the car reaching for my door Kyle stepped on the gas. My gaze went to his as we sped around the stone fountain. Surprisingly, he actually chased the vehicle. I didn't try to hide my pain from him, hell, at the point I couldn't if I tried.

"Journey! Wait!" He yelled as for a moment he ran beside the car beating on the window. He tried to reach for the door knob but couldn't grasp it. And then he did something that caused me to scream out. He grabbed unto the top of the car and leaped up unto the roof...

I yelled as he slammed his fist into the front window on Kyle's side.

"Stop this car you mutha f****!" He hit the window again and cracked it.

"Dear God!" I screamed. He was like a wild man. Kyle slammed on the brakes and Jo rolled off the hood unto the ground coming smoothly to his feet out of a flawless roll.

My mouth fell open. "What the world!" I don't know if I said that out loud or just thought it. Jo had just moved like some kind of robot or something. His suit wasn't even ruffled, must be his military training. Standing in front of the car he pointed at Kyle grinding down on teeth as if he really wanted to lay hands on him, but then changed his mind.

His pleading eyes came to me. "Journey baby, I'm sorry. I should have told you about Chloe." He shook his head. "I didn't tell you because I was planning on telling everybody tonight that I couldn't marry her because I want to marry you."

He reached in his pocket and pulled out a small black box. "See, it's ruby like the necklace I bought you." He made a sound in his throat that sounded like a half laugh half cry.

"I bought this engagement ring the same time I bought you that necklace…I carry it everywhere with me, trying to work up the nerve to ask you to marry me. I always knew you were the one."

I stared at him through a sea of tears. He opened the box and the ruby flashed red in the headlights. My hand flew to my mouth.

"Please baby, don't go like this. Just give me a second to make this all right. Please, J!"

My heart!

What was Jo doing to my heart? One minute he causes it pain like it's never felt before, and in the next complete fullness. As if it had a mind of its own, my hand went for the door. But right then Kyle stepped on the gas causing Jo to dive out the way. I turned to look at him.

"Kyle, what are you doing?"

"He's lying, Journey!" He growled as he clutched the steering wheel with both hands so tightly his knuckles turned white.

"How can you believe anything he says after what you went through tonight?" I turned to look back at Jo, instead of chasing after the car he ran across the yard yelling something in his phone. Several guards were running towards the guard booth and the gate that was beginning to close.

My eyes widened as we continue to speed towards it anyway. "Kyle, slow down, we going to crash into the gate!"

"We're going to make it." He mumbled concentrating on his task.

A scream froze in my throat as he slid past the gate scratching the side of his car. I put my hand on my chest as I collapsed back in the seat.

"Wow!" Was all I could say. He reached over and took my hand bringing it up to his lips to kiss my knuckles.

"I'm sorry I scared you, but I had to do something, I saw you falling for his silky lies again. It's the reason why I didn't tell you before now that he had a woman and you was the side piece."

My heart!

"What was the reason?" I asked my voice barely over a whisper.

He turned to look at me with sorrowful eyes. Opening his mouth to speak, but seemed to change his mind and shake his head.

He exhaled. "Listen Journey, you're young and some men prey on that fact. I didn't tell you because I knew that you loved him so much you wouldn't believe me. But now that you've seen it with your own eyes, please don't be foolish enough to call your own sight a liar."

I turned to look out my window so that Kyle couldn't see just how true his words were. After seeing the ring and hearing Jo declare he loved me and wanted to marry me, I called my eyes a liar for what they claim they saw.

He was right, Jo had played me for a fool. And I would be an even bigger fool to continue to fall for as Kyle say, his silky words. Had I known he had a woman I would have never agreed to this relationship. I would have never given him my heart. It was already too late to walk away from him without being heartbroken, but like my mama always said, time heals all wounds.

I chuckled through my tears. I didn't know if that was true or not, but I guess I was about to find out. I turned to look at Kyle.

"Yeah," I whispered. "You're right."

Chapter Eleven

The Other Side of Jo

Joseph

A sharp pain shot through my head as I came awake. I went to lift my hand to rub my temples, but couldn't because my hands were handcuffed to a bed. I tried to open my eyes to see what was going on, but my lids were too heavy.

"What the f*** do you mean, you don't know what is going on with him?" The sound of my father's raised voice caused me to relax back in the bed and pretend to still be out.

"You assured me that he would never become a danger to the public."

"Mr. Warren, need I remind you that he was created to be a weapon of the United States government? I didn't design him to be a civilian in any way. If he senses danger, his survival instincts are going to kick in, in which case, he won't strike to wound, he will strike to *kill*." I didn't recognize the voice of the man that spoke to my father, yet it sounded very familiar. What the hell did he mean design? And who was the he they were talking about?

"And need I remind you that Macon Cooperation paid three and a half billion dollars for him? And he's just single handily wiped out half of their elite force security."

"Pss, elite force my ass!" Whoever it was threw something down angrily. "Any one of the Law brothers will single handily destroy an army. And you want to cry to me about some candy ass *elite force*? Get the f*** out of here!"

"Now is not the time for you to do your peacock strut. You created these—these weapons of mass destruction! Three and a half billion dollars is a lot of money. You'll have to be a fool to think that something so valuable will not be insured. Those men he killed today was his owner's insurance policy." My father spat.

"And yet the fact remains, he's a three and a half billion-dollar *weapon*, that *you* decided without *my* consent to sell to the highest bidder, letting him loose amongst the public. Repeatedly I have warned of the risk we are taking with such an action."

"You assured us that he was civil, you said you can control him. He didn't respond to the cease and desist command. Now my wife is afraid he may kill us all in our sleep!" My father growled, so angry I could hear his teeth grinding together. Their raised voices came from somewhere out side of the room I was in or maybe they were inside the room.

Once again, I tried to open my eyes but couldn't. It felt as if I had been drugged. I was having a hard time determining if I was awake or still asleep. My mind felt sluggish, I gritted down on my teeth, I didn't like this feeling.

The strange yet familiar man chuckled. "If he finds out what is going on, your wife won't have to worry, because I can guarantee he's going to kill us all."

My father went on a cursing binge. "How can we fix this?" He asked when he had once again gained control of himself.

"I told you the program will work as long as nothing happens to disturb its hold on him."

"Nothing happened; everything was going according to schedule before he had some kind of war flashback and took out half of Macon's security team." My father fired back.

"Oh please, Mr. Warren! You don't think I know about the love interest? We discussed this. Strong emotions like love can interfere with the programming. His need to protect her will override everything we've trained him to do."

"We did not expect him to fall in love with her. He's never loved before. How were we to know this time would be different?"

"And what about the child?"

My father exhaled. "He won't bring her around and he has them under constant surveillance. You can't get close to them without him knowing. And if he's not with them then he has the old man who is now completely loyal to him with them, another one of your brilliant *weapons* gone rogue!"

"Hey! The old man was there as a safeguard because you and your precious wife was too chicken sh*t to be around the kid without one."

"It's like you said, *a weapon is a weapon*." My father said in a very patronizing tone.

"Either way, he was put there to keep him in order should you lose control. But once again, my instructions were not followed, and you allowed a bond to grow between the two." He paused for a moment.

"Listen, if you don't want this thing to crumble down around us, you had better find a way to cut those ties. Until then, he's uncontrollable; there is nothing I can do."

"Don't you give me that!" My father hissed. "I put my whole career on the line for you! Remember if not for me, you would have never gotten a chance to parade your little freakshows in front of the Secretary of Defense."

"How can I forget when you find a way to remind me every time we meet?" The man's tone sounded as if he was bored.

"Well since you're so good at hearing, hear this. If this thing crumbles as you so eloquently put it, I won't fry alone. I'm taking you and all your little monsters down with me."

Who were they talking about? My mind was so sluggish I couldn't comprehend what they were saying. If my father was so worried about this person, why didn't he tell me so that I could handle it? The pain in my head was beginning to drown them out. I went to lift my hand again, but the handcuffs prevented it.

What the hell was going on? I racked my mind trying to remember how I got here. The last thing I remembered clearly was seeing Journey clinging to another man. It had been the most painful thing I've had to watch in my whole life. I once was forced to witness one of my brothers-in-arms tortured and then brutally murdered, and it hurt less than that.

That poetry reciting bastard had the nerve to wink at me before he slid in the car and drove away with my woman. As I watched his car speed toward the gate, I swore that when I got through with him it will be awhile before he was able to see out of either of his eyes.

I went back into the house to get the keys to my car. At the same time, I turned on the tracker that I'd put on Journey's phone and saw that they were headed toward the house.

"Jo, where are you going? You can't just leave in the middle of your party!" My father growled as he and my mother burst into my old bedroom. I grabbed my keys out of my bag.

"How did Journey get here?"

"What do you mean, dear?" My mother began in her fake placating voice that only grated on my nerves.

"You know what I mean!"

"Joseph, don't yell at your mother!"

I balled up my fist. I didn't have time to deal with them right now. That bastard was with Journey and I swear if he so much as lay one finger on her, he was dead. My father grabbed my arm as I charged past him, but I snatched it away and angrily turned to face him.

He flinched. I shook my head, that's not the first time he's done that. Anytime I get angry he has to work hard to cover his fear of me.

"What about Chloe, son? If you walk away and leave her down there by herself it will disgrace her and her family." He spoke in a calmer tone.

"I don't give a damn about Chloe or her family. I'm not marrying her, I'm marrying Journey. You two need to get used to that fact." I turned to walk out the door, but my father grabbed my arm again.

"Please don't do this. The implication from this could be more than you or I are prepared to handle."

I chuckled. "No dad, the implication of this is more than *you're* prepared to handle. Me? I'm prepared to *die* for this."

His eyes rounded. "Prepared to *die*? What nonsense is this?"

I gritted down on my teeth to control the rage that was roaring inside me. "Journey and Ayana are mine and that's a fact I'll die for." I snatched my arm from him again and closed the gap between us, so that I was standing eye to eye with him. I needed him to understand that the words I now spoke were true.

"That's a fact I will kill for." I heard my mother's indrawn breath, but I didn't wait around to see her fainting spell.

"Joseph, what's going on?" Chloe cried meeting me at the bottom of the stairs. My mother's assistant was doing a great job of making sure the rest of the guests were good and distracted inside the ballroom. I could hear Senator Banks speaking on the mic about my accomplishments.

"Who is that woman you were chasing?" I forced myself to stop and give her a few seconds of my time. Like me, Chloe was just a pawn in our family's politics.

"Chloe, that woman is the mother of my child." Shock registered on her face. "I'm so sorry I didn't tell you sooner, but I can't marry you."

She shook her head. "Nonsense, you won't be the first man to have a child before marriage. The good thing is it happened before we announced our engagement, which means—"

"Which means," I said interrupting her. I did not have time for this conversation; this needed to be short and to the point. "If she'll have me, it is *her* I want to marry."

"Joseph, please wait!" My mother cried coming down the stairs. No doubt my father was in his study sulking over a glass of his eighty-year-old scotch.

"I will talk to you guys later once I find Journey." I told her, leaving Chloe in her capable hands. When I pulled into the gate at the cottage, I had to forcibly quit the anger in me. The last thing I wanted is for Abby to see me in savage mode.

As soon as I opened the door I knew something was wrong. Abby was sitting on the couch pushing a sleeping Ayana in her little chair swing.

"Where is Journey?" I asked using all my strength to school my voice. She stood and came towards me with a worried look on her face.

"What's going on? Journey ran upstairs crying and a minute later she came back down saying she couldn't sleep in this house or in you guys' bed. She asked me to look after Ayana for a couple of days. Jo, what happened? Are you guys fighting? Why was she crying?"

I clicked on my phone and saw that her tracker was still here.

"No J." I hissed as I took the stairs up three at a time. "F***!"

Sitting on the bed next to the necklace I bought her was the phone I'd gotten her and her credit card.

"F***!" Needing to vent some of the rage that was burning in me I turned and threw my phone into the corner of the room so hard it shattered. The slight gratification I got from it was cut short when Abby's concerned voice came from the bottom of the stairs.

"Is everything alright, Jo?"

"Yeah, Abby, everything is alright." I muttered as I sat heavily on the bed burying my head in my hands.

Damn, I messed up! Damn!

I was so angry I couldn't think clearly. I had to steady my heartrate and figure out what to do next.

I needed to get to my office where I had the materials to track her down.

Journey

Okay, so what I'm going to tell you guys next may sound confusing, and it's because I'm confused. Something happened to Jo. Something very bad. He's not what any of us thought he was. He's some kind of… I don't know.

Let me just tell you guys what I saw.

When Kyle pulled up in front of the cottage I asked him if he would wait for me. I knew that there was no way I would be able to sleep in the same bed Jo had just made love to me in without being ill. Plus, there was no doubt in my mind that he was on the way here, and as you guys can see I'm not that strong. Jo was clearly my weakness and I needed to get away from him so that I could think of what next to do.

So, I went in and asked my mom if she would watch Ayana for me for a few days. I couldn't stand the feel of that necklace around my neck, so I took it off. And the thought of spending another dime of his after he had told his father that he paid me for sex was just inconceivable.

I held back my grief as I talked to my mom, I wasn't ready to admit to her how stupid I had been. I held back my grief when I got back in the car with Kyle and asked him to drive me to a dinky motel way across town where Jo would never think to look for me. I was ashamed that I had to ask him to borrow money.

"Really, it's no big deal." He told me as he took a hundred dollar bill out his wallet. He reached in to give me another, but I stopped him. Let it not be said I went from being one man's whore to another.

"I don't think it's wise for you to be alone." He said when I reached for the door handle. I was so physically and mentally exhausted I could barely speak. Plus, the downpour of tears, I was holding back was now choking me.

"Please Kyle, I just want to be by myself."

"Okay, but promise me you'll call me tomorrow so that I can take you out to lunch. I don't want to see you suffer for something that is not your fault."

"Thank you, Kyle for being there for me." I whispered instead of a confirmation to call him tomorrow.

When I finally closed the door to the motel room shutting out the world, I walked to the bathroom and ran me a bath. As soon as my foot touched the hot water my tears ran free. Here in this bathroom I didn't have to hold back my sobs. And I'm not talking about baby sobs, I sat in that tub and had me a good ugly cry.

How could I have been such a fool? I told myself not to fall in love with him. My brother had tried to warn me about him. He wanted to tell me something, but just like Kyle, he didn't because he saw my nose was wide open.

Oh God!

This was my first time experiencing this kind of heartbreak. Nobody ever warned me about it. They never said that it made you feel so low to the ground you might as well be dirt. Nobody ever said that it felt as if someone punched you in the stomach leaving you breathless.

Why didn't I see this coming?

Not once since I've been back in D.C. has he invited me over to his place. He never took me to any of the dinners and events that he was constantly invited to. The only thing he wanted me for was sex.

I grinded my palms in my eyes.

The sex…

I had been blinded by it. How could I not? The man made love as if his very life depended on it. He wasn't satisfied until I'm left shaking and panting, begging him for mercy, yet begging for more. In all the lustful, sweaty nights, it never crossed my mind that it was the height of our relationship.

I looked at my pathetic reflection in the water. "What else does a man want with his mistress?"

He never lied. It was me. He had me sign a contract to be his mistress. It was me that started reading more into it than what was there. I had lied to myself. Groaning I hit my head with my fist.

I wanted to go home. I wanted to get on the first thing smoking back to Chicago. I should have never left my neighborhood or the protection of my brother. This is what he tried to keep me from. Alice was right, I didn't know how the game was played here in D.C.

This whole time he had a woman. This whole time he had made me feel as if I was his world. This whole time he had played me for the fool I am.

I had to do something. I needed to make some moves. But the only thing I managed to move was my body from the bathtub to the bed. And that is where I stayed for nearly two days.

I would have stayed longer, but Kyle showed up at my door.

"Who is it?" I muttered from the bed.

"It's Kyle."

I exhaled putting the cover back over my head. I didn't want to deal with him. I didn't want to deal with anybody.

"Journey, open up. You promised you would go to lunch with me yesterday. I waited all day, you never called."

I did not…

Throwing the covers back I sat up. My whole body protested the movement.

"Kyle, I'm not hungry." I couldn't even change the fact that I whined that.

"I know you may not feel hungry now, but once you get out into the fresh air and the sunlight, you will see that you are. It's been almost two days, you have to eat." He paused for just a moment.

"I know this really nice restaurant that have the best jerk chicken in town." I collapsed back in the bed just wishing he would go away.

"Come on, Journey. I'm not going to go away. You've been closed up in there too long. Queen, you don't deserve this."

Tears came to my eyes… Kyle called me his queen, but Jo made me feel like his queen. I sat up and dried my eyes.

"Okay, I'll be out in a sec." I told him trying my best not to cry. I was tired of crying.

"Okay sweetheart, I'll be waiting right out here in my car." I nodded wiping away another flow of tears. However, it did no good, as soon as I got in the shower they sprang free. What Kyle said was true. I could not stay shut up in this room forever, mainly because I had to check out today; the hundred dollars he had given me had reached its limit.

But the Heavenly Father knows I did not want to leave this room. I did not want to go home to my mother's questions and Jo's apologies. I did not want to deal with the fact that Ayana, who now loved her father just as much as she loved me, would not understand why her little family wasn't together anymore.

Now I had to be one of those mothers that had to share a child with a man I could barely stand to look at. Exhaling I pulled my black sweatpants and a t-shirt out my bag. Pulling my locs back into a ponytail I took one last look at myself in the mirror. I was presentable, but it looked as if I was on my way to identify the body of a loved one.

Oh well…

The sun burned my eyes when I exited my room with my bag on my shoulder. I wish I had thought to grab my shades.

"Hey Journey, you look amazing." Kyle said as he opened the car door for me. I tried to smile at him, but the smile may have come out a bit of a sneer.

Kyle drove some kind of sports car that sat low to the ground. I think it was a Corvette, but don't quote me. Leaning my head back against the seat I mourned the loss of the dark motel room. He got in and smiled at me and I wanted to yell at him. Instead I lifted one side of my mouth in what I hoped was a smile.

I didn't want to take my anger out on him. He's been nothing but supportive during this whole debacle.

"You're going to love this restaurant." He said as he put the car in reverse and pulled out the parking spot.

"Alright." I muttered as I watched my little escape slip farther and farther away. Leaving this place meant it was time to face reality. It was time to face my mother, Ayana and Jo. The fact still remains I was under contractual agreement to be his mistress. I didn't know how I could go on at this point. The thought of it sickened me.

I kept hearing his father asking me what was the going rate for my services. I never thought I could hate someone, but it was safe to say I hated Jo's parents. The both of them were evil as hell. I didn't ever want them around Ayana. I exhaled, we had some stormy days ahead of us. I was prepared to go to battle. They had no idea the monster I could become to protect my child.

I will fight them all! Jo, his parents…The f***ing Senate! All of D.C. if I have to!

Kyle's voice pulled me from a very dark place. "We're here."

I was so far into the sunken place I didn't notice how nice the restaurant was or even how the waitress looked that took our order. I couldn't even tell you what I ordered. Kyle sat across the table and talked to me and I couldn't repeat anything he said if my life depended on it. In my mind I was coming up with a way to get me and my child away from these vampires.

It was during these thoughts that I looked up and saw Jo, the head vampire walking through the restaurant door. Everything about him was proficient. The way he walked. The way he held the door for the lady going out. The way he looked at me and read how hurt I was in my eyes.

Several things happened. First, I disgusted myself because for just a moment my thirsty gaze drank him up as if he was a tall, strong, muscled glass of chocolate milk.

As always, he was well put together in a grey suit that had been custom made for him, his broad shoulders filling the jacket out in only a way that he could. On his feet was a pair of matching grey boots.

Damn it!

Kyle looked behind him to see what I was looking at and jumped up out of his chair.

Now…this is when things started to go south.

"What are you doing here?" Kyle asked using his body to block Jo's view of me.

"Man… look… just get out my way, okay?" At this point, it was no hostility in his voice. He sounded defeated.

"I've come to take Journey home. I need to talk to her." He reached his hand past Kyle towards me.

"Journey, come here baby, please, I need—"

Kyle, feeling impowered by the dejection in his voice slapped his arm away. "She ain't going nowhere with you man!"

There was a collective pause. It was as if the restaurant as a whole took a deep breath, everybody waiting to see what would happen.

When Jo struck, he did it so fast it took all of us a minute to comprehend what happened. He hit Kyle so hard in his face that the man's feet left the ground, but Jo was on him before his body could even land. His arm was moving like a machine as he punched Kyle over and over again in his face.

"Jo, stop!" I cried running to him. I tried to grab his arm to stop it, but the strength in his limb was beyond anything I had ever felt. The first punch took Kyle out; blood poured from his nose that I was more than positive was broken.

"Help me!" I yelled at all the people who were just standing around watching. Several of them even had their phones out recording it.

"My woman mutha*****!" Jo growled as he continued to pound Kyle's face.

One minute I was there on Jo's back trying to stop him from beating Kyle to death and the next I was grabbed roughly from the back, picked up and then slammed on the ground.

Pain shot through my body. Confused I looked up and saw that the restaurant was now filled with men dressed in black military gear that was roughly pushing and throwing the other customers into the kitchen. One of them had slammed me on the ground.

Were these the police?

It couldn't be, the way they were handling the people was illegal anywhere. A woman screamed out when her phone that she was using to record Jo was taken from her and then she was shoved through the kitchen door by her head.

Jo turned to look at where I had been slammed on the ground and I swear there was nothing in his eyes but death as he stood and took in the fact that we were surrounded by soldiers or something.

And this is the moment the Jo we know left the building and a terminator took his place.

And yeah… I know you're all like *terminator*? Really Journey? That's a bit much, isn't it?

Well let me tell y'all something, a shadow fell over his eyes. There is no other way I can describe it.

Guys, if I wasn't there witnessing what happened next, I would have never believed it had somebody tried to explain it to me. The man that slammed me on the ground faced Jo, holding out his hands as if he was trying to keep him calm. He began to say strange words to him, something about walking alone in a field of clovers.

But Jo's eyes came to me where I still lay on the floor one more time and then all hell broke loose. Moving like lightening he grabbed a spoon off the table before kicking the man so hard in his knees he collapsed forward, the sound of both of his legs breaking will be something I will never forget. I screamed because as his head was coming down, Jo used the handle of the spoon imbedding it into the man's chin and up into his head.

My eyes widened in horror as the body dropped next to me. I had to stifle another scream when it twitched and the all life left it. Blood begin to ooze from the hole in his chin. I gagged. It took all the strength I had not to vomit.

When the other men saw what happened to their leader, they came at Jo with all they had and amazingly I watched as he took them all out. This kind of stuff you only see on TV. The first man that reached him threw a punch but ended up getting his face smashed hard into the table causing the table to break in two.

No way he survived.

Jo did some kind of turn around the next guy taking his head with him; the sound of the man's neck snapping like the sound of that first guys legs breaking will be forever seared in my memory. He picked up a chair and bought it down on the head of another man that dove to take out his feet, the chair broke apart leaving him holding both the legs in his hands...

And I kid y'all not, Jo used them legs to beat the hell out of the rest of the men. One after the other, they dropped until he was left standing there surrounded by bodies. When he saw there was nothing more to destroy he threw the sticks down and walked towards me.

I tried to scoot back away from him but my hands were slipping in the blood of the dead man with the spoon rammed into his head. Completely ignoring the fact that I was terrified of him he leaned down and scooped me up in his arms carrying me out the restaurant. He put me on my feet next to his car.

"Get in." Was all he said after he opened the door for me.

I didn't argue, I didn't blink, I got in. The energy that was coming from him at that moment was astonishing.

"Are you alright?" He asked when he got into the car. With wide eyes I nodded. I was still not talking to Jo. As he drove he checked himself for injuries. He didn't talk to me, so I didn't talk to him. But I watched him.

Jo had checked out. This killing machine that now drove me was not sociable. He was like a robot.

What the hell?

He drove to a empty park and got out of the car. I sat there and watched him pace back and forward in front of the car. Several times he grabbed his head as if he couldn't believe what he'd just done. Seeing him in anguish was tearing me apart, I wanted to comfort him, but I was afraid of him.

I can't lie. What I just witnessed had freaked me out. Jo took out a whole army of men by himself, many of which he left dead. It was like he had been some kind of war machine.

After about thirty minutes he got back in the car and pulled off. Jo was back, he rubbed his hand down his face and I could sense him trying to figure out the best way to break the ice.

What the hell kind of Twilight Zone sh*t is this?!

"J—I…"

Looking straight ahead I waited for him to explain what I just saw.

"I'm sorry you had to see that."

"What are you, Jo?" My question was so low I feared he may not have heard it.

"I'm a man."

I shook my head. "No man can move like you did back there. You were faster and stronger than anything I have ever seen."

He shook his head. "I'm just a man." He clutched at his head as if he had a headache. Whatever it was going on with him, he was having a hard time reasoning within himself about it as well.

"You nearly killed Kyle." My words were still very quiet, the last thing I wanted to do was wake that killing machine back up.

"That bastard had it coming." He growled as he angrily drove down the street.

"Can you see that that's not alright?" I kept my voice low.

He turned to look at me then, his handsome face twisted in anger.

"Why aren't you yelling at me? Why are you talking to me like you think I will hurt you?" He hit the steering wheel and I damn near jumped out of my skin.

"J!" The anguished sound that came out his throat tore at my heart, but I still clutched the door handle for deal life. I couldn't help it. You guys have no idea what I was dealing with. I was shaking all over.

"Baby, I will kill myself before I ever hurt you."

I wanted to believe his whispered plea, but he wasn't stable. We didn't talk again until he pulled up in front of the cottage. He killed the engine.

"Tell me what I have to do to prove to you that I love you and I will never hurt you." This was my first time ever seeing him so vulnerable. It was a complete mind screw after seeing him destroy a whole army of men by himself.

Now he looked at me like a lost little boy in desperate need of love. If I didn't know any better, I would think that this powerful man actually *needed* me. Tears filled my eyes.

"If you love me, Jo," My voice quivered so bad my words were barely recognizable. I paused and gathered myself.

"If you really love me…tear up the contract."

Chapter Twelve

Letting Go

Journey

I almost believed the look of pain that came across his face.

Almost!

My heart had turned to stone. At least that's what I convinced myself. So, no matter what he said or what he did, I will not turn back.

"J please, ask me to do anything else. Anything. Just—" He paused for a moment, his eyes searching mine.

"Just don't leave me..." His words made him very vulnerable. He was taking a risk even uttering them. Vulnerable like I was watching him walk into his party with another woman on his arm.

"Do you love me?" My voice was cold.

"More than anything in this world."

Be strong, sista! He doesn't mean it!

"Then let me go."

He rubbed his hand down his face. I could see him wrestling with himself to do the right thing. He didn't answer right away, I began to get worried that he was going to force me to fulfill the contract anyway.

"I'll tear up the contract only under one condition." He spoke those words without looking at me. He stared straight ahead out his front window.

"What?"

"You don't leave D.C., you stay here in this house and allow me to continue to support Ayana and you." I began to shake my head, but he held up his hand.

"Just hear me out."

Although I didn't feel like I owed him anything I sat back in the seat and listened.

"I f***ed up. I know that. It's so many things I should have done differently. I have to own up to that. But a man needs to know he's taking care of his child and his wom—" He caught himself.

"His child's mother. So please, I won't force you to allow me to see Ayana. I would like to see her, but I won't force you. Just stay here close to me, so that at least I'll know you guys are safe."

I wanted to say no to his request, but my mother had raised me to have compassion. She called it the fruits of the spirit. If the roles were reversed and I could not see Ayana, I would go mad with worry. And yes, I would want her to be in the same town as me. I would want to know without a shadow of a doubt that she was safe.

But he wanted me to continue taking money from him. To me that was personal. It would make me feel like I was still his.

Well…there was a such thing as child support. And famous people like him paid a grip. Maybe I could look at it like that.

"If I agree to this, will you tear up the contract?"

Still staring straight ahead, it was clear he was not happy with my question, the muscle ticked in the side of his chin.

"Yes."

It took everything within me to school my features.

I was free! I couldn't believe it…

"Okay, deal."

I didn't wait to see how he took the news, I just opened the door and got out. Without looking back, I took my keys out my bag and went into my quiet home. After I closed the door I leaned back and listened as he started the car and pulled off. Only then did I exhale in relief.

"Oh God!" I whispered into the empty living room.

I can't believe it's over.

"Journey, is that you?" My mother called from upstairs. I could hear the gentle hum of her television. No doubt she was watching the afternoon news.

I began to head in that direction. "Yeah mama, it's me. Don't get up, I'm coming up."

Remembering I had blood on me I stopped at her bedroom door, so glad she was lying down in her bed and could not see the back of me.

"How are you feeling?" She asked sitting up in her bed. It looked like she had been napping.

"I've been better."

She smiled sadly at me as she patted her bed next to her. "You want to come lay down and tell me about it?"

"How about over tea a little later? I really need to shower and to get some rest."

She nodded as her eyes raked over me trying to determine in what condition I was in. More than anything I wanted to lie next to her and cry my eyes out, and if I wasn't covered in that man's blood, I would.

"Where is—"

"Not coming back." Tears came to my eyes as I waited to see how she was going to take the news. Surprisingly, she didn't say much, just nodded once again.

"Okay, baby. Ayana just laid down for a nap, so go ahead and get some rest." I nodded.

"Thanks, mama."

The first thing I did when I closed my bedroom door was strip out of my blood-stained clothes. I didn't bother putting them in the dirty clothes hamper, instead I put them in a bag and pressed it down in my trash can. I didn't want my mother to see them. She would ask questions that I was not prepared to answer.

I stood for a moment and stared at the shower. My hand lifted as if it had a mind of its own and touched the glass. Just the other day, Jo made love to me in this shower, I remembered the claw marks my fingers made in the steam as I grabbed onto the glass, needing an anchor or anything to let me know that I was not dying of pleasure.

Snap out of it, Journey! If you're going to get over him, you can't be thinking about how awesome the sex was...

I made quick work in the shower, not able to stand amongst those memories. The moans and the quiet screams that had come from my lips that day now haunted me. But that wasn't where the ghost of amazing sex past ended. I found myself standing in front of the bed staring at the sheets and blanket that still carried the scent of us.

How can I sleep in this big bed without him?

Tears filled my eyes as I angrily began to rip the sheets off the bed.

I hated him!

I hated him!

I hated him, because I loved him still…

Disgusted with myself I curled up on the empty bed in a fetal position and cried myself to sleep.

Joseph

My head felt like it was going to explode. It happened again. These black outs…or more like transferal of personalities. It used to happen a lot while I was in the military. And even a few times in the field.

God…Journey had to witness it!

She looked at me as if I was a monster. She was so afraid of me. I would do anything to turn back time so that she never had to see that side of me. I didn't even know how to begin to explain it to her.

Hell…I really didn't understand exactly what happens myself.

One minute I'm in control and if I sense real danger, it's like I step aside so that a more lethal version of myself can step in place. It's still me…sort of.

All feeling disappears, my emotions shut off so that I can do what needs to be done. During that time, I don't feel love, or anger or pain. I feel absolutely nothing. And when my emotions come back on I'm generally surrounded by a pile of bodies.

I pulled up to my lonely penthouse and just killed the engine. I did not want to go in there. I wanted to go back to the cottage where the warmth was. Where my heart was.

Damn, she asked me to let her go…

Of course, I said yes, I'd f***** up, what else could I say? But I had no intentions of honoring that. There was no way. I needed her like I needed air. She did something for me that has never been done. She made me feel love. She breathed warmth into my cold heart. There was no way I could give that up. I'd rather go back to the Navy and enlist for another forty years.

Getting her to agree to stay in D.C. was the first step. She'd gotten out of my car confident that she would be able to be this close to me and resist my pull on her. I chuckled, she actually thought I would behave. I don't know if that spoke more about the purity of her spirit or the absolute scoundrel in me. I would unapologetically do anything to keep her.

Lie, kill or steal….

That was the last thing I remembered thinking before I woke up, or rather came through to consciousness in handcuffs. I still could not open my eyes. Without a shadow of a doubt I had been drugged.

My father and the strange man that sounded so familiar continued to argue. Were they talking about me?

"You do your part and I'll do mine. If anyone even suspects that one of the Law brothers is becoming aware, they are going to start making sacrifices to save their own asses and guess who are the lowest men on the totem pole and just right to become the scapegoat."

"Speak for yourself, senator. This is not my first rodeo. I know how these bastards work, and I've prepared for it. If this thing goes south I am a ghost." The man my father spoke to had a very calm voice, it was so familiar, yet…distant

The memory of that voice seemed just out of reach. I racked my brain causing more pain in trying to place it.

"What about the oldest brother, has he been found?"

"No. I believe he's dead."

"What makes you believe that?"

"I have trained them to always come back to me, no matter what. If he was alive I would know."

"And what about his handler?"

"Also dead." The man paused for a moment. "Speaking of handlers, when you cut the ties, you've got to get rid of the old man, they've become too close."

My father exhaled. "I'll cut the ties…you regain control of him. If he doesn't announce his candidacy soon, Jeff is going to come for my head. Macon Technologies paid for a president and a president they're going to get."

God dammit!

They were talking about me. I balled up my fists, using all my strength to open my f****** eyes. What the hell was going on? Who was this man my father was talking to? And who the hell was the Law brothers? Where had I heard that name before?

Rome!

He'd asked me if I knew a man named James Bennet Law...my eyes opened.

"Ahhh!" I yelled as a piercing alarm went off inside my head. The pain was blinding. A door opened and my father and a man dressed in a lab coat stepped into the room. I went to look at the man's face, but the alarm got louder in my head.

"Ahhh!" Gritting down on my teeth I tried not to pass out from the pain.

"F***, do you think he heard us?" My father asked.

"It doesn't matter, when he awakes from this he will not remember a thing he's heard."

I cursed when I felt the sharp prick of a needle. Seconds later everything went black.

****

When I came to, it was to see Albert's ugly mug staring down in my face with concern. I frowned.

"Why the hell are you staring at me like I'm dying?"

He visibly exhaled. "You were in a car crash, kid."

What?!

It was then I noticed the beeping of a heart monitor. I was lying in a hospital bed with an IV in my arm.

What the hell?

"How did I get here?" I asked sitting up in the bed.

"Ahhh!" My damn head was killing me.

"Take it easy, man. What part of you was in a car crash didn't you understand?" Clutching my head, I turned so that my legs hung over the side of the bed. Confused I looked around.

"How in the hell did I get to the hospital? And what is this nonsense about a car crash?" Albert picked up the remote and turned up the news.

"Breaking News…Authorities say a drunk driver coming down the one way in the wrong direction crashed head on into newly retired Senior Special Agent Joseph Warren's car doing over thirty miles per hour. We are told that he was rushed to the nearest hospital to be treated for non-life threatening injuries."

Albert muted the television again.

"What the hell?" I was drawing a complete blank.

"You don't remember having a head on collision?"

"No."

"What's the last thing you do remember?"

I thought past the pain in my head. "Journey dumping me." I moved my arms rotating my shoulders. There was no pain anywhere else but my head. How could that be if I'd been in a head on collision?

Albert was now looking at me with a thoughtful look. But I was already one step ahead of him. Throughout my life I've experienced two kinds of black outs. One that seemed almost natural to me. Although, it was a change of personalities per say, I still remembered everything that happened.

However, there was another black out that have happened where there was a vague memory, but it was just out of reach. Always just out of reach.

"Anything in the news about me trashing a restaurant and leaving a pile of bodies?"

Albert shook his head. "Not a word… But then again, it never is. What happened?"

I exhaled. "One minute I was beating the sh*t out of that poetry reciting bastard. And the next I was surrounded by some cats dressed in full military gear. They didn't trigger my alter until one of them picked Journey up and slammed her on the ground, hurting her." I shook my head.

"The rest was history. When I came through again I was surrounded by bodies. Nothing new there. However, this accident." I shook my head again. "That sh*t didn't happen."

"What did happen?"

I rubbed my hand along my head to my neck, trying to rub away some of the stiffness. "I don't know…."

Albert slapped his hat against his thigh. "They f***en with your head, man! And I'm telling you, your dad got something to do with it. Something ain't right with them people."

For as long as I could remember, I've had Albert in my life. To a lot of folks, he appeared to be an old man enjoying his retirement years and before that, my driver. But looks were misleading. Albert was one of the deadliest men I knew.

Like me, he'd been a military man in his youth. He enlisted in the army at the age of seventeen. By the time he was twenty – three, he had been recruited for a hostage rescue and counterterrorism force, one of the "Tier One" units. They recruit almost exclusively from other SOF, in particular the 75th Ranger Regiment.

Now, he was what our government considered retired and extremely dangerous. The old fox liked to argue that he had a more impressive military career than I. Because of course in his day, the enemy was smarter, stronger and faster. Albert said the world wide web was turning the world into a bunch of pu*****. His words.

Although that was a bunch of poppy cock, I still trusted him with my life and the life of my woman and child. He has been telling me something has been going on with these black outs that I have no memory of for a while.

At first, I waved that away as nonsense.

But now…

Now, I was beginning to believe him. There was no way in hell I was in an accident. I sat for a minute and eternally checked my body again. Outside of my head I wasn't feeling any pain anywhere else. This accident story was a bunch of bull****.

He lifted his hand to rub his head. "I don't know, but whoever it is, they're messing with my head too."

Also something he's been saying for a while.

"Do you have pictures of the wreck?"

He took out his phone and scrolled through it. This is why I trusted him with my life. He'd heard I'd been in a crash and I don't doubt he's done a full investigation already, which is why he knows I spoke the truth when I say it didn't happen.

"They said the car came at you head on at thirty miles per hour." He handed me the phone.

Son of a *****! My damn car was totaled.

"It's only one problem with their story." He took the phone and scrolled through a couple more pictures before handing it back.

"Them bastards!" I hissed, feeling rage waking up inside of me.

Albert had taken a few close-up shots of the smashed-up hood. Deep in the creases were brick particles that who'd ever smashed my car into a wall missed when they were cleaning up behind themselves.

"You got to figure this thing out, kid. You can't keep pushing this to the back burner. You got a woman and child now that you need to keep safe. Whoever is playing with your head is now a danger to them. You understand that, right?"

I nodded balling up my fists wanting to destroy something. When it was just me and Albert was spouting what I thought at the time was nonsense that was one thing, but now things were not adding up. And there was no way I was taking a chance with Journey and Ayana's lives.

"You're not going to want to hear this, but I don't think you can trust your parents. It may be wise to hide your hand from them."

He was right, I didn't want to hear that. I mean it was true that I didn't come up in the warmest house. My parents weren't the type that heaped on the affection. I don't think I could ever remember them telling me they love me or me telling them for that matter. They often spoke about how proud they were of me, but that was about as far as their endearments went.

Still, they are my parents. What Albert was suggesting was unimaginable.

"You probably shouldn't trust them noodle necks down at the bureau either." He grunted. "Hell…you're in a tight spot, kid. I don't know where you should even begin your search."

"I do," I told him, as my soul cringed at the thought.

He chuckled. "Journey's brother…"

I nodded. "I'd rather work with a leprechaun than work with that bastard. But if it means keeping my family safe, I'll do what I have to do."

Albert nodded. "I never doubted you would." He paused for a moment. "So, she left you, huh?"

I exhaled shaking my head. "Yep."

"And what? You gon' give up?"

I chuckled. "Hell no, I already got a plan." I pulled the IV out my arm coming to my feet. "I'm going to need your help to pull it off though."

He didn't budge out of his chair, just looked up at me with a skeptical look. "You do know I'm trying to get her mother to the altar, right?"

I made my way over to the closet where my clothes had been hung. "Good for you, old man. But what does that have to do with me asking for your help?"

"Don't give me that sh*t, I didn't just meet you yesterday. You're up to some kind of trickery. You damn politicians are as crooked as the letter S and you want to pull me into your f*ckery!"

I laughed as I slid my legs into my pants. "Oh, don't pretend like you've never participated in my shenanigans. Now that you've found you a good woman you're suddenly a saint, huh? If she knew half of the things you've done in your miserable life, she'd be on the first thing smoking."

It was his turn to laugh. "Whatever you say, young buck. Unlike you, I know how to play the game. You let your girl catch another woman on your arm. My Abby Cat know I only got eyes for her."

Damn his words stung. I couldn't believe I'd let that dumb sh*t happen. I thought I had time. Chloe was the furthest thing from my mind. She wasn't even important enough for me to dump as soon as I knew Journey was the one.

But that's alright. I'm not the kind of man who wallowed in my mistakes. I don't accept defeat and I never give up. Albert knew me well. I was desperate and not above trickery. What ever it took to get my woman back in my arms I was willing to do. Period!

"The way you going, I'm gon' end up married to the mama...before you can even get a ring on her daughter's finger." He still chuckled at his own relic a** humor.

I shook my head. "Don't bet on that, pops...Like I said, I have a plan. Get ready to sit back and take notes, I'll show you how to tuck your tail and plead with your girl to come back like a boss."

Albert erupted in laughter.

Chapter Thirteen

The Overlay for The Underplay

"Misery won't touch you gentle. It always leaves its thumbprints on you; sometimes it leaves them for others to see, sometimes for nobody but you to know of."

-Edwidge Danticat

Journey

They say when depression falls on you, you can feel it all the way down to your bones. My mother says depression is a demonic spirit that's attracted to your pain. She says that it grabs a hold of you and feed off your grief. And to keep its food supply coming, it continues to feed you lies and doubt so that you can sink further and further into its greedy clutches.

I don't know if that's true or not, but I do know when I opened my eyes the next morning, my whole body was in pain. I had to drag myself out of my bed to tend to Ayana. As I fed her my mind raced with thoughts of failure. It was just me and Ayana before Jo came into our lives and I was doing just fine. So now, why does it feel like I'm going to crumble and fall without him?

And what the world did I witness yesterday? I was a hundred percent sure that Jo had a split personality, one that was deadly. What the hell was I supposed to do with that information? And what about all the men that he killed in the restaurant? I'm sure that once the press got wind of it, self-defense or not, his chance for running for office was shot.

I gave Ayana her bowl of cherry puffs and put my head in my hands. Goodness! Everything was a mess. And poor Kyle, when Jo was done with him his face looked like ground beef. Oh! Man!

"Wow, Journey, you look like your best friend has died." My mother said coming into the kitchen to fix her a cup of coffee.

"I feel like my best friend has died. Well…at least dead to me." I muttered without taking my face from my hands. It hurt to even hold my head up. I felt like I was drowning. Life without Jo was unthinkable.

"You ready to talk about it?" She asked as she took two mugs out the cabinet. One she prepped for chamomile tea and the other she prepared for her coffee.

I took my hands down sitting back in my chair. "Nothing to talk about. Found out Jo had a fiancée, got embarrassed out of my life, ran and hid in a motel room and cried my eyes out for two days."

My mother sat a steaming cup of tea in front of me. I leaned over and just inhaled. The smell of chamomile is so very soothing. Yet this morning, it did little to soothe me.

"How do you know it was his fiancée?" She asked sliding down in the chair across from me with a cup of coffee in her hand.

I just stared at her for a minute. What kind of question is that? Did she think I was making this up?

"Because he came into the party with the heffa on his arm, and then the news reporter asked him if they were going to be announcing their engagement soon!" Even though I tried to school it, my words came out a little snappy.

My mother wasn't fazed one bit. "Soooo… they're not engaged?"

I looked at her as if she had grown a building out her head.

"Don't look at me like that! You the one that just said the lady asked when they were going to announce their engagement, which means something that has yet to happen."

I exhaled, letting my head drop back on my shoulders. "Ma, they're engaged!" I yelled at the ceiling.

"Well did you talk to him and allow him to explain why he lied?"

I jerked my head back up and looked at her amazed. "Why would I do that?"

"Because you don't know what's going on. At least give the man a chance to explain himself."

"I don't need him to explain, I got the message loud and clear. I was just too blind to see the signs."

She looked at me doubtful. "What signs? I've been here for a while now and the only sign I saw was of a man that was in love for the very first time." She paused for just a minute giving me that look that heralded her saying something otherworldly.

"You know I can read people. I'm not saying Jo is innocent. He's a politician for heavens sake, which means he's not above doing *whatever* he has to do to get what he wants, even if it means using trickery. However, he's not a fool. He will not risk losing you and Ayana for some hilly head floozy his mama probably picked." She pointed at me.

"Now his mama…" She shook her head. "Snake, reptile…can't be trusted with a piss filled bucket. But Jo…naw, there were no other signs except that of his love."

I held up my hand and began to tick them off for my mother, who was obviously team Jo all the way.

"He never invited me back to his place. Did you notice that, old spiritual one? It don't take a rocket scientist to figure out why. He never invited me because his place is her place too."

"He never takes me anywhere where cameras or the press will be."

"He never takes me to any of those fancy restaurants where his peers mingle. You know why, Yoda? His peers know about his fiancée."

She shook her head at me. "You said all that to say nothing—" her phone rang cutting her off. Looking down at it she smiled when she saw who it was.

"Hey, baby. Mama was just thinking about you." The smile disappeared off her face. "Boy, calm down, what are you saying?" She stood as she listened.

"Ma, who's that?" I asked coming to my feet as well. She held up her hand shooshing me.

"Okay baby, I'm on my way." She hung up the phone and headed towards the stairs. I scooped Ayana out of her high chair and followed.

"That was Rob, he says Rome done gone crazy."

"What!? Why?"

She shook her head. "That girl done left him."

Bewildered, I sat on her bed as she began to pack. Ayana slid out of my arms and began jumping on the bed like a bunny rabbit.

"What girl?"

"His babysitter."

"Ohhh! Why is he going crazy 'cause she left?" My mother stopped packing to stare at me as if I was the slowest snail in the race.

"Because he loves her Journey, just like you love Jo. Go figure, both of my children are being idiots at the same time. Now I got to go and try to rein this boy in before he does something stupid and end up in jail."

I stood. "Me and Ayana will go with you."

She held up her hand stopping me. "No, you stay here and try to clean up your own life. This child need her father. He a good father. What you gon' do about that? Or are you gon' be one of those women that deny him a relationship with his daughter 'cause your feelings hurt?"

My mouth opened, insulted. "That's not fair. I didn't ask for any of this!" Tears came to my eyes. "How is this my fault?"

She exhaled sitting on the bed pulling me with her. "I'm not saying this is your fault, or that you asked for this. What I am saying is this is the hand you've been dealt whether you asked for it or not. How you choose to play it out is what counts." She chuckled dryly.

"Hell, I've seen some beat the game working with less."

As she spoke she rubbed my arm, my head dropped to her shoulder on its own accord needing her comfort. Poor mama, her children were a wreck and she was the only one keeping them together.

"You can make it through this, baby. If you ain't never listened to mama before, listen to me now. I know it may seem as if the ultimate betrayal has happened, but the devil is busy, and he wouldn't be doing his job if he didn't blow things up and magnify them in our heads till we feel like we're drowning."

I grunted. That was exactly how I felt right now.

Her voice gentled. "That man love you, and if I know Jo like I think I do, he's going to show you. Just continue to be your amazing self. He's addicted to that."

I looked up at her and frowned. "What?"

She smiled. "Yeah, he's addicted to you. I know an addict when I see one. You silly girl, if you think he's going to give up, you're lying to yourself. Men like that..." She shook her head. "They don't stop till they get what they want. And he wants you. Just don't give in too easy." She kissed me on the forehead and continued to pack.

I didn't bother telling her she didn't have to worry about me giving in too easy, because I wasn't giving in at all. It was over between Jo and me. He will never get a chance to hurt me again. But to my mother I just nodded and helped her pack. I didn't want our last words to be that of a disagreement. She was team Jo because she didn't know him like I did. If I told her about his alter ego that can kill as easy as normal people spread butter on their toast, she may have a different opinion.

Joseph

I sat back in my home office chair and watched as Journey helped her mother into a cab. She thought the reason I haven't brought her here to my place was because Chloe was here. That was the furthest thing from the truth. I haven't brought her here because her place was better. Simple.

But of course, there was never anything simple when it came to women. Or maybe it was that they just couldn't believe us men were just simple creatures. We were always at her place because it was warmer, brighter…always smelt like good food. There was laughter there and love.

I exhaled. *That's okay, my sweet J, I'll ease all your worries and soothe your pain. I broke it, I was damn sure going to fix it.*

But first…

I picked up my new phone and sent a text.

Me: Need to talk to you on a secure line

It took about five minutes for my text to be answered.

Punk Kid: Where are you?

Me: Home office

Several seconds later my computer screen went completely blank before it rebooted. When it came back online I had a view of Rome sitting in a chair made for a king, his loft apartment behind him. This son-of-a-b****, hacking bastard. So much for my goddamn hundred-thousand-dollar firewall.

"You just hacked a system I was told was un-hackable." I told him dryly.

His lip lifted in a half smile that didn't reach his eyes. Eyes that were blood shot red. It looked as if my statement had generally amused him, taking his mind off of his problems. According to what Abigale told Journey, Rome had fallen in love with Nak.

Poor fool, back during our Seal days, Nak's code name was Black Widow, a name she had earned a hundred times over. Her beauty is deceptive. It is all things alluring, soft and warm. Many of unsuspected victims have fallen under its spell, only to be drawn in enough to receive her deadly bite.

Outside of Albert, Nak was the only other person I trusted with my life. She has always had my back and I've always had hers.

"Oh yeah?" He asked responding to my statement. "Is that what the brochure told you?"

"That's what the man who cleaned out the little bug you left in my system told me."

He chuckled without any humor shaking his head slightly. He looked tired.

"Yeah well, he lied to you. Once I'm in, there is no getting rid of me."

Damn, I hated this kid. It really grated on my nerves that I needed his help.

"I knew you were going to come groveling sooner or later." He said as if he'd heard my thoughts.

I chuckled. "Having a rough day, kid?" The muscle in his chin ticked, letting me know I'd hit the mark.

He exhaled rubbing his hand back across his head. He was tired of the small talk.

"What can I do for you, chump?"

"James Bennet Law…who is he?"

"Where does Nak live?" He answered my question with a question.

I sat back in my chair surprised. How did he know her name? Nak would have never told him that.

"Who is that?"

His lip twisted in an angry snarl. "She told me her name. But even before she did, I learned an awful lot about her from your *personal* computer. In fact, I learned about your whole team. Now, answer my question! Where does she live?"

I put my hand underneath my chin lifting one eyebrow. "It would seem if you know so much, oh mighty hacker, you would have that information."

He growled before he slammed his fist on his desk. "I—" He paused to regain control over his rage. "I don't have time for this. The longer she's gone the less likely it will be that I will find her. And I need to find her!" He spit his words out through clenched teeth.

I exhaled taking pity on him. Hell, he and I were two peas in a pod. I understood exactly what he was going through.

"Look kid, I don't know where she lives. Nobody does." I shook my head. "She's what we call a phantom, she'd enlisted with a dummy address and gave the agency the same one."

He breathed out frustratingly through his nose, letting me know he'd already been to that address.

"How could she be your right arm and you not know where she lives?"

I held up my hands. "She was uncomfortable with anybody having that information and I respected that."

My words were true. Nak never kept it a secret that when she decided to disappear, she was gone and nobody would find her. I understood. I never had a reason to question her loyalty to me, so I never insisted she reveal her retiring destination. She had paid her dues and deserved her peace.

But what amazed me even more is that the kid nodded, not questioning whether or not I spoke the truth. He was a damn human lie detector. It was just mind boggling to see the brain that hid inside that hoodlum's body.

"My turn, James Bennet Law? What do you know?"

He exhaled, shaking his head a bit. When he spoke, he did it in a manner that said he really didn't feel like talking to me. His mind was on finding Nak, probably already thinking of his next move. If anybody will be able to find her, I'm sure it would be him.

"Man, I'm going to be honest with you, you're involved in some serious sh*t, and I don't have the full picture to begin to explain to you how serious. This kind of incriminating information is constantly on the move. But that's alright, I have chaser program I designed on it and it won't be long before it catches it. I need a few days though. However, you need to either send my sister and my niece back here so that I can keep them safe, or you need to protect them." He paused for a moment as his weary eyes took me in, judging me.

"It's wilder than I initially thought. If my suspicions are correct, this thing goes all the way up to the top. They've been experimenting on people. This sh*t so wild that once it comes to the light, a lot of folks are going to have to die because of what they know. You're going to have some real big enemies. And so will I for being the one that uncovered this sh*t."

"Protect my sista, I wouldn't be surprised if they start trying to do damage control now. I'll holla at you in a few days." The screen went blank before my initial screen came back up.

F***!

He said a mouthful and nothing at all. What the hell did he mean, *this thing went all the way to the top*? What thing? He said he wouldn't be surprised if whoever this proverbial *they* were, didn't start trying to do damage control.

Is that what this recent blackout was about?

Damn! His cryptic message has left me back at the starting point. Because I didn't know who I could trust outside of Nak and Albert, and now, as much as I hated to admit it, Rome, I was pretty much grounded until he got back to me.

However, his warning about protecting Journey and Ayana only solidified my plans. I picked up my phone and dialed Albert.

"Yeah boss…" he said into the receiver.

"I'm going to need two days to prepare everything. Stay close to them till I give you the go."

Journey

It's been two days since I saw or heard from Jo. Two gut wrenching, horrible days. The fact that he hasn't called or tried to come by only solidified what I've come to learn about him. He didn't care about me, all this time he was only using me. As soon as I called it off, he was out the door and hasn't even looked back.

I expected him to at least try to come by and see Ayana. Nothing! I'll never admit to the fact that I missed him something terrible. I missed his warm body next to me at night. I missed him always trying to talk me into doing something nasty with him. I even missed when he came up in my greenhouse and pretended to be interested in my plants.

I was suffering so bad y'all. If not for Albert, who surprisingly had been here for the last two days, I don't think I would have made it. Poor Albert, he was missing my mother, although they talked on the phone with each other all the time. Heck, I don't know who was more blue, him or me, which is why when he fell asleep both nights downstairs on the couch. I just covered him with a blanket instead of waking him to go home.

Truth was, I was glad he was here. He kept me distracted so that I didn't do anything stupid, like pick up the phone and call Jo, telling him Ayana needed something just so I could see him. Plus, it allowed Albert and I to talk about some things that I couldn't discuss in front of my mother.

The morning after the first night he slept over, he and I were sitting at the table having coffee and tea. I'd had Jo's split personality heavy on my mind and I knew that if anybody knew what was going on with him, it would be Albert, seeing as to how Jo said the older man had practically raised him.

"Albert?" I asked as I stirred a little honey in my tea.

"Mmm?" He didn't look up from the paper he was reading.

"Something strange happened the last time I was with Jo, and I don't understand what I saw."

He looked up then. "Oh yeah? What did you see?"

I took a sip of my tea. "Jo was different. Something happened to him. He changed."

Albert chuckled. "You're going to have to be a little more descriptive than that, little lady."

I sat my tea cup down and looked him square in the eye. "I saw Jo fight and defeat nearly thirty men, leaving more than half of them dead. He did it in record time, moving like some kind of—of…" I searched for the right words.

"Machine! I don't know, he was fast and strong. Deadly!" I shook my head. "I've never seen anything like that. Not even on TV." Albert didn't speak right away, so I continued.

"And you know what the crazy thing is? I haven't seen or heard about it on any news outlets. It was like it never happened."

I hit the table. "And Kyle! Oh, my goodness! He beat the hell out of Kyle!"

Albert chuckled. "First of all, you can forget about seeing any of Jo's dirt on the news. His family has the best cleaners in their employ, and they've been cleaning up after Jo for many, many years."

"Cleaners?"

"Yeah, fixers…they go around and tidy up crime scenes, erasing all incriminating evidence. You'll be amazed at some of the things the very wealthy do that will never come close to the news. And as for the dweeb Kyle," He shook his head.

"He had it coming. He better count his blessings, Jo took it easy on him."

I held up my hand. I didn't want to discuss Kyle. I knew that everybody around here disliked him.

"I know your opinion of Kyle. Tell me what's going on with Jo."

He exhaled settling back in his chair. "Jo was in the Navy for a long time." I nodded.

"Yes, I am aware of that."

"Our government has sent him into some real sh*t holes. And when you're in situations like that, you have to do what you have to do to survive. I've seen cases where men or women have blacked out in temporary insanity to pull their way up out of the hole, having to do things that their minds cannot justify."

He gazed down into his coffee cup remembering the horrors. "Something very similar happens to Jo, when he feels threatened or if his loved ones are threatened…" He snapped his finger. "It's as if his emotions shut off like a light switch. And by some mysterious reason, it causes him to be faster, stronger…" He looked across the table at me. "Deadlier."

"What you witnessed is the reason he was of such value to the United States Government." He chuckled again. "They sure hated to see him go."

"But is he dangerous to me or Ayana?"

Albert looked at me as if I'd lost my mind. "Are you kidding me? That boy would chew off his own arm before he ever hurt either of you. Trust me, I've known him his whole life. He will never hurt you. Now... I can't say the same for anybody that ever does hurt you."

"Think back to that day. Can you remember what happened to set him off?"

"Ummm..." I frowned, now that I thought about it, when he had first went in on Kyle, he still felt like my Jo. After the man had slammed me on the ground he felt different. That's what had set him off.

I told Albert.

"You see what I told you? A threat to you or Ayana will feel like a threat to him, and that will trigger his alter."

"Alter?" I asked.

"Yeah, it's what his brothers-in-arms took to calling it."

"Wow!" I sat back in my chair floored. Albert had given me a lot of information to mull over. I was relieved in the fact that he was convinced Jo was not a danger to Ayana and me. I had been battling with letting her go and visit her father without me. Before that incident happened in the restaurant, I would have done it without a second thought.

Now thanks to Albert, I can let my heart be at ease that my daughter will be okay on unchaperoned visits. Only...

He hasn't even called. And I know it's only been a day, but dang...shouldn't he have at least called by now?

"Albert?"

"Hmmm." He asked from where he had gone back to reading his paper.

"Have you…" I cleared my throat, feeling like a weak female for even asking this, but I had to know. "Have you heard from Jo?"

He shook his head without looking up from the paper. "He probably went somewhere to lick his wounds. A break up can be hard."

Hmmm…

Yeah right!

I know men stick together. And no doubt Albert knew exactly where he was and just didn't want to tell me. He was probably back with his fiancée apologizing for stepping out on her with the little young ghetto college girl, taking her to all of those fancy restaurants that he couldn't take me, and cooking his stupid gourmet spaghetti for her on his state-of-the-art stove. They were probably even now as we were speaking sitting down at some fundraising banquet with fifteen-hundred-dollar lamb chop plates, giving phony smiles to their future constituents.

Goodness! I had become a bitter woman.

That realization didn't sit well with me. I didn't want to be a bitter woman. I didn't want to be sitting on the sidelines sending hateful vibes through the air.

I squared my shoulders. I loved Jo. He'd really hurt me. I deserved time to grieve. But I was only going to give myself so long. And then it was going to be time for me to get my life back on track.

I had to keep moving. It wasn't too late for me to achieve at least a few of my dreams.

On that third day, I woke up with a new attitude. Although my heart still hurt, I was determined to do something other than moping around the house. I began my day with a pause moment. It had been a while since I'd had one. With everything that's happened, I hadn't taken the time to stop and reflect. After loading my misters with my essential oil blend, I stood under them with my head thrown back as the sun began to rise and enjoyed the gentle mist that rained down on me and my plants.

Stopping to reflect is healing. In this moment, there isn't anyone but you and the Creator.

In this moment, there are no worries, only possibilities

In this moment, the devil's lies are quieted. The tricky imagination of your mind is abolished.

Only facts are on the table.

It is a blessing to be alive.

It is a blessing to still have your right mind.

It is a blessing to have another chance to get it right.

This is the moment to give thanks for all the things we constantly take for granted.

When I came out of my reflection, I was ready to start a new day. I began with trying to find out if Kyle was okay. So I called Michelle. Since I didn't know what I could or couldn't say to her, I tried to keep it light and ask her if she had heard from him.

"Girl, Ben says Kyle and his family left town."

"What?" The surprise in my voice was genuine.

"Yeah, apparently their catering company got an offer in New York that was too big to refuse. They packed up and left practically overnight."

"What?"

"Why do you sound so concerned? Don't tell me you've started vibing on Kyle." I opened my mouth to deny that, but right then, Albert rushed through the front door with a strickened look on his face. Without knowing what put it there, my heart dropped.

"Jo has been in a horrible car wreck!"

Chapter Fourteen

Little Brown Lie

Journey

"Oh, my God!" I cried out as Albert began to show me the pictures of Jo's mangled car. I clutched his arm. "Where is he? We have to go and see him!"

"He's home resting. But a caretaker couldn't be found for him on such short notice. So, he's going to need round the clock care. I can do it sometime—" I shook my head cutting him off.

"No, I'll do it…" I paused surprised at the words that had just flown out my mouth.

What about his fiancée? And his mother? Surely, they are before me in line to see about the task.

Albert's face brightened. "Oh, that would be perfect! He could really use a helping hand. I know he feels so alone right now."

I nodded and shook my head at the same time, I was so torn. "Of course, I'll do it, just give me a second to get Ayana and my things together."

My mind was rushing so fast. I had an overwhelming feeling of guilt trying to choke me. This whole time I had thought the worst of him and Albert said he had been in the hospital fighting for his life.

I ran towards the stairs, but then paused, 'cause I had no idea what I was doing. He said Jo was at his place. I couldn't go to his house, his fiancée was there.

"What's the matter?" Albert asked, wondering why I had stopped.

"You said he's at his place, I—I can't go to his place… can I?" He looked at me as if I'd lost my mind.

"Yeeess!! Journey! Hurry, he's been in an accident!"

"Right…Okay--Right!" I was a nervous wreck…I didn't know what the right move was to make… I stalled again.

"Sweet baby Samuel." He uttered under his breath. "What is it now?!"

It was clear he was losing patience with me, which was not helping, because my mind was already frazzled. My first instinct was to rush to help Jo, but there were so many issues with that. Was his fiancée there with him? Would I go there and run into his parents or her? Would there be pictures of her on his wall? Should I just go for the day and then come home? I had absolutely no idea what to do!

"I don't know how to pack, should I pack for the day or two…a week?"

Albert must have heard the distress in my voice, because when next he spoke, his voice had gentled.

"You may want to pack for a long stay, sweetheart. Who knows what condition the boy is in? He's going to really appreciate you helping him out."

I nodded. "O—okay."

I packed for Ayana and me as quickly as I could, then I ran upstairs to the greenhouse and set the timer for my sprinklers, so they could water my plants while I was gone. I had no idea what a long stay meant. I wish I would have just kept my mouth closed and not offered to look after him.

But how could I do that? It was my love for him that spoke. The thought of him laid up in his bed with a bunch of tubes running from his body that was weak with pain, barely clinging to life was tearing me up. The pictures of his car were horrendous; it was a miracle he'd survived.

I couldn't help but wonder if the wreck happened after he and I broke up. And if so, would that mean it was my fault?

That thought put me into something of a slump. If I had been kinder would it still have happened? Maybe I could have gently called it off and given him a little hope for tomorrow.

I shook my head. It was a waste of time to ponder what could have been. We are here now and I just had to deal with it.

I sat silent as we drove into a part of town that I had only been to a handful of times. This area reminded me a lot of Chicago's Gold Coast, except where the Gold Coast had Lake Michigan, this area had the Potomac River. This was the part of town that housed all the elites of D.C. On the outside, Jo's building looked like something from the future, all glass and stainless steel. On the inside, it was a world of luxury.

Albert had to pass two check points in which he had to identify himself to park his car. I was so nervous as we rode the mirrored elevator to the top floor I was shaking. By the time he used his key card to open Jo's door I was drowning in my guilt, because I had somehow convinced myself this was all my fault.

"Jo, my boy!" He called out as he carried Ayana into the huge foyer of the penthouse. As soon as the bright light hit me, I remembered what stood out to me most the one time I was here. The windows. He had huge floor to ceiling boxed windows with a startling view of the Potomac River and the Hill outside.

"In here!"

For just a moment I closed my eyes as that deep voice caused a shiver that took my breath to run down my spine. I know it's only been two days since I'd last heard it, but it felt like a life time. His voice sounded strong and clear, it wasn't the voice of a sick or injured man.

I inhaled as we rounded the corner into the massive living room, but all my breath whooshed through my lips at the sight of Jo looking simply scrumptious sitting on his couch. He was dressed in a white t-shirt that clung to his muscled chest and ripped lean stomach just right with a pair of white basketball shorts. His rich dark skin contrasted with the white of his clothes in a way that made his beautiful melanin pop.

I brought my hand to my belly as an involuntary flutter of arousal shot through it. His dark gaze swept over me with the same hunger, no...starvation that mine was doing him. My body was betraying me.

We are no longer allowed to have these feelings for him! I screamed at myself. But then it seemed like time just slowed down as he licked his lips before lifting those beauties in a killer smile aimed at me.

Speak for yourself! My body yelled back at me.

"How is that leg?" Albert asked breaking the spell Jo had cast over me.

Y'all, I had been so distracted by his chocolaty goodness I didn't even notice that his left leg was propped up on an emerald green ottoman that matched his couch, and it was wrapped in a cast. Next to him on the couch were a pair of crutches. In his hand he held a remote control that he used to turn down the volume on the football game he was watching.

I disgusted myself. I never thought I was a weak woman. Growing up, I witnessed so many of my friends get their hearts broken by guys who thought they were playas, and I always swore that would never be me. But now look at me, one six foot plus chocolate brotha with a banging body has proven me to be a liar.

I lifted my head on my shoulders. Damn that! I will never forget the hurt he caused.

Ayana began to buck in Albert's arms. She had spotted Jo and she wanted him.

"Da-da!" She yelled, causing that sexy smile on his face to grow.

He reached for her. "Come here, baby!"

Ayana was so excited to see him she was practically vibrating with joy. When Albert put her in his hands she actually wrapped her little arms around his neck and squeezed him for dear life.

"How is daddy's little lady?" he asked kissing her on her fat cheeks in the way that she loved.

Tears burned the back of my eyes. She'd missed her dad and if I was telling the truth to myself, I'd missed him too. I had come expecting to see him weak and in bed. So, you can imagine the shock at seeing him sitting here looking as good and as capable as the last time I'd seen him.

Better even!

He chuckled before his deep smoky voice washed over me. "Do I look that bad?"

It was then I realized I had just been standing there staring at him. I shook my head.

"No…no, it's just that I thought you were hurt."

His spirit seemed to deflate right before my eyes, he laid his head back against the couch. "I get spurts of strength, but then I burn myself out and I'm tired again." Even his voice suddenly sounded weaker.

I cleared my throat as my guilt washed over me again. "Umm—would you like some help?"

With a pair of serious puppy dog eyes, he nodded. "That would be great. That's if you don't hate me too much."

I took a few steps closer. "I don't hate you, Jo."

He lifted his head. "You don't?"

"No, of course not. I—"

"Ma ma ma ma!" Ayana suddenly yelled out pointing to something behind me.

I turned my head to look and see what had caught her attention, turned back, but then whipped back around clutching the arm of the couch to keep from falling.

"What the hell?!" I put my hand on my chest.

There was a huge picture of me on the wall. I'm talking floor to ceiling. The thing had to be at least twenty feet. It was the picture my brother Rob had painted from a sketch he'd done of me while I sat in the window watching the leaves fall to the ground. I hadn't even known he was sketching me.

How in the world did Jo get this? Only I knew that my brother sold his paintings on eBay. He didn't want anybody else to know in fear that it may hurt his street cred. However, I know for a fact he didn't sell anything this big, which meant somehow Jo got a hold of a copy and had this made.

Joseph

She was so damn beautiful! I struggled to remain sitting and not cross the floor and wrap her in my arms. I've missed having her warm plush body pressed against me. I've missed her taste. I felt starved for it.

My body instantly reacted to her, needing her in a way that left me in pain. During our time apart, I discovered that I couldn't sleep without her, so for the last two nights, I've sat at my desk watching her sleep. To trick my body into resting, I had to lay my head on my desk next to the computer screen and listen to her deep breathing, imagining that she was lying next to me.

Noticing her mother on the wall, Ayana began to bounce on my leg pointing at the painting.

"Ma ma ma ma!" She cried.

Journey turned and glanced behind her, it must have taken her mind a moment to register what she'd just seen, because her eyes came back to mine before she whipped back to face the painting clutching the arm of the couch for support.

I had to press my lips together to keep from laughing. The look of amazed horror on her face was priceless. It was very similar to the look on my father's face when he had come by to check on me earlier, only there was no amazement, just horror.

"Son, have you gone insane?" He'd asked as he stared at the painting. I sat where I was sitting now with my fake cast on my foot and smiled at him.

"Yes, I've gone insane."

For just a moment, fear flashed in his eyes before he got himself together, he seemed a bit edgy all the way around. However, after I'd informed him that I would be working from home for the next couple of weeks till my foot healed, anger took its place.

"Dammit, boy! You can't keep putting off your responsibilities!" I blinked at him innocently.

"Whatever do you mean, father? I was in a *horrible* car crash. Surely you don't expect me to come back to work so soon. Plus, I have a doctor's note." I held up the papers that said I should stay off my foot for six weeks. He'd snatched the papers out my hand, balled them up and stormed out.

Frowning at the stricken look on Journey's face, Albert turned to see what had caused it. I hadn't told him about the painting. It was just installed this morning.

"Oh sh*t!" He actually jumped, not expecting the in-your-face picture. When his startled gaze came back to me, I winked at him with a huge goofy grin on my face. I told the old bastard I was going to show him how it's done.

The painting was frighteningly huge. No sane individual would have such a thing on their wall. I'd like to see her argue that my place is Chloe's now.

When I saw that she was turning back to face me, I quickly lay my head back on the couch and sighed pitifully.

"Jo?" She sounded winded. "Where did you get that picture?"

As if it pained me, I lifted my head off the couch to look at her, pretending I didn't know what she was talking about.

"What picture, sweetheart?"

She used her thumb to gesture behind her back. "That one."

"Oh…that old thing? I've had it for a while now. I forget where I found it." I rested my head back against the couch. I could hear Albert off to the side pretending to cough in a napkin to cover his laugh. I nearly smiled myself. It's true what they say about politicians. We have no shame.

"You've had that for a while?" Her question was quiet and unsure. Everything she had assumed was being shot down.

I nodded turning to look at her with sad eyes. "It saved my life."

The shock that was now on her face was well worth the exuberate amount of money I paid to have the picture blown up and a frame made for it in the time that I had. It was true, I've had the original print for some time now. In investigating her brothers, I discovered Rob's little shop on eBay. As soon as I saw the pic I bought it. I tried to get the original, but he wouldn't sell it.

She bit her sexy bottom lip as she battled within herself. She didn't want to have good thoughts about me. She didn't want to ask how the painting had saved my life.

I've got news for you, my sweet Journey, when I'm done, you'll never question my love again.

"How did the painting save your life? I've got to hear this." Albert muttered dryly, relieving her. She exhaled, gently blowing her breath through her thick plush lips.

Show time. "The doctors told me I died on the operating table." I paused for a moment so that could sink in. "And all I could remember was…was walking toward the light."

Albert erupted in another fit of coughing.

"Are you okay, old boy?" I asked trying to cut eyes at him without Journey noticing. If he didn't get a hold of himself, he was going to give me away.

"Yeah, yeah…I think the acrylic," He waved his hand around looking up in the air. "Is choking me up. Go ahead and tell us what happened next." He was barely holding it together.

"As I was saying." I smiled at Journey. "I was walking toward the light, feeling at peace. And I heard a voice calling. A sweet voice, soothing to my soul. And when I looked back over my shoulder, the only thing that was there was that painting."

Her eyes raked over me, before she frowned slightly. "Operating table? But it looks like only your leg was injured."

Oh sh*t! That one got away from me.

I cleared my throat. "Yeah—well yeah they had to operate on the leg." Albert just stood behind her shaking his head.

"You saw the light from a leg operation?" She asked.

"Well…babe, there is no such thing as a safe operation. You can ask any doctor. But the good thing is, this painting is what called me back." She turned her head and looked at the painting before she looked back at me.

"Hmmm…okay." It didn't sound as if she was really buying my story, I looked up at Albert for a little assistance.

He stepped forward taking her bag out of her hand. "Here darling, let me show you where you and baby girl rooms are."

She didn't follow him right away. She just stared down at me through narrow eyes. Ayana, bless her soul jumped up and wrapped her little arms tightly around my neck as if she feared her mama was going to take her away from me.

That got Journey's feet moving, but as she passed me she still looked at me with eyes full of suspicion. When they were gone my gaze went back to Ayana, who was now sitting in my lap staring up at me as if she too was waiting to see what other ridiculous thing was going to come out of my mouth.

"I don't think your mama bought my tale." I whispered. She erupted in giggles falling against my chest.

Journey

Jo was full of crap!

"He saw the light?" I asked Albert as he led me down the long hall to the wing of the penthouse for the bedrooms.

Albert chuckled, shaking his head. "That boy... he's been that way since he was a kid. No shame... he'll do and say whatever it takes to get what he wants."

I stopped walking and folded my arms. "I'm glad you think this is funny. I don't see the humor."

Albert took my arm and quickly guided me into a guest bathroom.

"Okay, little lady, before you get upset just hear old Albert out." He was talking very low.

I can understand the whispering, but I was drawing a blank as to why he'd pulled me into the bathroom. Maybe sound traveled good in the hall and he didn't want to run the risk of Jo hearing his words.

Hmmm...this should prove interesting.

"Jo hurt you, didn't he?"

I nodded. "More than I care to admit."

"Wouldn't you like to get a little revenge?"

My eyebrow lifted in interest. It's a shame how good that word made me feel. "Revenge?"

He nodded.

"How so?"

"As you can see, the boy will do just about anything to get you back." He gestured towards the living room and the ridiculously big painting.

"Yeah, that painting is a little crazy."

He nodded. "Of course it is, and if I know Jo like I think I do, it's only the tip of the iceberg. He's prepared to humiliate himself, beg, borrow, and apparently lie to prove how much he cares for you." He shrugged. "

"So why not have some fun while giving the poor fool a chance to prove himself? I know you love him. I've heard you in your room crying for him at night." He grabbed my upper arms in both his hands giving them a warm squeeze.

"Us men, we mess up all the time. We're dumb that way. But ain't many of us willing to go far and beyond to correct our mistakes like Jo. Give him a chance, daughter. It breaks my old heart to see y'all this way."

I bit my lip as I thought about his words. I must admit, I was expecting to see pictures of his fiancée on his wall, not a wall-size picture of me. So obviously, this was not her home. There was no woman in the world that would stand for her fiancé having a huge painting of another woman on his wall.

I guess it was a little cute that he would do such a thing, even if it was a bit ludicrous.

"Plus," Albert continued. "If you want to really see him suffer, watch him try to keep up with his fake injury for longer than three days. He can't keep still that long."

"Are you telling me there is nothing wrong with his leg?"

He shook his head. "The boy is as strong as a bull."

"Oh, my goodness! He is such a con artist!"

"We like to call it politician around these parts. Come, let me show you your rooms."

There were three bedrooms at the end of the hall, one big door in the middle and two doors off to either side of it. He opened the one to the left of the middle door, then moved to the side so I could step past him. My mouth opened in surprise.

It was a beautiful nursery with so many toys that it almost looked like a toy store.

"How beautiful!"

I walked into the room, completely floored at what I was seeing. There was a huge wooden baby crib that looked as if it had been hand carved against the wall. This room didn't have the big square windows that were in the others. It looked as if the O shaped windows faced the back of the property, but they were covered in pretty pink and purple curtains.

The room looked as if it belonged to a royal princess.

"When he first laid eyes on Ayana, he had this room prepared for her." Alfred said quietly from where he stood by the door.

"Are you serious? Don't lie to me!"

He held up his hands chuckling. "I guess I deserved that for helping Jo get you here. But I'm not generally a liar."

I believed him. Albert is a solid, dependable person. I've grown to love him like a father. And no, it's not because it looked as if he and my mom were getting really close. It's because ever since I've known him, he has always had my back. For some reason when he's around, I feel safe, just like when I'm with Jo

I continued my perusal of the nursery. It was fully stocked with diapers and clothes for Ayana. Jo had thought of everything. There was even a potty for her. She wasn't quite walking yet, but it would be any day now. I was just telling Jo last week that I was thinking about starting to potty train her. And look…there was a potty.

Stunned I shook my head, I couldn't help but think about my mother's words she said to me before she left to go back to Chicago to check on my brothers. I don't know what kind of fiancée Ms. Chloe was to him, but she wasn't the type that came to his house.

I brought my hand to my head. "I think my mother may have been right." I muttered.

Albert snapped his fingers. "Don't you just hate when that happens?"

I looked up startled that he had even heard me.

He nodded his head. "Come on, check out your room."

I followed him out of the nursery and expected him to cross the hall to the door that was on the right of the big room, but he didn't, he headed toward the big wooden door in the middle.

I froze. "What are you doing?"

He nodded again. "Come on, this is your room."

What?!   .

When he opened the door and moved to the side so that I could come in, I had to grab the wall for support. Somehow Jo had managed to get the feel of my cottage inside this room. There were sheer curtains on the big boxed windows that was parted very artfully. But what brought out the beauty of the windows were the beautiful plants that adorned it.

This room was a stark contrast to the rest of the penthouse; it was all whites and greens, where the rest of the penthouse was very state-of-the art modern decor. However, inside this space was a little slice of heaven. I took off my shoes, because the carpet was pure white and soft. It felt like I was standing on a cloud. In the center of the room sat a big four poster bed that was surrounded by a beautiful sheer canopy.

Plants had been placed perfectly throughout the room to heighten my senses and bring joy to my spirit. I turned back to look at Albert.

"This is my room?" I whispered.

He smiled. "Why are you whispering?" He whispered back.

"Because I'm having an endorphin overload." I put both of my hands that slightly shook to my lips to keep from screaming out.

This room was perfect!

Joseph

I smiled as I watched her take in my home that I had made hers. Lifting my finger, I touched her cheek on the screen of my phone.

"There is nothing I won't do for you, J...."

Chapter Fifteen

Her Worth

Journey

Albert left me to unpack in *my* room. I eased down on the bed sitting my bag by my feet. What was I doing? Was I really thinking about staying? I chewed my bottom lip. Can I sit here and pretend that there is no danger in being here alone with Jo?

Albert and my mother think I should give him a second chance, but they didn't know how painful it was to cry out my heart in that motel room. They didn't know what it was like to look into the eyes of someone you trusted to realize this person had lied to you and betrayed you, and everything you thought to be true was not.

I know that knowing how to forgive is important, especially when we wanted the Heavenly Father to forgive us, but I am a flawed individual and just didn't know if I could. I will always remember the pain of seeing another woman on his arm. That is something I don't think I can ever forget.

I shook my head.

I couldn't do this…

I was just going to have to tell Albert it wasn't going to work, I wasn't quite ready to forgive him and put my heart at risk again. The wound was too fresh.

I stood and reached down for my bag, but right then a gentle breeze blew through a glass door that was ajar. I hadn't paid much attention to it earlier because it was covered with a sheer curtain that matched the ones on the windows.

Curious, I quickly crossed the plush carpet and gently opened the door.

I sucked in my breath as the smell of my oil blend wafted around me, stimulating my sense of smell, instantly sending the message to my brain that everything was going to be okay, because my Creator had me in his embrace.

Walking farther into the space, I was able to see it was a partial greenhouse that opened out to a beautiful private balcony that overlooked the city. There was a clear breathtaking view of the White House.

In the center of the balcony sat an in-ground hot tub that was surrounded by beautiful palm trees that sat in huge multi-colored flower pots. The greenhouse was empty of plants, but there were shelves and stands set up and ready to be used. There was also a little metal table and chair set like the one I had at home, where I liked to drink my tea sometimes.

I walked to the shed-like cabinet and opened it. It was stocked full of brand-new supplies, all the stuff that I used.

Dear God, all that time I'd thought he'd been pretending to pay attention to me as I went on and on about my plants, and he had actually listened.

I gave him this long spill about the organic fertilizer blend I liked to use. I made my own from a number of products. And do you guys know he had all the products here in the cabinet, including cartons of egg shells?

On the wall was a button with a note written in Jo's handwriting that said, *Pause for A Moment.*

No!

He didn't!

Closing the cabinet, I pressed the button and cried out when my blend began to gently mist me.

I laughed because right then a breeze blew in from the balcony and once again a strong feeling came over me, a feeling of protection. A feeling that my Creator was watching over me and would never let anything happen to me.

Tears came to my eyes; I couldn't believe Jo did all this for me. He'd made his home mine; including giving me his bedroom and getting it reconstructed to appease my taste. All this stuff was new I could tell. This had to have cost him a fortune.

Albert stuck his head out the bedroom door. "Hey, little lady, we're going to order a couple of pizzas is there anything special you want on them?"

I was so full of emotion I could barely talk, the only thing I could do was shake my head. "No, whatever you guys get is fine."

"Are you okay?"

I nodded. "Mmmhhhmm, I'm just going to put my clothes away and then I will join you."

"Okay, take your time, it's no rush."

Trying to hold back my tears, I nodded again. "Okay."

After he left I went back into the bedroom picking my bag up off the floor and carrying it to the closet. I opened the door and my mouth hit the floor. This closet was huge. It was damn near the size of my bedroom at the cottage. My little lonely bag of stuff was going to look silly hanging up in he—

"Oh my—" I turned on the light to make sure my eyes weren't playing tricks on me. The closet was packed full of new clothes.

Women's clothes!

Women's clothes that were my size and style!

Expensive women clothes that were my size and style!

One whole wall was a shoe rack and it was packed full of brand-new shoes, shoes and boots that made my feet itch to try them on.

That was it!

I dropped my bag and ran out of the room and down the hall. I came to a stop in the living room and I didn't care that I probably looked silly. Albert had been saying something, but at my sudden appearance he paused. However, my focus was not on him, it was on Jo.

Casually as if he didn't know he'd just rocked my world he turned to look up at me. A smile appeared on his handsome face.

"Did you find everything okay?" I nearly closed my eyes as that deep voice washed down my spine.

"Jo, what's going on? I-I don't understand." My voice was barely over a whisper. He had stimulated all of my senses at once and it was too much.

"Come on, baby girl, let's see if there are some of those little nasty plain baby cookies your mommy likes to give you in the kitchen. Tomorrow I'm going to sneak you a cookie with real sugar." Albert said scooping Ayana up from the floor where she had been playing with some of her new toys. My gaze went to the toys and I gestured toward them.

"Why are you doing all this?"

He turned off the television and sat up. "Come here, baby." He took my hand, pulling me down on the couch next to him.

Goodness, he looked so good. *Be strong, J!*

"I know there's not much I can say in the way of an apology." He shook his head. "I don't think I will ever forget the look of pain in your eyes. It tore me up on the inside." He placed his hand against his heart.

"I felt it like it was my own."

His intense gaze was pulling me in, I felt myself drowning in it.

"Some pain can't be spoken away. Some pain must be physically removed. And all that I ask is that you give me a chance to do that. I won't try to tell you how sorry I am, because you deserve so much more than my words. I want to *show* you how sorry I am." He reached out and gently took my hand in his.

"I want to show you how much you're worth to me." He gestured toward the bedroom. "That stuff is nothing. It doesn't even begin to encompass your value. Just give me the six weeks it's going to take my leg to heal to show you how much you mean to me. And if at the end of the six weeks, you still feel as if you're not my whole entire world, my very reason for breathing, then I'll let you go and I'll never bother you that way again."

"What about your fiancée?" My voice quivered.

"I called it off. My right hand to God! I called it off that same night. The only thing I could see was your tears. I—" I put my finger on his lips. I wasn't ready to have this conversation with him. It was all too much.

He took my hand in his and kissed my palm. "Please baby, just give me the six weeks. I don't deserve your kindness. It's your mercy I'm begging for."

Biting my lip, I looked away from his drugging gaze to think about his words, but then he kissed my palm again and I damn near moaned.

"Please, baby!"

Goodness! He begged so sweetly. I looked back at him. "You want me to stay here with you for the six weeks it's going to take your leg to heal?" Sensing his victory, he tried his best to suppress his smile and nodded his head.

I looked at his leg in the cast skeptically. How many stories had Albert told me about the rascally side of Jo? They were all funny stories and I must admit that I was a little jealous that I hadn't seen that side of him. I had only seen the serious Jo or the horny Jo. It appeared as if I was getting ready to get my chance to see Jo the trickster.

"And how is your leg doing?"

As if on cue, he lay back against the couch and groaned. "It's killing me!" He lifted his head and looked at me.

"Did I tell you I damn near lost the whole leg?" I inhaled loudly.

"Nooo!" Two can play at this game; I had two older brothers. I wore a look of astonishment on my face. "You didn't! Wow! That must have been horrible!" I got on my knees next to him and began to fluff the pillows behind his back.

Y'all should have seen the lecherous look that came into his eyes, his nearly amputated leg forgotten.

"Well I don't want you to worry. I'm going to take really good care of you for the next six weeks." Looking like a little boy he nodded.

"I sure do appreciate it." I had to look away from him to keep from laughing. This man was a mess.

The phone rang. Albert answered it in the kitchen. A few seconds later he brought Ayana to us.

"Pizza's here, I'll get it."

That night we ended up having a really good time. I was glad Albert stayed as long as he did, because I wasn't going to lie and say

I wasn't nervous. And of course, Albert, being Albert made me laugh so hard I almost peed my pants.

Needless to say, he helped me to forget all about my nervousness, especially when he told a story about the time he'd convinced Jo as a kid that he had VD. Of course, Jo didn't want him to tell that story, which only made me want to hear it more.

"It was clear he was going to be something of a lady's man very early. When he was in third grade his teacher caught him with a little girl in the coat closet."

"Alright, old man, next story." Jo interrupted.

I sat on the couch with him. Ayana had fallen asleep on the pillow between us. Reaching over I swatted at him to shoosh him so that Albert could finish the story. But as I did it, he reached up and caught my hand bringing it to his lips kissing my palm.

I inhaled as my heartrate increased. He didn't let my hand go, he just lowered it in his lap and used his thumb to rub that spot just above my palm where my pulse beat was. I wondered if he could tell it was now beating faster?

"So, he gets in the car with a note from the teacher. Now this kind of stuff he never took home to his parents, he always brought it to me to sign."

Bless Albert's soul, he was a master at removing tension from the air.

"I read the note and I asked him what the hell he was doing with the little girl in the closet. Do you know this kid looked at me and said, *I was handling my business, what you think I was doing?*"

"What?!" I screeched. "In third grade?! Oh my goodness! How old were you?" I asked Jo. He had an embarrassed smile on his face.

He looked over at me with his sexy gaze. "Old enough to handle my business."

I held my head back and erupted with laughter. I could see his little bad butt saying something like that.

"So, I knew I was going to have to teach him a lesson." Albert continued. "I say boy, what are those spots on your neck? And I'm really selling it; I got a look of horror on my face and everything. He starts freaking out yelling, what spots?" By this time, Albert is barely able to talk around his laughing.

"He's literally climbing the seats of the Town Car crying, saying he just kissed the girl, he promised. I said it don't matter, kid. She gave you something, just look, you got more spots." Albert had to pause because he was now clutching his sides laughing.

"He screaming, *what she give me?! Al, what she give me?!* I leaned in close and looked at his neck. I say, it look like she gave you VD, buddy. As soon as I pulled the car up in front of his house, he shot out the door and ran straight to his father's office, who at the time was meeting with the Governor of Florida. He didn't knock or nothing. He just burst through the door yelling, *dad help me, help me, dad! I got the VD!"*

Both Albert and I nearly slid out of our seats laughing at him. Jo let us laugh for a minute, although he didn't join us. He just wore that *yeah you got me look on his face*, but then he turned to look at me.

"It's really not that funny." And of course, that just made me laugh harder.

Albert helped me clean up after dinner and then told us he had to go. I hugged him good bye and thanked him for all he'd done. I'm telling you, I don't know where I would have been without him. When I came back into the living room Jo was sitting there looking like raw uncut temptation. Ayana's little feet were on his lap, he was relaxed back on the couch.

He watched me with those bedroom eyes of his.

"Did you have fun laughing at me all night?" He drawled.

I bit my lip and nodded. "I did, it was quite funny the way Albert chose to have the talk with you."

He shook his head. "Funny to *you*. He scared the hell out of me. Because of him, I didn't touch another girl for the next sixteen years."

I tried to hold on to my laugh, but I couldn't. Just picturing a young Jo freaking out at the thought of getting VD is comedy gold.

"I sure do miss the sound." He said so low I barely heard him.

"What sound?" I asked sobering.

"The sound of your happiness…"

Danger! Danger! Danger!

The warning bells were going off in my head. I cleared my throat. "Umm…I'm going to lay Ayana down, jump in the shower and hit the bed. It's been a long day. Do you need anything before I go?" It took him awhile to answer.

I could have kicked myself for my choice of words.

Finally, he put me out of my misery and shook his head. "Naw, I'm alright."

I picked up the baby. "Okay, goodnight."

I practically ran out of the living room. Now, I know a lot of you guys are looking at me as something of a coward. Well, call me what you like. My mama said not to give in too easy. Had I stayed in the living room a second longer I'd been a goner. You guys do remember how aggressive Jo is, don't you? He had a way of forcing himself past all your safety walls.

As I got Ayana settled down for the night, I thought back to how excited she had been to be in the presence of both her parents. She had spent the whole time crawling from Jo to me, then back to Jo and then Albert, who she loved like a grandfather.

How could she not when he was always there and spoiled her right along with Jo and I, and my mom? I leaned over and kissed her fat cheek. She was tuckered out.

Although she had been sleeping through the night lately, I left the nursery door cracked a bit just in case she did wake up and freak out from being in a new room.

After I took a shower, I had to laugh out loud when I saw that Jo had stocked damn near a year's supply of cocoa butter in the bathroom cabinet. I shook my head as I moisturized my skin. It was hilarious how much he enjoyed the smell of it. Poor baby, to be black and not know anything about cocoa butter until he met me.

With a towel wrapped around myself I went to my bag for my pajamas. However, my eyes strayed to the pretty nightgowns in all colors that hung there in the closet, pretty silk and soft to the touch nightgowns. I took a cream one down from the hanger and slid it over my head. It felt as if the material caressed my skin as it slid down my body to fall mid-thigh. There was also a pair of matching panties.

Standing in the mirror I looked at myself. With my skin glowing from the cocoa butter, it looked as if I was on the way to join my lover in the bed.

I exhaled. Oh well, there is no rule against looking lovely to bed alone.

Before I slid between the sheets I opened the canopy on the bed so that I could have a clear view of the Hill, hoping that amazing view would help lull me to sleep. However, after an hour of tossing and turning I gave up on sleep.

Kicking the covers back I just kind of sat propped up with my back against the pillows and just enjoyed D.C. after dark. I think Jo was suffering from sleep deprivation as well. I heard him go into his room earlier. A little while later, he came back out. Then he'd gone back in.

Throughout this whole break up, I think the nights were the worst. You'll be surprised at how quick you get used to that warm body sleeping next to you or being wrapped in a pair of strong arms.

The sound of gentle knocking broke through my thoughts. I turned toward the door wondering if I was hearing things. A few seconds the barely there knock came again.

"Come in!" I called.

Jo opened the door. I smiled at him standing there looking adorable with his fake cast on and unneeded crutches.

"Having a hard time sleeping?" I asked.

He shook his head. "I haven't slept in week and I'm exhausted."

I bit my lip. It had been a week since last we slept in the bed together. "Why?" My question was so low I didn't think he heard me.

"Because I can't sleep without the smell of cocoa butter against your skin."

Cocoa butter against my skin? What the world does that smell like?

I cleared my throat trying to quiet my nervousness. "That's not good for your healing. You need rest."

He looked at me with those puppy dog eyes. "What do you suggest I do? I am your patient for the next six weeks."

I put my finger against my chin. "Hmmm, maybe you can use a little sleep therapy."

He looked skeptical. "What exactly is that?"

I had to bite my lip to keep from laughing. "It's when the nurse allows the patient to sleep in the bed with her, so that he can get the proper amount of rest."

A huge grin spread across his handsome face. "I think that is the perfect prescription." He nearly tossed his crutches away before he pulled his t-shirt over his head.

Give me strength!

He half limped half hopped towards my bed. I held up my finger as he leaned over me.

"Just sleep."

He nodded. "Yeah, of course, just sleep."

I gasped when he didn't continue to the otherside of me, but settled between my legs. His big hands closed around my waist sliding my nightgown up until my panties were showing and then he laid down resting his head against my center, moving it till he got good and comfortable.

My mouth opened in shock. After he found the spot he liked the best, he wrapped his strong arms around my waist holding me close and sighed.

"How I've missed that." He muttered.

It took a minute for my shock to wear off, but when it did, I realized I still held my hands in the air over him. Slowly I lowered them and began to gently rub his head, holding him close.

Moments later, I kid you not, he was out. However, his heavy breathing was causing all kinds of havoc against my girlie parts.

Even still I found myself smiling. I think I liked the rascally side of Jo. And you know, although I thought there was no way I was going to be able to go to sleep in this position, it wasn't long before I joined him in slumber.

He and I must have been tired because neither of us moved till the next morning and he not even then. I carefully slid from underneath him and looked down at him sleeping. He wasn't lying about not getting any sleep. Jo was generally a light sleeper, but it looked as if his body was making up for the sleep he'd lost.

It felt good to know that our time apart had affected him just as much as it affected me. I stood there and allowed myself a moment more to visually enjoy the sight of his muscled chocolate body lying on my white sheets before I hurried into the washroom to perform my morning rituals. If Ayana wasn't awake yet, she would be up shortly, and I didn't want her to cry out and wake her father.

Once again, I chose to bypass the clothes I had brought from home and instead chose a beautiful yellow summer maxi dress that had caught my attention last night. I don't know why, but I felt amazing and today, I wanted to be the girl in the yellow dress.

I even took extra care with my locs, moisturizing, re-twisting, and then piling them high on my head in a messy bun, allowing a few tendrils to escape down my neck and back. Barefoot, I tip-toed past Jo and out of the room. When I eased opened Ayana's door, it was to find her standing up in her crib looking around wide-eyed at all the toys in her room.

When she saw me she reached for me. "Ma ma ma ma."

"And how did you sleep, precious heart?" I asked her as I laid her on the changing table and changed her diaper. In a language that only she understood she began to tell me how she slept. In fact, she talked while I got her dressed and brushed her little hair into a ponytail on top of her head.

She continued to talk to her mama as I took her into the kitchen, sat her in the high chair Jo had gotten for her and prepared her a little bowl of baby cereal. She talked in between spoonfuls. The only time she stopped is when I sat on the couch and began to nurse her.

She still liked to nurse a little after meals. But since she was in fact eating solid foods, she was nursing way less. I had worried that the weaning process was going to be difficult, but surprisingly it was happening quite naturally.

"I am such a damn idiot." Jo said startling me. I had been looking down at Ayana and didn't hear him come into the room. He stood there in the entrance to the hall that led to the wing of the penthouse where the bedrooms were watching us. And honestly, I had no idea how long he had been standing there.

He was dressed in only his basketball shorts leaving his muscled chest and stomach on display to torture me. He must have decided to skip the crutches this morning, because they were nowhere in sight.

I chuckled. "What do you mean? What did you do?"

"I almost lost this." He said gesturing toward me and Ayana. "I've been blessed with the two most beautiful girls in the whole world and I almost lost them."

Blushing I looked away before my gaze came back to him.

"It's a good thing the Heavenly Father is merciful, huh?"

He grinned at me. "Yes, indeed it is."

Chapter Sixteen

Sealing the Deal

Journey

"Are you trying to kill us?!"

Jo yelled as he clung to the door of his brand-new Range Rover that had just been delivered this morning for dear life.

I clutched the wheel with both of my hands, my adrenaline was pumping overtime. The last time I'd drove was when Rome was teaching me so that I could take my driver's test. His temperament at the time had been very similar to Jo's now. It was the only time I had ever seen my big brother afraid.

Okay, so maybe driving wasn't my strong suit. And I may or may not have failed my driver's test the first time I took it. But I eventually passed. And do y'all know Rome never let me drive his car a day after that? He said he would've bought me one, but he feared if he did, I would kill myself or someone else.

"Don't be a baby!" I told Jo as I jerked the wheel to change lanes. "I just need to get use to how this car drives that's all."

And boy did it drive. I barely had my foot on the gas and this baby was moving.

Jo threw both of his hands out, drawing his body up and screeched like a girl when I was forced to slam on the brakes because some butthead had decided to turn at the last minute. The car in back of me laid on the horn.

"Come on, people!" I yelled hitting the steering wheel. "Drive like you have some sense! A signal would have been nice!"

Jo looked over at me with real fear on his face. "I've made a horrible mistake." He whispered. It looked as if he was close to tears.

Nobody was as surprised as I when his Albert phoned upstairs and told us to come down to see Jo's brand-new truck that the dealership had just delivered. Talking about a beauty. It looked like something that belonged in a museum for luxury cars. Jo spared no expense on the extras. There were several televisions inside. The seats were real leather and felt like heaven to sit on.

The inside was lined in a wood trim that matched the tan seats perfectly and contrasted beautifully with the sparkling black paint job. There was even a matching car seat for Ayana. I didn't even know car companies made custom made car seats.

Then Jo had looked at me and asked if I wanted to go for a ride.

I shrugged. "Sure."

But then he handed me the keys. "You want me to drive?" I tried to keep the excitement out of my voice.

He gestured to the cast on his foot. "I can't do it. I know this really nice bistro; we can go grab something to eat."

I had to bite my lip to keep from smiling as I took the keys from his hand. This was so cool. Albert even agreed to baby sit

Ayana so that Jo and I could have some alone time. I'm telling y'all, it's something about wearing the yellow dress. This day was turning out to be AWESOME!!!!

Well…awesome for me. By the time we pulled up to the restaurant, Jo practically jumped out the car, thanking the Heavenly Father for not letting him die.

I folded my arms and shook my head at the heathen.

"You're moving pretty good for just having your leg *operated* on."

He didn't even miss a step. "You'll be amazed what a man can do when faced with death."

I smacked my lips. "Being a little dramatic, aren't we?"

He took his keys out of my hands. "Dramatic my a**, you are never driving again. You're a menace to the road!"

My mouthed opened. "That's not fair—"

"Mr. Warren, it's good to see you up and about after the accident. May I have a second of your time?" The voice came from behind me cutting me off. Jo looked over my head.

"Dusty, the gossip extraordinaire? Whose life are you going to attempt to ruin today?"

The man Jo had just called Dusty held a microphone in his hand, standing next to him was a man with a camera that was pointed at us.

My heart skipped a beat. Oh no! It's the media! I went to step away from Jo, but right then he took my hand in his pulling me back towards him as he handed the keys off to the valet.

Dusty chuckled. "If I promise to keep it clean, will you answer a few questions, sir?"

Jo pointed at him. "No questions about the campaign and you only have till I get to the door." With my hand firmly in his he started toward the door. He had ditched his crutches all together, claiming he could walk better without them. I don't know who he thought he was fooling; he didn't even try to walk with a limp.

Excited that Jo was going to give him the interview Dusty fell into step with us.

Joseph

I chose this bistro because I knew the media liked to linger here in hopes of catching an interview with some of the legislators that frequent the spot. My baby felt that I was hiding her. After today, she will no longer feel that way.

Although I wasn't going to allow Dusty to talk to her, I didn't want to feed her to the piranhas. I am going to allow him to capture her on film. This would send a message to all parties involved about my feelings for her.

"Can I start by asking who this lovely lady is you're holding so close?"

Sometimes you had to love the media. I couldn't have asked for a better question. Journey squeezed my hand.

"This is the woman I hope to make my wife very soon." She sucked in her breath sharply. Her nails were now digging in my hand. I doubted she was even aware of it.

Dusty chuckled. "You say hope, like there isn't a woman alive that wouldn't kill for the honor of being your wife and maybe one day becoming the first lady of this great nation. "

I chuckled. "I wish that was true. It appears I found the only one that's immune to my charms."

"What do you mean?" Dusty asked as he hurried around a group of business men and women as they left the restaurant.

"Well, I asked her to marry me and she turned me down." I felt Journey's gaze fly to me as I ushered her through the door.

"What are you going to do now?" Dusty called after us.

"Keep asking till she says yes!" I said over my shoulder as the doorman closed the doors behind us.

Journey

"Why did you tell him that?" I had to physically keep myself from screeching. My heart was beating so fast. Joseph Warren, only son to Senator Warren and future president of these United States, if his parents had anything to do with it, had just told PMZ, a well-known celebrity gossip television show that he proposed to me and I turned him down.

Oh my God!!!

I put my hand on my chest trying to calm my breathing. He smiled down at me, lifting his finger to push one of my locs that had fallen in my face behind my ear.

"Because it's true."

I opened my mouth to say that it wasn't, but never got a chance because a booming voice came from within the restaurant.

"Joseph Warren, just the man I came back to Washington to see."

"Bill, you son of gun. Where have you been? The Hill has been a boring place without your theatrics." Jo said shaking the older blond man's hand.

Bill chuckled. "I heard about the accident. Is your foot okay?"

Jo waved away his concern. "I'm faking it to get all of this one's attention." He said reaching for my hand bringing it to his lips.

Bill laughed again, taking Jo's words for the joke they were attended to be. Only I knew that the scoundrel was actually telling the truth. When I looked at him skeptically he had the nerve to wink at me.

This man is a trip. He is such a damn *politician*!

"And who might this lovely lady in the yellow dress be?" Bill asked reaching for my hand lifting it to his lips.

"This is the woman I hope to someday *soon* make my wife." Jo said easing my hand away from the older man's before his lips could touch it. "So, keep your lips to yourself, you geezer."

This caused Bill to hold his head back and roar with laughter. He patted Jo on his back. "This is why I love you, kid. Come, join me for lunch. I would love to get to know the woman that has captured the heart of a legendary rake like yourself a little better."

Jo opened his mouth to refuse his offer.

"Oh, come on man, I've come all the way back to Washington with a blank endorsement che—" He didn't even have to finish.

"You know, Bill, I think my lovely lady and I will join you for lunch to catch up on old times of course."

My goodness! See what I mean? Politician…

"Sorry about this, my love, I will make it up to you later." Jo said low as he guided me through the restaurant to Bill's table.

"No problem, do what you have to do."

He looked down at me for a moment before he nodded once. There was something else in his eyes that I couldn't quite peg.

He pulled out my chair and as I went to sit, he leaned over till his lips gently brushed my ear. "I appreciate you understanding."

I sucked in my breath at the feel of his tongue against my lobe. A shiver ripped through me from the unexpected caress. I looked around with startled eyes to see if anybody had noticed what he'd done.

Nobody had, not even Bill, who was still jovially going on about how good it was to be back on the Hill and how he'd missed everyone. But at that point I was having a hard time focusing on anything he was saying.

Yeah sure, I was smiling and appearing to give him my undivided attention, nodding here and there, but something had shifted in the air between me and Jo, and I ain't gon' lie, I was losing hold of my willpower to fight.

The lines were beginning to blur. I didn't even know what I was fighting anymore. Ever since he'd laid his head against my warmth and slept there last night...

Ughhhh!!!

Now, I had to force myself to think about something other than sex, which was hard to do because everything Jo did made me think about sex. He had a way of licking his lips sometimes before he spoke, and there was the way he opened the button on his suit before he sat, revealing just how well his shirt fit against his well-muscled stomach and chest.

And whenever he laughed his Adam's apple moved up and down in his strong neck, making me just want to crawl in his lap and lick it. I groaned biting my lip.

Dang it, I'm in a tight spot.

Jo looked over at me and smiled. It was as if he could sense what I was going through because right then, he put his hand on my thigh, gently moving my dress aside so that his warm palm was against my flesh.

As the lunch progressed his hand got higher and higher and I knew I should stop him or push his hand away, but for the life of me I couldn't.

However, I did manage to get through lunch without jumping Jo, thanks to Bill, who was hilarious. Jo and his son had attended college together and were pretty close in those days. Like Albert, he had plenty of wild stories about Jo's shenanigans that had me in tears. And of course, Jo shook his head denying the things Bill said were true.

Several people stopped by our table to talk to Jo. I was amazed at how many people wanted to be a part of his world.

"It's always been that way." Bill muttered to me reading my mind as Jo stood to shake hands with the Supreme Court justice. "The kid has charisma."

I nodded and was going to tell him I was beginning to see that, but right then Jo reached for my hand and introduced me as the love of his life, the woman he soon hoped to make his bride.

You see, this had been the fourth time he'd said this today. I didn't want to read more into this than what it was. Jo was a smooth talker; he would say anything to get what he wanted, but what could he possibly want from me that he hadn't already gotten?

So why keep saying that he wanted me to be his bride if he didn't mean it?

The one time he'd said anything about marriage had been the night of his party. He hadn't uttered another word about it till today. Now I couldn't tell if it was something he really meant or something he was just telling his peers.

And oh my goodness! These were his peers. He was introducing me to them and that just confused me more. Could I have made a mistake by assuming all those things about him?

I know what I saw at his retirement dinner. But how can I explain this?

"Jo, my wife is driving me crazy." Bill said after the Supreme Court justice had moved on. "She's really concerned about climate change."

His words drew me out of my thoughts.

"I don't know what nonsense she's been watching, but she's convinced the damn planet is dying. Claims she can't grow anything in our soil anymore without adding crap to it."

I wiped my mouth with my napkin. "With all due respect, sir, she is not speaking nonsense. What she said is a fact. You only need to study any data collected by the Unites States Department of Agriculture of the nutrient reduction in the soil from 1981 till now to know she speaks the truth."

Bill looked at me surprised, up until this point, I hadn't said much. I had been too busy trying to hold my composure and not start doing a happy dance because Jo was telling all his peers that he loved me.

"Journey received a scholarship to Georgetown for their Botany program. She was single handily courted by the head of the department. So, if anybody would know whether your wife speaks the truth, it would be her." Jo surprised me by saying, I wasn't even aware he knew that information.

Bill exhaled. "Okay, young lady. Give me the spill. Should I be as worried as my wife says I should be about the condition of our planet?"

"Mr. Bill, you should be more than worried. In fact, you should be terrified."

Then I spent the next thirty minutes telling him about my studies and the studies of others in the field. When I was done he wore a look of astonishment on his face.

"You marry this woman and you'll have my endorsement." Bill told Jo as we were leaving.

"Okay now, I'm going to hold you to that."

Bill chuckled as he patted Jo on the back. "I've always told you, I'd rather see you sitting in that seat." He paused for a moment as his eyes grew sober.

"If you choose to run, young man, you don't have to worry about finances. There are a lot of us waiting to back you." He patted him on the back one more time. "We believe in you, kid."

"Thank you, Bill, that means a lot."

Bill took my hand and brought it to his lips before Jo could stop him. "It was an honor meeting you, Journey. You're good for him. Out of all the years I've known him, I don't think I've ever seen him in love. You make him want to be a better man." He nodded.

"With you by his side, he will succeed in whichever path he chooses."

Tears burned the back of my eyes. "Thank you, Bill." My words were barely over a whisper.

Like yesterday, my emotions were on overload. I couldn't quite compute all that had happened in the last few hours, although God knows I was trying. I had been so lost in my thoughts when we left the restaurant that I didn't even pay attention to the fact that Jo was driving till we were halfway home.

You see, there was something I needed to know before he and I went any further.

"Jo?"

He reached over and turned down the music. "Yeah, baby."

"Why didn't you tell me about Chloe?"

He exhaled, shaking his head slightly. "I was stupid. I let my anger rule me. I told myself the only thing I wanted from the woman who had ran away from me without telling me she was pregnant with my child was sex. There would be nothing more. I got the house for

Ayana, the money…it was all for her. I—" He paused, shaking his head again.

"I didn't think I would fall in love. It's never happened before. I didn't know…" I turned to look at him, amazed he was telling me the truth, his anguish was real. It was like he was trying to figure it out as he answered my question.

"I don't know when I started loving you, but I did. And at that point I didn't know what to do. On one hand, I had my parents pressuring me to fulfill an arrangement that was made when I was in grade school and on the other hand, I have the woman who brought warmth and color into my life. This woman in the yellow dress, who takes a moment out of her day just to give thanks for her blessings and taught me how to do the same thing. This woman, whose laughter makes me feel like the luckiest man on earth."

He rubbed his hand over his head. "I really didn't know how bad I'd messed up until I lost you and realized I'd lost my heartbeat."

He turned to look at me. "How can a man survive without his heartbeat?"

His gaze searched mine, looking for an answer to his question.

I shook my head. "I don't know." My words were low.

"He can't, J…he can't."

"What about now? What about your parents and Chloe?"

It took him a little while to answer that. "You know, I was raised to follow a certain pattern. It seems like my whole life has been about me trying to rebel against it. When I was a kid my parents couldn't handle me, so they brought in Albert to do their dirty work for them. I didn't feel free till I went to the military. There, I felt like

I could be me, like I could release all the frustration and the anger that's been building up in me."

"What were you angry about?"

He shook his head. "I was angry because I was moving in a direction I didn't want to go, and no matter how I bucked and protested against it on the inside, my body continued to go in that direction. But something happened when I met you. For the first time, I saw a different way and I wanted it...I wanted it so bad I could barely think about anything else. You became the light at the end of the tunnel."

He paused for a moment. "I told my parents and Chloe the night of my party that I couldn't marry her. I called it off. And it felt great. For the first time I strayed away from the path that had been set out before me and it felt great."

I wanted to tell him about what his mother had done in the beginning when she found out I was pregnant and the afternoon of his party, but for some reason, I held my tongue. She was evil, but maybe she was just trying to do the best thing for her son. I mean, should Jo decide to run for office, I'm not really first lady material. I could be the reason America would never accept him.

Maybe that's why his parents were so set on him marrying Chloe. She was definitely first lady material. It was clear she was mixed raced. She didn't have natural hair like me; she had long processed hair, not a curl in sight. And she didn't favor the loud bright colors I did. She was definitely a black and navy-blue suit kind of gal.

"Did they choose her because she would make a good first lady?"

He chuckled. "Hell no. They chose her because she's Jeff's daughter."

"Who is Jeff?"

"The head of Macon Technologies. The man whose money put my father in office. Jeff is the puppet master, that's who he is." He paused for a moment.

"He's also the man that's going to try and put me in office. The man whose noose is around my father's neck and soon will try and be around mine, if I allow it."

As a woman in a man's life, you must be careful what you say to him. Your words can impact him to be great or to be a failure. My mother said that no matter how angry she got at my father she never said words that degraded him, because life had degraded him enough. The job he's forced to work to get paid less than he deserves.

When he walks out the front door he's faced with the knowledge that depending on the whelm of the authority of this land, this could be his last day alive or able to support his family that depended on him to be the lead and the head.

She said the Heavenly Father has given her a super power. She had the power to build him up and the power to break him down.

So, here I sat while my man, the man that so many wanted to one day become president of these United States, spoke to me of the agony of his life. What was I to do? A simple word from me would encourage him to continue on the path that is causing him anger and rage. And a simple word from me could help him choose the path that leads to his freedom…

"If this path that has been chosen for you upsets you so, why do you continue to walk it? It seems to me that you have been chosen to help people. Maybe the way in which you always assumed this mission would be accomplished is not the way the Heavenly Father prepared for you."

He turned to look at me then. He didn't speak, he just studied me, taking in my words and digesting them. See what I mean?

"Sometimes we do a disservice to ourselves when we try and buck against his will." I chuckled. "My mama calls it the vanity of man. She says it's completely vain of us to assume we have our whole lives figured out when there is one that sits high and looks low."

I took his hand that rested on the seat next to me.

"It's okay Jo, you're going to know soon enough which path you should choose. And I have all the confidence in the world that when you find your path, you're going to make a difference in a lot of folks' lives, including me and Ayana's. But no matter what you choose, we got your back, bro."

Chapter Seventeen

Sweet Surrender

"There is nothing in nature like it. Not in robins or bison or in the banging tails of your hunting dogs and not in blossoms or suckling foal. Love is divine only and difficult always. If you think it is easy you are a fool. If you think it is natural you are blind. It is a learned application without reason or motive except that it is God."

~~~Toni Morrison

Journey

A week later I was in a desperate state. Jo was torturing me! I wanted sex! And the man pretended as if he couldn't even tell. He continued to sleep in my room, in my bed, holding me close to him, giving me just a gentle peck on the neck and nothing more. He was always touching me just outside of the places I needed him to touch most.

He'd palm just underneath my breasts or rub his hand on my thigh just outside of my hot center.

Oh! Oh! And this one takes the cake; he'd placed his hand at the base of my back, just above my butt. He was going to force me to jump on him and just take what I wanted!

Now that I've gotten that off my chest…like I said, it's been a rough week. Let me tell you guys that I have been fighting fire with fire. That fake cast was driving him mad. He was scratching at it and kept banging it against stuff. The other day he went into a full cursing fit about how stupid the thing was. He cursed that cast out like it was a grown man that had robbed him or something.

I know he wanted to take it off for a minute, but I never gave him a chance. He knew what he was doing to me, those little kisses on my neck and never on my lips, and those little gentle brushes of his hand.

And yes, I knew what I was doing as well. He'd try to go into his office, claiming he had work to do, I would wait a minute and then just barge in. Several times I caught him in the act of taking the cast off.

"Jo, your leg needs to heal; you had a big operation on it, one that caused you to see the *light*. You can't pull at the cast like that. You don't want to end up *flatlining* again, do you? Here, let me help you get it back situated."

"Thanks baby, you're so good to me." He'd mutter dryly.

I would have to bite my lip to keep from laughing. I could tell he wanted to pick me up and physically throw me out his office.

I had gotten to a point where I was tired of playing games with him. I was ready for us to come clean about everything. Him and his fake injury. And me that I forgave him and was ready to have a good round of makeup sex.

The perfect opportunity presented itself that Tuesday when he informed me a few of his brothers-in-arms were going to come over to work out with him. He said it was something they did at least twice a month.

"That's perfect, I need to go and speak with my professor about some new data I'd gathered. Once she and I get going we can go for a minute, so I probably won't be back to just before dinner."

I could tell he didn't want me to go; of late, he's barely let me out of his sight.

"Okay, as long as you take Albert with you. If you want, you can leave Ayana here, I'm not going anywhere."

I nodded, my mind already putting together my plan. "That will work. Have fun with your friends." I told him.

"*Brothers*, baby...these are my brothers."

I chuckled shaking my head. "Sooorrrryy...have fun with your brothers."

Before I left the house, he surprised me by pulling me close and taking my lips in a kiss my body had been feening for over the last week. Standing on my toes I wrapped my arms around his neck and moaned as I tried to deepen the kiss.

But Mr. Tease only pulled back, making my moan turn into a growl. That's okay, I let him go. But tonight, he was mine, just watch!

After we left the cottage, I told Albert to run me back to the penthouse because I'd forgotten my notes. I didn't fill him in on my plan because Albert was only loyal to me to a certain extent. His complete loyalty belonged to Jo, make no mistake about it. Had I told him what was going on in my head, I wouldn't put it past him to send a warning text.

When we got back to the penthouse Albert used his key to open the door. I could hear the men in Jo's home gym. Albert went to the kitchen because I told him there was some blueberry muffins left over from what I made this morning, I continued down the hall.

Without making myself known I looked in at the men. They were all dressed in cargo pants and wife beaters. Some of them wore gym shoes while others wore military boots, including Jo. They all had on their dog tags and sported the same tattoo in the same spot, which meant like Jo, they were all Navy SEALs.

And what do you know. The cast was nowhere to be seen. For a moment I allowed myself to study him as he lifted weights and joked with his brothers. This is the real him. Jo is a warrior. He wore this more comfortably then any suit. When he was finished his set, he bent down and scooped up Ayana, who had been sitting in her little chair waiting on him. A big man with red hair and freckles walked up to her and tickled her.

"What's going on, scrubs?" Albert called walking around me with a muffin and a cup of coffee in his hands.

When Jo looked up and saw me, the con-artist didn't even miss a beat. He grinned holding up his free hand.

"Look, baby, it's a miracle!"

I folded my arms across my chest as I stepped in the room. Albert held his head back and barked with laughter when he noticed Jo was wearing a pair of boots instead of the cast.

The other men looked around puzzled, wondering what they were missing. So Albert being the wonderful story teller that he is, filled them in on what Jo had done.

"Okay, I can explain." He said approaching me with Ayana in his arms as the other men began to join Albert in laughter.

I shook my head. "You ain't got to explain. I knew you was faking." His mouth dropped.

"And you let me suffer this whole time, when you could have put me out my misery?"

With my hands still folded across my chest, I took a step closer to him closing the gap between us. Then I lifted an eyebrow at him.

"Ditto, playa…"

The devilish sexy grin that appeared on his face let me know he had been torturing me on purpose.

"There's a method to my madness." He whispered.

"And what is that?"

He winked. "I'll tell you later. Come and meet the boys."

Jo introduced me to all eight of his brothers. Surprisingly, he was the only black man amongst them, but there was no racism between them. Whatever they had gone through had caused these men to form a bond that was unbreakable. They said only one was missing from their group, a female soldier named Nakhti.

With them, Jo was free to be himself. He laughed and talked crap. And oh my goodness…they teased him so bad about the huge picture of me on his living room wall.

Guess who led the charge. Mmmmhhhmm, you got it… Albert.

And it didn't help that PMZ aired Jo's little interview the other day and that somebody uploaded it to YouTube, giving Albert even more fuel. Of course, he just had to play it for the fellas. Now he didn't just press play on his phone. No, that wasn't enough for Albert, he had to set it up on the big screen so that I could once again be embarrassed out of my mind.

The producers of the show had spliced the interview in a way that threw major shade at Jo's ex-fiancée and apparently, I was now famous. That kind of frightened me a bit, but Albert assured me that the public was fickle, and I would only be famous for a day.

He pressed play on the video as the fellas settled down to watch. I eased down on the couch next to Jo.

"So, do you guys remember when just last week the media was trying to get an engagement announcement to the lovely Ms. Chloe out of Jo Warren, as well as the announcement of him running for his father's senate seat?" The host of PMZ asked his staff who all sat around the office waiting for the latest gossip.

"Well, it appears as if Dusty found out why Mr. Warren has been so tight lipped." The screen cut away from them to me killing it in that beautiful yellow dress trying to step away from Jo and the cameras and he taking my hand pulling me back close to him.

Jo's brothers-in-arms actually began to cheer at this point.

Dusty asked Jo who I was and he looked at the camera and smiled like a man in love before he told them I was the woman he'd hoped to one day make his wife.

Kurt, the soldier they all teased for being super short patted Jo on the back. "Good job, man."

The screen went back to PMZ's office, they all wore shocked faces. One of the black girls on the show nodded her head enthusiastically. "Wow, she is the complete opposite of Chloe. He went and found him a *real* sista." The host of the show and the other employees laughed and asked her what she meant by that.

"You can just tell she is down to earth and proud of her culture. I like her. And if he runs for president, he definitely has my vote."

Jo leaned over on the couch and gently kissed me underneath my ear. "You're good for business." He whispered before he turned back toward the television. I bit my lip to try and tame the super cheesy grin that tried to take over my face.

"But get this," The host told his employees. "She turned him down."

All of their mouths dropped. "What do you mean she turned him down?" His co-host asked.

The host smiled deviously. "I mean, he asked her to marry him and she turned him down." He spaced the words out so that all the world could understand what he was saying clear as day.

Another one of Jo's brother's hit his lap. "That explains the big a** picture. He's begging." This caused the rest of the men to chuckle.

"I don't believe you." Another female employee said on the show. "There is no woman alive that would turn down a marriage proposal from Jo Warren."

The host chuckled. "Well, apparently he found the only one immune to his charms." He said stealing Jo's words. "Roll the clip."

The television cut away from their office back to us. Jo was ushering me through the restaurant door that was being held open by the doorman.

"What do you mean?" Dusty asked.

Jo turned to look back at him over his shoulder. "I mean, I asked her to marry me and she turned me down."

In the bottom of the screen, a photoshopped picture of Chloe appeared. She was cheering and clapping, glad about what Jo just said.

"What are you going to do now?" Dusty called.

"Keep asking till she says yes!" Jo called back over his shoulder. A big foot appeared next to Chloe, who was now crying hysterically to kick her off the screen. What made it so bad, they made the little doppelgänger of her scream as she flew across the screen.

I held my head in my hand shaking it as Albert paused the video. Jo's friends…I mean, his brothers all congratulated him.

"It's good to see you finally standing up to your old man." Tad, the one they teased because of his buck teeth told him. They all nodded in agreement.

"We thought you were going to end up dying miserable like him."

"Y'all can get off my boy. You know y'all whole generation is little weak." Albert told them, picking right back up from where he'd left off in his crap talking.

He claimed Jo's generation of soldiers was soft compared to his. And of course Jo and his brothers couldn't take that sitting down. So they spent the rest of the night in a heated debate over which war was the worst, Vietnam or the war America has been fighting in the Middle East.

And get this…At some point in the middle of this fierce debate, my mother called Albert's phone. He looked down at it and smiled like a school girl before he hurried to the balcony and talked to her for a good while. Jo and his brothers teased him about that. They accused him of being curled up on the settee clutching the pillow close, pretending it was his Abby Cat.

By the time all those men left, I had laughed so much my throat was raw. I still chuckled to myself as I cleaned up after everyone. When I was finished, I came out the kitchen to see Jo standing in front of his living room window staring out at the Potomac River.

"Did you finally get her to sleep?" I asked, straightening the pillows on the couch.

Our deal had been I clean and he try and get Ayana to sleep. All the activity of the evening had left her buzzing with way more energy that we liked to see at bedtime. When last I saw her, she was literally bouncing up and down on the couch singing her da-da song.

He chuckled. "Yeah, I had to pretend to be asleep in the chair next to her bed."

I shook my head as my gaze fell on that ridiculous picture of me. I stood for a minute studying it. While his friends talked about him for being what they called p**** whipped, he'd just sat there grinning proudly.

"You guys are just upset because I've found the kind of girl that helped me tap into my inner artist."

Alec, the redhead all his friends called the Scotsman shook his head. "No, buddy, you found the kind of girl that helped you tap into your inner Norman Bates."

He turned to look at me. "Listen to me, lass, if you come to a man's pad and you see something like this on the wall, kindly excuse yourself to the bathroom and then call the cops and tell them if anything happens to you, to check his freezer."

That had caused all the rest of the men to erupt with laughter. And so it went, one after the other they talked about him shamelessly.

Now I stood shaking my head, something had to be done about this thing.

"Jo, what is it going to take to get rid of this picture?"

"Marrying me."

I jumped because I hadn't heard him come up behind me. As I turned to face him he was going down to one knee. In his hand he held that box he'd shown me the night of his party. When he opened it, the huge ruby winked at me.

"Oh My God!" I felt like my heart was getting ready to beat out of my chest. I put my hand over it. I think I was going to have a heart attack!

"If you marry me, I will get rid of the picture." His voice shook as if he was extremely nervous.

Tears came to my eyes as my mouth opened, but I was such an emotional wreck no words came out, all I could do was nod my head.

"Yeah?" He asked, not sure he saw correctly.

"Yes!" I cried as I threw myself at him, wrapping my arms around his neck. "Yes!"

He stood lifting me off my feet as he held me close.

"Thank you, baby. Thank you so much."

He put me back on my feet so that he could put the ring on my finger, but my hand shook so bad he had to hold it still long enough to get it on.

The ring was so beautiful, like the necklace he had bought, it was a rose gold band designed to be a flower. And just like the necklace, there were small diamonds on the leaves that looked like rain drops.

"It's so beautiful."

"Not as beautiful as you." He whispered before he was kissing me.

And not those teasing kisses of the last few days, he was kissing me in a way that fed my need, and my need was strong. He was kissing me in a way that let me know the past few days had affected him as well.

"Jo...I need you!" I moaned, reaching for his shirt pulling at it, not caring that I seemed desperate.

"Damn!" He growled as he stepped back enough to rip it over his head.

His back muscles flexed under my hands as he lifted me pressing my body against the painting. My legs wrapped around his waist as he snatched my shirt over my head. With hands as desperate as mine he pulled my bra down until my breasts popped out.

"I've missed your pretty breasts." He whispered.

I had to bite my lip to keep from screaming when his strong arms flexed as he lifted me even higher until my sensitive tips were level with his hungry mouth. My nails scraped across his back as he feasted on me.

Then I felt his hand under my skirt ripping my panties. Seconds later he was filling me. I couldn't hold back my cries; they filled the living room to mingle with his heavy breathing, making beautiful music to my ears.

"I told myself I would not make love to you again until you agreed to be my wife." He whispered in my ear as he drove into me.

I screamed out as my world exploded violently, snatching my breath away. He carried me to the couch where he continued to make love to me until he caused my world to shatter again.

Oh, how I've missed this. This man made love like his alter ego destroyed…utterly.

By the time he found his release, my entire universe had shattered three times. I felt depleted of everything I had left, so much so, I didn't protest when he stripped away the rest of my clothes and carried me to our bathroom where he ran us a hot bath.

I relaxed back against him as the warm bubbles rose around us, happier than I've ever been in my life. Holding my hand up I took in my ring. Gently he traced it with his finger.

"It's so beautiful." I told him, if I wasn't so drained I'd be crying right now.

"I wasn't lying, I've carried this around with me ever since I gave you the necklace."

"Why didn't you propose before now?"

He chuckled. "I was afraid you would say no."

I lifted my head and turned in his arms. "What?"

He nodded. "See, I'm not as cocky as you accuse me of being. Even I doubt myself sometimes."

I ran my hands gently through his beard before I leaned in and kissed his lips. "You don't ever have to doubt when it comes to me."

A sexy grin came to his face. "Dare I hope that you are finally going to say the three words my heart longs to hear?"

I bit my lip trying to tame my smile. "Maybe."

A look of false hurt came upon his face that was so cute I held back my head and laughed. When my laughter died, I kissed his lips again.

"If tomorrow I wake up and this is not a dream, I will tell you that I love you. And not only that, I'll tell you just how much I love you. But something tells me this is too good to be true and that I'm going to wake up and you're not going to be there."

He gently moved the locs that had fallen in my face behind my ears. "I'm going to be here tomorrow, and the day after, and the day after that for the rest of our lives. You don't have to worry about that."

Joseph

The sound of my phone dinging woke me. That was a special ring that only meant one thing. My father had gotten into trouble and now emergency damage control was needed. I eased from underneath Journey. There were still a couple of hours until the sun came up and I was careful not to wake her.

My business phone was in the room next door that I had temporarily made my bedroom. Quietly, I slipped on my pants and left out gently pulling the door closed behind me. My phone stopped dinging for just as second, only to start right back.

F***

That meant something really bad was happening. I frowned down at the number. It was my father's assistant.

"Tim, why are you calling me so damn early in the morning?" I growled into the phone, not even pretending to be civil.

"Mr. Warren, you have to come quickly. Your father has locked himself in his office with a gun. Your mother is afraid his going to do something to hurt himself."

I was already moving to get dressed. I could hear my mother in the background screaming for my father to come out of his office.

"I'm on my way." I said hanging up the phone to slide my feet in my boots.

Damn it!

Damn it!

Leave it to my father to pull some sh*t like this…

As I grabbed my keys and headed out the door, I dialed his number.

You bastard! You better not kill yourself!

Chapter Eighteen

In the Blink of an Eye

Journey

I woke up the next morning alone.

For a half second, I lay there and thought about that. And I guess I can say that was the first clue as to how my day was going to go, that and the fact that something was not right with me.

However, I was only allowed that half a second to ponder over it because I could hear Ayana talking to herself in her bed. Groggily, I used the bathroom and did my morning rituals before she started demanding my immediate attention.

"Jo." I called when I left out of the bedroom to head to the nursery. Outside of Ayana's babbling the house was completely quiet.

"Hmmm." He must have had to run out for something.

"I guess it's just me and you, baby girl." I told her as I prepared a bath for her.

There was something off about me this morning, but I couldn't quite put my finger on it. Speaking of fingers, I took in my engagement ring.

"Your daddy asked your mama to marry him last night." I told Ayana as I got her dressed.

She fingered my ring before she tried to bring it to her mouth. "No, sweetheart, you can't eat that. Come, I will make you some breakfast."

I picked her up putting her on my hip and had to clutch my stomach as a slight cramp shot through it.

Uh-oh! That explained that off feeling. My period was coming. It would pick to come *now* after not showing its face for three months.

As I stirred my daughter's oatmeal, a thought came to me. The last time I felt like this, I had been pregnant with Ayana and didn't know it, then right behind that, another thought came.

When was the last time I took my birth control pills? My hand slowed.

Oh God!

I couldn't even remember the last time I took those pills!

This knowledge instantly caused my body to tense with stress, drawing more attention to the fact that something was definitely going on with it.

I told myself not to panic, but I couldn't help but think that if I was pregnant, Jo was going to kill me. I mean, preventing pregnancy must have been something that was important to him or he wouldn't have added it in the contract.

"You're not pregnant; it's just your period. Stop tripping."

Yeah, I know what my lips said, but my body was telling me something different.

Now of course I couldn't relax, because I had to know for sure. So, after I finished feeding Ayana, I called Albert and told him I needed a lift to the drug store to pick up a few things and then to the cottage so that I could check on my babies.

The whole way to the store Albert gushed over how proud he was of Jo for finally getting his ring on my finger. I smiled and nodded, but my mind was a hundred miles away. If I was pregnant, would Jo be so angry that he'll change his mind about wanting to marry me?

If he did get that angry, would I still want to marry him? Children are beautiful and a blessing from the Most High. If he didn't want this baby, then he didn't want me. I buried my hands in my face.

I can't believe how quickly my ultimate happiness shifted, not to say that if I'm pregnant I wouldn't be happy. It's the anxiety of worrying about what Jo will think that was eating me up.

Damn it, Journey, calm down, you don't even know if you're pregnant yet!

"Everything alright, little lady?" Albert asked looking back at me through the rearview mirror as he pulled into the drug store parking lot.

I nodded smiling at him, although I didn't feel like it. "Yeah, just a little tired, we had a long night."

He chuckled, "I bet you did."

As he took Ayana's car seat out the car and sat it in a cart, I bit my lip trying to think of the best way to tell him I needed to go into the store alone. But right then his phone rang.

"Did you tell your mom about the engagement?" He asked smiling down at his phone.

I shook my head. "Not yet."

"Okay, I won't tell her, I'll save it for you. Go 'head in, I'll talk to her out here."

I exhaled with relief as I took the cart from his hand. "Okay, we'll be right back out." He nodded already lost in his conversation with my mom.

Perfect timing, Abby-Cat...

I made quick work in the store, putting unnecessary things in the cart to mask what I'd truly come to buy. I told the store clerk to double bag the pregnancy test. After she did, I still folded it up in the bags and stuffed it down the side of another to make sure it was good and hidden.

She lifted her eyebrow at me, but didn't say anything about my strange behavior. I was so far gone in my worry I didn't even care, I just took my receipt and thanked her. Instead of pushing the cart out the store I unclipped Ayana's car seat and grabbed my two bags.

Albert looked up from where he was leaning against his car talking to my mom and began to approach me when he saw us coming out of the store. However, he hadn't taken but a few steps towards us before a black Tahoe came to a screeching stop between us.

It was the look on Albert's face that alerted me to the fact that something was terribly wrong. The next few seconds would feel like a life time.

My hearing magnified. I could hear my breath flowing threw my lungs, and the blinking of my eyes that too seemed to slow down.

This is the moment I learned that Albert was not who I thought he was. In the blink of an eye, he tossed his phone through his car window and in the same motion, pulled a gun from somewhere in back of him.

When I blinked again, the windows of the truck had let down and a scream froze in my throat when I saw the barrel of a gun pointed at me. I could remember thinking before the first shot was fired that the eyes of the man holding the gun did not match the way he was dressed.

He dressed like one of the brothas from the hood, but his eyes were missing the hunger. They were missing all evidence of coming from the gutta. It's strange how observant one gets in the moment they are faced with death.

The blast from the gun brought my thoughts to a halt. I jerked when I felt the impact in my chest. Looking down, my eyes widened with shock as blood began to soak through my shirt just above my breast.

Ayana's wails filled my ears.

I blinked and looked up just in time to see Albert slide across the hood of the truck and fire two shots, both shots finding their mark in the head of the driver and in the head of the man who had just shot me.

Damn! Albert is bad a**!

He reached me just as my knees gave out, picking me up in one arm and grabbing the car seat with the other.

"Hold on, little lady, I'm going to get you to the hospital. It's okay, baby girl!" He told Ayana, who was now screaming her lungs out.

"Pa-pa Al is here and I'm going to keep you safe."

I smiled. Was he actually trying to comfort the baby in the midst of all this?

As he quickly carried us to the car, I fought the blackness that tried to claim me. I had been shot in my chest, but I didn't feel any pain. I wondered if this is one last mercy God grants the dying.

Painlessness…

Another Tahoe pulled into the lot just as Albert got Ayana and I in the backseat. I screamed when they began to shoot at us too. Albert fired back as he ran around the car and jumped in the driver seat. He threw the car in reverse and stepped on the gas, ramming the vehicle that was shooting at us.

"Stay down!" He yelled at me before slamming the car in drive flooring it out of the lot.

I covered Ayana's car seat with my body just as the back window exploded in on us from the bullets that were coming through it.

"F*** this!" Pa-pa Al yelled slamming on the brakes.

I opened my mouth and screamed as once again time slowed down. Albert cut the wheel hard to the right, causing the car to spin in a way that I was positive was going to lead to all of our immediate demise. He pointed his gun out his window and as the car whipped back past the Tahoe, fired at the truck's wheels causing it to spiral into a death roll that sent it crashing into several parked cars, eliminating the threat.

And as smoothly as if he was turning into an intersection, Albert straightened the wheel, joining regular traffic like it was just another day. I stared at him with shocked eyes.

What the hell kind of Bourne Identity?!

However, the sight of blood gushing out of a wound in his neck caused me to reach for him.

I opened my mouth to tell him that he had been shot, but no words came out...only grunts. It was then I realized I was more hurt than I thought.

Albert reached back and grabbed my hand that was shaking very badly. "Don't try to talk, sweetheart, we're almost there."

Letting my hand go, he picked up his phone and pushed a button.

"Meet us at St. Lutheran. Journey's been shot!"

I blacked out...

****

When I came through again, I was in a hospital bed surrounded by nurses and doctors; the light was so bright it was blinding me. I reached up and tried to stop them from cutting away my shirt.

"Stop! What are you doing?"

"Relax, ma'am, you've been shot, we have to get you out of this shirt." A nurse said taking my hand. But her worried gaze shot to the corner of the room. There was a commotion over there.

Although it hurt like hell, I turned my head to see what was happening. Albert sat in a chair in the corner of my room holding some kind of bandage to his neck while clutching Ayana's car seat in his lap. He didn't look too good. There were several nurses and doctors telling him that they needed to see about his neck.

"No, don't worry about me, just help her. Do you hear me, dammit? Help her!" His eyes looked delirious.

"Sir, you're going to pass out if you don't let us stop the blood loss!" Another doctor told him as he tried to take Ayana's car seat from him. Albert reached into the back of his pants and pulled out his gun pointing it at him.

"Nobody touches this baby." His voice was calm and deadly. "Now help her before I blow your damn head off."

Chills went down my spine. My goodness, Albert is a beast. That was the last thing I thought before the beckoning blackness claimed me once again.

Joseph

"He's sleeping it off." My father's psychiatrist said as he joined Tim, my mother and me in the study.

My mother stood and hurried to him. "How is he?"

"He's fine, just had one too many last night, that's all."

I lifted my scotch to my lips and took a sip. "Thank you for coming over on such short notice." I told the doctor from where I stood by the window.

"I don't have to tell you to keep this confidential."

The doctor nodded his head empathetically before assuring me I'll never have to worry about him leaking anything to the press. I didn't respond, just turned back to gaze out the window watching as people headed out to work.

I was sick and tired of this life. This was not my father's first time pulling a stunt like this. In fact, it was becoming his norm. I don't do what he wants me to and he goes and does something drastic to get me back in line.

Well, not this time. There was nothing he could do to get me to change my mind about making Journey my wife. She was a part of me and my parents had to get used to the idea.

"Joseph, you can at least pretend to give a damn about your father!" My mother cried after the doctor left.

I drained my glass, placing it down on the windowsill before heading towards the door. That was just it, I was tired of pretending. I wanted to go home to what was real. Being here made my skin crawl.

She grabbed my arm. "Where are you going?"

"Home." My gaze went to Tim. "Call me if anything changes."

It was as I was turning the key in the ignition that I got Albert's call. He said three words that stole the breath from my body.

JOURNEY'S BEEN SHOT!

Whipping my truck around, I raced towards St. Lutheran. I didn't call him back; it sounded as if he was driving fast and needed to focus on what he was doing.

Something stirred in me.

No!

Not yet!

I began to take deep calming breaths. It was critical that I keep my head until I found out what was going on. I knew from experience that if I got too emotional, the other part of me would take over, but I needed to see what was going on before that happened.

My other half was not the type that reasoned. It didn't barter, negotiate, or compromise. It didn't value anything, let alone human life. It is a destructive force that once released, will not stop until all it perceived as a threat was eliminated.

Although it was true that I've learned to depend on The Politician to help me escape the pain that comes from making certain choices, for Journey's sake, I had to keep my head.

Ten minutes later I pulled my car behind Albert's at the emergency room. There were two police officers searching it.

"What the f***?!" I growled when I got out and saw that all the windows had been shot out.

Rage!

Pure uncut rage shot through me. "What the f***?!"

Somebody was going to die for this. My woman was in that car, my child. I balled up my fists as I walked through the emergency room doors. I could feel the killer waking up inside of me. My rage was almost blinding.

"Where is she?" I asked the nurse who was rushing towards the front door. She looked as if she was heading for the police officers.

Her eyes came to me with real fear before she realized who I was.

"Oh my God! It's you—" She began, but I was in no mood.

"Where is Journey?!" I yelled.

She jumped. "Who?"

"My wife and child, they came here in that car!" I pointed out towards Albert's car.

The killer in me was awake, and he was coming to the surface whether I wanted him to or not.

Instantly, relief washed over her face. "Come quickly, you're just in time. I came up here to get the police. The man that brought them just pulled a gun on Dr. Yung. They're in the operating room."

"Don't worry about the police, just take me to him." She nodded and pushed a button that caused two doors to open. I followed her down a very long hall before we went through another set of doors. When they opened I could hear Albert telling them not to worry about him, just help Journey.

"No one is allowed in the operating room." The nurse told me as we hurried towards the commotion. "But this man refused to leave."

As soon as I stepped in the room, Albert exhaled in relief lowering his gun.

"Thank God you're here, kid." Was the only thing he muttered before his limbs went lax.

"He's fainted!" The nurse who'd led me to the room cried.

"Help him!" I yelled to the doctors as I took Ayana's car seat off his lap and the gun out of his hand.

My gaze went over to the operating table; it was hard for me to see what was happening because Journey was surrounded by doctors and nurses. I tried to go to her, but two nurses jumped in front of me pushing me away. One of the doctors lifted his hand and it was covered in blood.

"F***!" I was losing it!

"Please, Mr. Warren, wait outside, so that the doctors can do their job." One of the nurses said.

"How is she?" I asked, needing something to grasp on to.

The nurse shook her head. "We don't know yet, please, just wait outside."

"No!" I growled.

Please God! Help me! I was losing it…

The nurse backed up from me afraid.

"Mr. Warren, I don't know what to tell you." Big tears came to her eyes. "Just let the doctors work and pray for the best."

I understood they had a job to do, but I needed... "Just give me something." I begged her.

She must have taken sympathy on me then. She smiled. "Dr. Yung and Dr. Phillip are two of the best doctors in the city. Just let them work, you'll see." I nodded and let her close the door in my face.

They had taken Albert to the operating room across the hall. With Ayana's car seat in my hand, I paced back and forward between the rooms, using all my focus to keep the killer inside of me quiet. I wanted to let him loose to get relief from the pain inside me.

But I couldn't always control The Politician. The last thing I needed was for him to sense some kind of threat and start killing people here at the hospital.

About forty-five minutes later, the doctor who had been working on Albert came out to give me an update.

"Mr. Warren, it is so nice to meet you." He said reaching for my hand.

I could see in his eyes that he was star struck. I wanted to yell at him to just get to it, but knew I could get better results with honey than I could vinegar.

I shook his hand. "Nice meeting you too, so about Al—"

He nodded. "Oh yes, luckily for him it was just a flesh wound, the bullet just grazed his neck. However, he did lose a lot of blood and needed quite a few stitches—"

I tuned him out after that. I was relieved to hear that Albert was going to be okay, but it was bittersweet. I haven't heard anything from the room across the hall. The nurses ran to and from it, but had no information for me.

I had taken Ayana out of her car seat when she began to fuss and held her in my arms, promising her that her mommy was going to be okay. Thankfully my constant pacing lulled her to sleep.

"Mr. Warren, about the gun incident. I'm going to have to—"

"Don't worry about the gun incident. I'm going to have someone from my office contact you to discuss compensation for all of your troubles. Albert is the head of my security. He was simply doing his job. Maybe he was a little delirious from all the blood loss."

Just like I knew it would, at hearing compensation, the doctor's whole disposition changed.

"Oh yes, that is quite understandable, thank you for clearing that up for us. We are going to be moving him to a recovery room really soon." I nodded as I paced away from him, my eyes going back to Journey's door.

I was going to go crazy if I didn't hear something soon. I couldn't take the waiting. I didn't know if she was fighting to take her last breath right now or what.

Please God... please, if you just bring her back to me. I promise to...

To what? I am ashamed to say that prayer wasn't my strong suit. If the roles were reversed and it was me in there and my Journey out here, she would know what to say to God.

What should I promise?

To be a better man, maybe?

Do your will?

I nodded…yes, all that. I promise to do all that. Just bring her back to me.

About thirty minutes later, one of the doctors who was working on Journey finally stepped out of the room.

"How is she, doc?" I didn't give him a chance to procrastinate.

"Stable." He took off his glasses and massaged the red spot they left on his nose. "We removed the bullet from just underneath her clavicle; it was embedded inside the muscle tissue there." As he spoke he pointed to the left side of his chest just underneath his shoulder.

"The good thing is it just missed her lungs." He paused for a moment. "It's a miracle actually."

"So, she's going to be alright?" I asked, needing to know. I began thanking God for this blessing.

He exhaled shaking his head slightly. "She's going to be just fine, however—" He paused as he tried to figure out the best way to give me bad news.

I felt the chill come over me as I realized God had let me down.

"Mr. Warren, she's eight weeks pregnant."

No!

No! I wanted to tell the doctor to shut up!

I was losing it. The rage inside me began to build at an alarming rate, this rage that had never let me down.

"The likelihood of the child surviving is very slim. When the mother's body is fighting for survival itself, it will cut off—"

I lost it….

My blood ran cold as my emotions shut off like a light switch.

The Narrator

Dr. Yung's words halted as he watched the change come over the senator of Florida's son. He really hated when he had to deal with the elites of D.C. They had the power to make your life heaven or bring on hell.

He cleared his throat and continued to tell Joseph about the child's slim chances at survival. Even now, the baby's heartbeat was very faint, he doubted it will be long before it ceased to exist. However, the eyes that now stared back at him were so very cold, they no longer felt human.

Wanting to be far away from this man who somehow felt…different. He quickly finished his report.

"The nurses are cleaning her up and then we will move her to a recovery room. Once there, you are welcome to visit her."

"Do me a favor, doc and put Albert and Journey in the same room."

Dr. Yung nodded his head, willing to agree to anything to be on his way. "Yes, absolutely." Even Joseph's voice seemed different.

Deadlier.

"You have a good day, Mr. Warren."

The being that now inhabited Joseph's body almost opened his mouth to tell the doctor his name was not Warren. But he didn't bother, the doctor was not important.

Instead he nodded. "You too."

The doctor hurried away. But before he rounded the corner he turned and looked back one more time, confused at the change that had come across the senator's son.

Joseph Warren was gone. In his place stood The Politician 373493…

The Politician felt no fear…

No Pain…

And no love…

He felt nothing at all…

Chapter Nineteen

Vengeance Shows No Partiality

The Narrator

Rome was on a mission. He was going to destroy Macon Technologies, the company responsible for putting his little sister in the hospital. Had they had their way, she would have been dead. He balled up his fists as his mind raced with a million ways to bring down his enemy.

Most people battled with weapons. Rome's mind is his weapon. Don't doubt he could defend himself physically if need be, but he did the most destruction with his brain. Macon Tech made a fatal mistake assuming Journey was a nobody, whose life was disposable. A mistake they will pay for in the most painful way he imagined.

At this very moment, he is the reigning chest champion of the world, a feat he did not accomplish by not knowing how to stay at least seven moves ahead of his enemy. Although he didn't care for Joseph, his sister loved him, which made him family whether Rome wanted to admit it or not.

And even before he was at the point to accept that fact, the things he'd learned about the other man had garnered his respect for him. Joseph was not aware of a quarter of things he'd gone through and even Rome only knew the half.

Still, they now shared a common enemy, an enemy whose demise Rome had designed weeks ago. But first, he needed to stop by the hospital to make sure his baby sister was okay.

As soon as he entered her room he knew that it was Joseph's alter that stood at the window looking over the two resting patients. Still dressed in his black cargo pants, military boots, and a tank top, he stood with his arms crossed behind his back, legs spread apart as if he was prepared for war.

Instantly Rome took some of the aggression out of his movements. He'd spent the last few months learning about these alters. Because they had no feeling, they were the perfect weapons for the United States government.

The fact that he is Journey's brother had kept Joseph from killing him. However, it would not stop the Politician, which was the name that had been given to Joseph's alter. If he felt in the slightest that Rome was a threat to him or to the three beings he was guarding in this room, he would kill him without batting an eye.

"Journey!" His mother called as she and Robert pushed past him to enter the room. When her eyes fell on the man asleep in the bed next to her daughter's, she put her hand over her mouth to stifle her cry.

Rome wanted to stop them and warn them to move easy, but it was too late, they'd made their way to Journey's bed and was leaning over it kissing her head, tears of relief running down both his little brother's face and his mother's.

They'd all thought the worst when his mother had run upstairs to his place yelling that Journey had been shot. After he'd calmed her down enough to get coherent words from her, she'd told him that she'd been talking on the phone with Journey's driver when somebody had started shooting at them.

She said she'd heard the driver tell Journey to hold on and that he was going to get her to the hospital before the phone went dead. Angry with himself for not following his first mind and insisting Journey come back to Chicago where he could protect her, he called in a favor from the mayor of Chicago, who'd allowed them to borrow his private jet and pilot, who'd gotten them here in a little over an hour.

He shook his head, he was making careless mistakes because his mind of late has been occupied with hunting down the woman Joseph had sent to spy on him. The woman who had somehow become his very reason for breathing. The woman who had left him, taking his heart with her.

However, he could not think about that now. Now, he would seek vengeance for his sister. And then he would continue to hunt Nak until he found her. And so help him God, when he found her, he will never let her go again.

Carefully, he made his way to Journey's bed to see with his own eyes that she was okay. As he did so he kept a leery eye on the alter. Although he didn't want to, if the Politician made one move toward his family, he would not hesitate to empty a clip in its head.

Next to the alter's feet sleeping in her car seat was Ayana. Rome wanted to get his niece away from the being, he didn't know how stable he was. From what he'd seen from the old footage he'd hacked from the CIA database, the alters were quite deadly.

"Oh Jo, what happened to my baby?" His mother cried right before she threw herself into the Politician's arms.

"Ma! No!" Rome called as he carefully approached them preparing himself to go for his gun.

The Politician stiffened at first, surprised by the sudden contact. But when he saw how uncomfortable the young cocky one was that his mother was embracing him, he slowly lifted his arms to hug her close.

Joseph didn't care much for the kid who stood across from him, and the Politician decided that he didn't care for the kid either, he was too damn cocky. The little bastard felt that he was smarter than everyone. The whole time he hugged Rome's mother, with his eyes, he dared him to go for the gun he knew he carried.

Make my day, punk. Give me an excuse to snap your neck.

"There, there, mom." He told her in a soothing voice, although he still looked at Rome with the eyes of a killer.

Rome bit down on his teeth not liking the fact that the thing called his mother, mom. As if he sensed his irritation, the Politician smiled at him. Figures, the alter would be just as irritating as his original personality. Although Rome now had respect for Jo, it didn't mean he cared for him. And now he'd decided he didn't care for either of them.

"Everything is going to be alright." It continued to speak to his mother as he gently rubbed her back. "I'm going to find who did this and I'm going to kill them."

He said that so matter-of-factly, Abigale looked up startled. However, the Politician just smiled down at her.

"I need you to do me a favor, sweetheart." He said gently.

She nodded sensing something was different about him, but not being able to put her finger on exactly what it was.

"Your granddaughter is going to need you when she wakes up. Can you sit here with them till I get back?"

He spoke gently to her, but Rome wasn't deceived. This was why this alter was called The Politician. Rome had studied hours and hours of footage dealing with this particular alter alone.

A six-year-old Joseph had unwittingly been a part of a group of test subjects whose minds had been shattered to create alters. In that group, Jo's alter was the only one that displayed sociable skills. So, they'd dubbed him The Politician 373493.

"Thank you so much, mom." It purred as he walked past her and Rome.

Stopping at Albert's bed he turned to look down at the sleeping man. Pursing his lips, he made a sound that none of them could hear. However, the man lying in the bed jerked before his eyes began to move under his lids.

The Politician made the faint noise again and the man's eye snapped open. He groaned as his hand lifted to finger the bandage on his neck.

"What happened, kid?" He asked the alter, his voice barely over a whisper.

"Flesh wound, just a graze."

When he heard the voice that spoke back to him, his facial expression sobered as he struggled to sit up a bit to see better.

"Politician... how long have you been here?"

"A little over an hour."

Albert nodded as he took in the other occupants of the room. When his eyes landed on Abigale they brightened.

"Abby Cat." He called opening his arms.

With a cry of relief Abigale ran to him, gently falling into his embrace.

"What the f***?" Rome hissed as his angry russet gaze landed on the man that was holding his mother.

"Watch your mouth, Romeo!" She admonished from where she still lay in Al's arms.

"This must be the famous Rome I've heard so much about. It's good to finally meet you and your little brother."

Rob had not left Journey's side. He still sat in the chair next to her bed holding her hand. He didn't even look away from her; he just stared at her through tear filled eyes. He and Journey were very close and he was not handling the thought of almost losing her well.

"Why are you talking to me?" Rome's question was filled with so much contempt Abigale cringed. She opened her mouth to admonish her older son some more, but the Politician's deep deadly voice cut her off.

"Old man, I need you to protect these civilians." He removed Albert's gun from the back of his pants and handed it to him.

Albert nodded. "Where are you going to begin to look?"

The Politician shook his head. "I don't know, see if I can get an I.D. on the men you killed and start there."

"I know exactly who did this to my sister and why." Rome muttered as a plan began to come together in his head.

As with most Tech Companies, it was *almost* impossible to get into their system from the outside. He can use the alter as the weapon he'd been created to be. While he handled Macon

Technologies *Elite Security Force*...Rome could get into their server room and plant his little bug he'd created especially for them.

"Who did this?" The alter asked gesturing towards Journey's bed.

"Your handlers."

The Politician didn't even blink. "Handlers?"

"You may know them as the people pretending to be your parents."

Abigale sucked in her breath appalled. Albert cursed. "Goddammit I knew it!"

"They had to get rid of those that caused you to feel love because it was—" The Politician held up his hand cutting him off.

"I don't need the break down, save it for Jo, I'm sure he'll be interested."

Abigale looked up at Albert puzzled. "I'll tell you about it later..." He whispered.

"Just show me where they are and I'll take it from there." The Politician continued.

Rome smiled big. "My man."

Rob looked up then as he swiped his hand across his face drying his eyes. "I'm going with you."

Rome and Abigale both said no at the same time. Rob stood from the chair, not prepared to take no for an answer.

"You see what they did to my sista?!" He yelled.

Rome held up his hands trying to calm the youth before he rattled this killer standing next to him.

"Bruh, let me handle this. You already know I'm going to make them pay. I can do my job better if I don't have to worry about you while I'm out there."

Rob shook his head. "You've trained me for this. I'm ready. You always tell me I can go next time. Well, there is no next time." He pointed to the ground in front of him.

"This is the time that matters!"

"What if they come here while we're gone?" The alter's deep voice filled the room. "Who will be here to protect your sister?"

Rome turned to look at the Politician surprised at his swiftness. Rob thought about his words before he swiped at his eyes again.

"Yeah…you right. I need to stay here just in case they come and try to finish the job."

The Politician nodded once before he turned and exited the room. But right before he did, his knowing gaze went to Rome as he gave him the, who's-the-smart-one-now? look.

For a second Rome just stared after him. Was the damn alternate personality trying to get under his skin? Really?

He shook his head, following him out of the room after assuring his mother and his little brother that he was going to be alright and would be back in no time.

He exhaled. *It was going to be a long night.*

****

"Hell no, you uncivilized bastard! I'm not going down in the damn sewer!" Rome hissed at the maniac.

The Politician shrugged. "Fine, stay here." He muttered before disappearing down the sewer like smoke.

"F***!"

Rome was really starting to dislike this chump. The alter made Jo look like a stand-up guy. Securing his book bag with his precious cargo in it on his back, he slipped down the manhole quickly sliding the heavy lid back in place.

While the Politician drove back to Jo's place to gather the tools he was going to need for the job, Rome tapped into the senator's phone and together they listened to his panic phone calls to Jeff, the CEO of Macon Tech.

"Goddammit Jeff, you need to send some men to my place right away. The hit on the old man and the girl was a miss, it did nothing but trigger the Politician!"

"Have you lost your mind calling me on an open line like this?" Jeff growled.

"I had no other choice! I can't get in contact with that bastard Baxter to deactivate him. My sources informed me that he's flown the f****** coup and gone into hiding. Not only is all we've invested in crumbling down around us, I am certain the Politician knows who we are and is coming for us!"

"Us? I don't know what you're talking about, senator, I am just an investor in your campaign. How you choose to run it is your business."

"You son-of-a-b****, I'm not going down by myself. If you don't send protection for my wife and I, I will call a news conference and tell the world everything I know about your shady dealings."

"Calm down, senator, there is no need for such haste. I will send a car for you and your lovely wife and bring you back here to the lab, where we can secure your safety."

Rome pulled up the blueprints of Macon Tech's Lab. The place was practically an eight-story vault, there was no way in except through the sewer system. He'd told the Politician that all he needed was about fifteen minutes to override the codes for the doors, but of course the alter did not want to wait.

So here he was trudging through waist high filth with his laptop on his back that had over 75 million dollars' worth of modifications. To say he was pissed was an understatement.

"I'm telling you." He grumbled to the back of the Politician as he followed him through the murky water. "If something happens to my equipment, I don't care what kind of super powers you have, I'm gon' take you out."

He grimaced as his Jordan covered foot stepped down into something slimy and squashy, not to mention that it smelled horrible too. "You can try and Karate chop my tech nine, mutha f****."

The Politician chuckled. "Stop acting like a b**** back there and man up."

Rome balled up his fists as he seriously considered trying to take him down.

"It's a suicide mission, kid." The alter muttered as he quickly climbed up the ladder that led them out into the lab's boiler room. Rome followed behind him moving with just as much agility.

The Politician would never admit it, but he was impressed with the young man's ability thus far. He had wondered when he'd first agreed to go on this joint mission if he was going to have to carry him most of the way.

Amazingly, the kid kept up very well and could no doubt handle his own should the sh*t hit the fan.

"Give me a sec." Rome mouthed as he took his bag off his back removing his laptop.

His hands flew across his keyboard as he took control of the building's security feed. Once he'd artfully cloned the last hour of footage, he put it on repeat for the guard's eyes. Then he went back to the original footage that now only he and the Politician could see.

"Jeff and your handlers are on the top floor. I took control of the security footage, so if you can take out all that get in your way quietly and with finesse, you can do it without raising the alarm. They have a fairly large group of guards stationed here, here, and here."

He hit a button pulling up the building's blueprints. "I need to go to the server room located here. When you're done I will meet you back here in the boiler room. Put this on…"

He handed him a small device to go in his ears. "I will be your eyes."

The Politician nodded once as he placed the device in his ear, this kid may be of good use after all.

By the time Rome placed his computer back in his bag, the alter had disappeared into the shadows. Now he knew why the alters had been a part of ghost recon, the man moved like the wind, silently, but deadly.

He quickly made his way to the server room. There was one guard standing outside the door. Silently he came up behind him putting him in a choke hold and didn't stop until he heard the satisfying crunch.

Before he could get into the door he heard rapid fire in the distance before the blare of the alarm.

"F***"

What part of finesse didn't the Politician understand?

Rome drew his weapon, there were about eight people in total manning the computers, whose jobs ranged from IT personnel to computer programming.

"All right, everybody, exit with your hands up and your mouths shut and today won't be your last."

When they looked up and saw him standing there in Jordan's, jeans, a white tee, and a gold watch, they froze in fear, instantly assuming they were being robbed by a gang-banger.

"Here, take my wallet!" One man said reaching for his pocket. Rome shot at the floor by his foot causing the man to wet his pants.

"I don't want your wallet, nasty bastard. I want you and these other geeks to get the f*** out!" He didn't have to ask again, they nearly trampled each other running out the door.

Chuckling he quickly set up his arsenal. But first...

He killed the alarm and put on some working music...The sound of Bone Crusher's Never Scared filled the building speakers.

"Alright killa, you got twelve minutes before them boys in blue have the place swarmed, let's see what you can do."

"I like the music." The Politician's deep voice came back at him as he used the body of one of the guards to block the array of bullets that was coming his way.

Rome pulled the security footage up on the big screens in front of him and watched as the alter did damage.

"I bet you do..." He told him as for a second he watched, enthralled as the man made quick work at breaking bones and just smashing sh*t. No wonder the alarm had begun blaring. The Politician was not trying in any way to be discreet.

He'd taken the stairs three at a time to the top floor gunning for his targets, plowing through the guards like King Damn Kong. Bodies were flying everywhere. Rome cringed as he watched the alter throw a man in the air before catching him and bringing him back down hard across a railing. He imagined he could hear the sound of the guard's back breaking.

The Politician had the guards so shook they were firing at him, not caring that they were shooting each other. The alter was like a ghost, he moved so fast they could not aim quickly enough to take a good shot at him.

"That mutha f**** is a beast..." Rome muttered to himself as he inserted his jump-drive directly to the company's mainframe and uploaded the bleeding program he'd designed especially for them. It will take his little bug eight minutes to do its job, he settled back in his chair and kicked his feet up to continue watching as the Politician destroyed.

****

He was not the only one watching as the destructive force came for them. Disgusted, Jeff looked over at the senator and his wife, who clung to each other shivering in fear. Quickly he set up the shields he'd programmed to prevent anyone from getting through the doors of his office area as he tried to shut down the mainframe.

"Dammit!" He yelled when he saw that something had taken control of his system and had locked him out.

Grabbing the phone, he called down to his server room.

"Joe's poolhall…eight-ball speaking."

All the blood drained from Jeff's face as he stared at the phone in shock. "Who the f*** is this?!" He yelled once he'd found his voice. "And what the f*** are you doing in my server room?!"

"I am death, you punk mutha f****!" The voice came back to him. "Your world is over." The phone went dead.

With hands that shook, he grabbed the remote to change the footage on the security screens from that of the hall that still showed the guards standing there silently chatting amongst themselves to that of the server room that showed his overnight tech team still busy at work.

"Dammit!" He yelled again throwing his remote control into one of the screens causing it to darken.

"What is it? What's happened? Are they not able to stop Jo?" The senator asked as he tried to quiet his wife's weeping.

"We've got bigger problems than your freak show of a son. Somebody has hacked into my system and is bleeding out all of my information—" Before he could finish, there was a loud crash at the door.

Mrs. Warren screamed as another loud boom followed. Jeff smiled, pleased that his shields, that thank God, was not connected to the mainframe still held.

Rome sat up in his chair as he watched the Politician throw guards toward the door to Jeff's office and the guards being electrocuted by some kind of invisible gate.

"A little assistance." The alter's voice came to him.

"Give me a sec." Rome said as his hands flew across his laptop. "Looks like our little buddy Jeff has a few tricks up his sleeve."

It didn't take Rome long to find Jeff's back up system and power down his shields.

"Should be good to go."

As soon as Jeff saw that his back up computer had been taken over he called for his helicopter to meet him on the roof. He didn't want to leave before he could at least set the self-destruction program for his lab, the last thing he needed was for this information he had here to get into the wrong hands, it would be the end of Macon Tech for sure.

But from the sound of it, Jo was at the door and right now, he needed to save his own life. He had a team of lawyers that he was paying a fortune for, at the very least he knew they would make sure he didn't serve any jail time.

However, it was time for him to shed some dead weight.

"I will be right back, senator, I need to activate the self-destruction program." He told them as he closed his laptop and slid it in his briefcase.

"What!? What do you mean?"

"Relax, senator, he can't get through the shield I have surrounding this office." He lied as he slipped into the joining office that had a trap door that let out to the stairs that led to the roof.

Jo's parents…or shall I say handlers ran after him, but when they got to the office, they were stunned to see Jeff had seemed to just disappear.

"Oh no!" Mrs. Warren cried as her frightened gaze went to her husband. Right then, the office door crashed in. The sounds of Bone Crusher Never Scared filled their ears before the Politician walked through the door.

Senator Warren held up his hands. "Now son, let's not overreact and do anything that you'll later regret."

The Politician smiled at them. "That's just it, pops, I don't regret anything." He slowly began to stalk them.

"It's time for you to walk alone in the field of clovers." Senator Warren said with a shaking voice.

The alter grinned, "Not before I snap that b****'s neck and throw you out the window." Both their eyes widened.

Senator Warren, in a last-ditch effort to save his own life, pushed his wife into the alter's arms. She didn't even get a chance to scream before the sound of her neck breaking filled the room.

The senator turned and took two steps toward the door, but he was grabbed roughly from the back and flung towards the window with such strength he died on contact. However, the window shattered and he flew straight through it falling to join the bird poop on the cement.

The Politician walked to the now open window to watch the helicopter fly away. Jeff smiled down at him as he gave him the finger.

"Count to three, chump." Rome's voice came through the device in his ear.

Three seconds later, the helicopter seemed to just shut off before it began to spin wildly out of control. Jeff's frightened gaze came back to him seconds before the chopper crashed to the ground, exploding into a fire ball that lit up the night's sky.

Jo nodded as a grin came to his face. "Good work, kid." He muttered as he stepped over his mother's dead body.

The sound of the police sirens could now be heard. It was time to vacate the premises.

Chapter Twenty

The Dawn of a New Era

We must be willing to get rid of the life we've planned, so as to have the life that is waiting for us. The old skin has to be shed before the new one can come.

--Joseph Campbell

Journey

"Wake up, daughter of Sarah." The deep voice penetrated the darkness around me, pulling me from its clutches.

"Journey, it's time for you to wake up now."

I frowned, I don't want to wake up; the place where I am is comfortable. Only pain awaited me from where that deep voice was coming from.

My eyelids felt heavy, I had to struggle to open them. The first thing I felt was the dull pain in my shoulder, but then the bright light that bled through my cracked eyelids was causing my head to hurt.

I moaned in pain, but right then, a big dark hand passed over my lids before the warm palm touched my head. I couldn't describe the feeling that came over me, it felt like cool water washing over my burning skin. Instantly the pain in my shoulder and head began to abate. Slowly I opened my eyes fully to take in the man standing over my bed.

I had to be dreaming.

"Are you a cowboy?" I asked.

He chuckled as he removed his hand.

"No, nothing so spectacular."

"But you look like a cowboy."

And he did. His long hair was braided in cornrows, their tips rested just below his massive shoulders. On his head he wore a black cowboy hat. I could smell the leather of his black coat. His skin was as dark as Joseph's. But it was his eyes that made me pause.

He looked down at me through a set of eyes that seemed…I don't know, they seemed ancient.

A horrifying thought came to me. "Am I dead?" I whispered.

This man must be an angel coming to take me to my place of rest. Again, he chuckled.

"No, child, far from it."

Carefully I sat up in the bed. Amazingly, my shoulder no longer troubled me, so I was able to move easily. Looking around the hospital room I was surprised to see my mother sleeping in the bed next to mine in Albert's arms. My little brother Rob asleep in the chair with Ayana fast asleep on his chest, neither of them woke from their slumber.

My gaze went back to the dark stranger. Now that I was sitting up in the bed, I could see that he wore a long black duster, underneath it the gleam of a sword handle winked at me.

Oh My God! Who was this guy...?

"I am the Qoheleth, nothing more, nothing less...but everybody calls me The Preacher."

I nodded, surprised that I didn't feel any fear of this man, who I doubted was a man at all.

"I've come to wake you and to commend you."

"Commend me? For what?"

"The wise words you told your husband. It is true that he and his siblings have work to do. They have been chosen to help mankind, but not in the way they always thought."

I frowned. "Siblings? Jo is an only child."

The Preacher shook his head. "Jo is one of five children. Each born to be warriors in a very special army."

I gasped. "Are you talking about his alter?" I whispered.

Again he shook his head. "In the coming years, Jo, like the rest of his siblings will come to learn that the alters are standing in the way of true power. They will find that some demons are harder to defeat than others."

He reached down and took my hand. "You, daughter of Sarah are a precious gift, given to calm a raging storm. You see, every warrior needs to know that after the battle, calm awaits them."

For some reason, his words caused tears to come to my eyes. He reached up and dried them.

"You will be alright, dear one. You, and the little warrior you carry deep in your womb. A time is coming where life as you know it will change drastically. There is a thin, almost nonexistent line between normal and paranormal. Some people live and die without ever knowing the difference. You, my child, are not one of those. Be brave, little one, continue to have unwavering faith in the Ancient of Days…He knows your works. He hears all your thoughts. He will send you the Helper."

He smiled at me one more time before he began to walk out of the room.

"Wait!" I called after him.

He paused and turned back to face me. As he did, the long duster swept across his powerful legs, I wasn't surprised to see that on his feet was a pair of black cowboy boots, spurs and all.

"Will I ever see you again?"

He nodded, but there was a sadness in his eyes. "You will, daughter. But the world will be on fire when you do." And after that, he was gone.

Joseph

Rome and I had made it back to my father's office on the Hill. We were here because he said that he needed a secure place to show me the things he'd found. And my father's office was the most secure. I told him that we had about an hour before someone tried to contact me about my dead parents. Or shall I say the people pretending to be my parents.

Rome sat on the couch in the office opening his laptop on the table in front of him. I paced back and forward as I tried to search inside of me for one shred of guilt over what I'd just done.

There was none…

Not an ounce…

I rubbed the back of my neck. Every time my personality changed, I felt like it killed more and more of what made me human. How long before I didn't change back to Joseph? How long before I became the monster that lived inside of me?

"Alright, buddy, you might want to have a seat to listen to what I'm about to tell you."

I paused in my pacing looking down at Rome. This had to be bad if he was speaking to me in such a placating tone.

I shook my head. "Naw, I'd rather stand."

He shrugged. "Suit yourself. Okay, so you obviously know that those wasn't your parents?"

I nodded. "Yeah, I figured that out along the way."

He chuckled, but he still seemed uncomfortable about what he was getting ready to say. His russet gaze rose to my face.

"Jo, you're a triplet."

"What?!"

"When you were born, there were two other boys born with you." He spoke as if he was talking to a mentally unstable individual.

What was it about this kid that constantly made me want to choke the life out him?

"I know what a damn triplet is, man!" I growled.

He shrugged. "Hell, I don't know that you do, you looked confused."

"Get on with it, will you?"

"You also have an older brother and a younger sister."

I eased down in the chair across from him. "How is this possible?"

"James Bennet Law is your real father. He enrolled in the United States Army in 69' during Nam." Rome shook his head.

"In our government's never ending quest to achieve the super soldier, they were allowing all kinds of sick sh*t to happen to some of the soldiers. James Bennet Law and Albert were best friends. Both of them had been taken and their minds experimented on."

"Albert? So he knows my father?"

"I doubt he remembers much. The doctor really did a number with his head. Without his knowledge, he was hypnotized or some sh*t and then sent in to handle you for your handlers. He just thought he was taking a job as your driver. In reality, they needed someone that was skilled in combat to calm you down should you lose it. Which is why the first thing I need to do is break up whatever that is he thinks he has with my mother."

I didn't rise to the bait, Albert could handle himself.

"Who is this doctor?" He typed something on the computer.

"Thus lies the mystery whose answer keeps evading me. I can't find anything on the man that experimented on them. Only that he had you guys call him Father."

"Wait? How did he end up with us instead of James Law?"

"He'd discovered a gene in your dad that he would later call a super human gene. The gene was laying dormant. He found a way to spark it to life in your dad, but he was too old, already set in his ways, so although it would spark to life, it would shortly sizzle out. Evidently, it's a mental thing. He figured he could have a fresh slate in your dad's seed. His mission then became trying to orchestrate James into having as many children as he possibly could. Children whose brains were young and fresh and easily programmable."

He shook his head again. "Man…this punk was so involved in your pops life without him knowing it was ridiculous. He knew everything about yo' oldman. Where he liked to drink, where he liked to buy his dope."

"Dope?"

"Oh yeah! It was the 70's, everybody was doing dope. Especially them boys who came back from Nam, they were real messed up in the head, including your pops. Which was how the doctor controlled him because he was going back and forward to the VA to get pills to help him deal with his PTSD."

Rome's phone began to vibrate on the table next to his laptop. Without looking to see who was calling he turned it off.

"Now because your dad couldn't get right in the head, my guess would be thanks to the help of the good doctor, he hopped around from woman to woman. But what he didn't know is the doctor was setting it up, so that he ran into certain women. Women who carried an X chromosome that in all sense and purposes made the superman gene in your dad more potent."

I sat back in my chair, floored. There is no way this happened.

"I know this sh*t sound wild." Rome said as if he could read my thoughts. "I felt the same way when this information first came to me. But it happened. Your mother had gone to the local clinic thinking she was getting another prescription for birth control pills. The good doctor had set it up so that the handsome James at the time was in her ear. Only she had not left with a prescription for birth control, but fertility drugs. So, when her and James lay together, she ended up having three of you instead of one."

I used my fingers to massage my head. It was too much; this kid was rocking my world. How in the hell?

"James stayed around long enough to name you boys, but not much longer. And when he left, your mother was conveniently talked into giving you guys up for adoption. And that's how you three ended up in the doctor's hands. He studied everything about you." Rome typed something on his computer before he turned it around to face me.

There was old footage of three little dark boys who all looked like me sitting in an all white padded room at a little round table drawing pictures. To the far right of the room was a one-way mirror, where I was sure we were being watched.

"Wow! Why is it I can't remember any of this? I remembered being a small child growing up in my home with my par--...The Warrens."

He shook his head. "All programmed thoughts. He put you guys through hell. He found that the only way to activate the gene in you and your siblings was by fracturing your minds and creating the alters who don't feel." He paused for just a moment. "Without emotion, brotha, you have superpowers."

It took me a moment to process all of this, I had so many questions.

"So all my siblings have alters?"

He nodded. "And this is the truly fascinating part. The five of you all shattered in a different way. In studying your particular alter, they saw that he was approachable and could communicate quite well with people. He could even convince those around him that he cared for them and was even concerned. They named him The Politician 373493."

"In studying one of the other triplets, they noticed a bully nature in both him and his alter. If he wanted something that you or your other brother had, he would simply take it, the same with his alter. His alter did things in true bully fashion. He didn't just kill, he made one look bad while doing it. If he was thirsty he would just take a drink out of someone's hand. They named his alter The Bully 373492."

"The last triplet was something of a loner in many ways, he was quite the mystery to the doctor. Although he stayed close to you and your other brother, he was quiet and kept to himself, read a lot, even seemed to think very deeply on different matters. His alter was something of a ghost. It killed before you even knew what happened, they called it The Loner 373491."

"What about my little sister?"

"Now your sister was the doctor's greatest achievement, he became obsessed with her. Her mother was the last woman to be with your father before he was murdered in a car accident. The doctor pulled Debra from a juvenile detention center."

"Debra?"

Rome nodded. "Your father had named you all after biblical characters. As I was saying, Debra got locked up for life for killing her mother's boyfriend who stabbed and killed her mother while trying to rape Debra."

I frowned. "No court in America would send her to jail for life for such an offense."

Rome chuckled. "It would if the Doctor had something to do with it. It was how she ended up in his grasp. You see he was having trouble with you boys. Although he could get you to do what he demanded, there was always a rebellious streak in all of you. He could sense your hate for him. In his fear that you all would one day kill him, he erased himself from you and your brothers' memories and then sold all three of you to the highest bidders, but not Debra. He splintered her mind and her alter didn't show any disturbing qualities like you boys."

"Her alter was able to blend smoothly into society, thus making her the perfect weapon." He continued.

"What is the name of her alter?"

Rome smiled. "Black Beauty 373901." He typed something into his computer and pulled up an image of a beautiful dark-skinned woman dressed in full military gear.

"It is rumored that she's the deadliest weapon the United States Government have at the moment."

The hell she is, I was going to find her. "Where is she?" Rome shook his head.

"Nobody knows.

"Can you find her?"

He shrugged. "I'm sure, if I had a little time."

I nodded, but then another thought came to me. "You said we had an older brother. What's his deal?"

Rome sat up on the couch resting his elbows against his knees. "He was the doctor's greatest failure. The one he called the Unbreakable."

"What do you mean?"

"He tried everything to break his mind. But no matter what he did, nothing worked. It was as if your older brother was born with the personality of the alters. Like them, he was not approachable or sociable. The doctor spoke of him as if he was a little more than a wild animal. The only thing the doctor could figure was that somehow the drugs he'd been giving your father caused his first-born son to automatically inhabit the genes that lay dormant in your dad. Get this, he claims that your oldest brother is the strongest out of all your father's children, the fastest, the deadliest." He sat back in his seat.

"In the CIA database, he's labeled unstable and extremely dangerous. But that don't mean sh*t, those are the ones they typically liked."

"What happened to him?"

"He went rogue and became the world's most wanted. Agencies across the planet linked up to try and take him out. The doctor believes he's dead."

Damn, I felt grief for a brother I never met, just imagining what he must have gone through. I was aware that our government was involved in some nefarious things. There are more ghost departments than I can count. However, I never imagined there was a department designated just for my family.

I didn't like it. In that moment I came to a decision. I am going to find my siblings. All of them! And then I was going to find the one called Father and kill him. He had to die for what he did to us.

"What was his name?"

"Judah Law 373001." The deep scratchy voice came from behind me. Rome and I both shot to our feet turning to look at the interloper.

The Politician stirred as I sensed that the man standing at the door was extremely dangerous. He stared at me through a pair of dark eyes that were a lot like my own, but that was the only thing we had in common.

He stood at least six inches taller than me, his shoulders broader. He skin was not dark like mine, it was about two shades lighter. His hair fell down his back in long dreadlocks and he had a huge shaggy beard as if he hadn't shaved in years. It hid more than half his face. He looked like a wild man.

However, he was dressed like me in a pair of army green cargo pants, military boots and a tank top. He wore a brown leather bomber jacket over it.

Without a shadow of a doubt he's a military man.

"Who are you?" I asked, preparing myself to spring into action if he made one hostile move.

His cold gaze fell on me and The Politician shifted again. I could feel him brushing my brain, tempting me to let him free.

The stranger didn't speak right away, he just stood there taking me in. When finally he spoke, his voice sounded as if he didn't use it much.

"I'm your older brother."

"The Unbreakable one!" Rome said low from the side of me.

I relaxed my stance a bit. "I thought you were dead?"

He chuckled. At least I think that's the sound he made. "For all parties that matter, I am."

"And what parties are those?"

He stepped farther in the office, causing both Rome and I to stiffen, readying ourselves for battle. I hated to be this way, but that's the kind of vibe this brotha threw off. He was pure violence in the flesh.

"Easy." He said shutting the door behind him. "If I wanted you dead I would have done it the day you graduated from high school and got sh*t faced drunk before passing out in your front yard. Or the day you lost your virginity and sat on your porch writing love songs to the chick."

Rome chuckled, relaxing his stance a little more. "I knew it. I said this chump Jo is the kind of sucka that sit around writing love songs and sh*t. That's probably how you got my sista."

I lifted one side of my mouth in a grin. "Yeah, but I have my lady, where's yours?" I blinked innocently, waiting patiently for his answer.

The grin left his face and a frown replaced it. "Won't you write one of your corny ass songs so that I can give it to her, cake boy!"

I'm not going to punch my future wife's brother in the nose. I'm just not!

My gaze went back to the wild man. "What? You've been spying on me?"

"I've been watching over you, as well as Naphtali and Levi."

"Are they the others?"

He nodded as his gaze went back to Rome. "I don't know how you managed to gather information in a few months that's taken me years to obtain…"

Rome the peacock gave him a look that said…well, I'm a genius.

"But there was something you got wrong. Something you couldn't have learned from Father's notes. Our dad was aware of what was happening to him. He was not schizophrenic. The things he said was happening were in fact happening to him. He made me promise before Father murdered him to look after his children and I have. Even if it meant breaking myself before Father ever could."

"What about Debra?"

His face fell. "I lost her. But so has Father. Whoever has her now have enough power to stay off the radar. But I'm not going to give up. Even if it kills me, I'm going to find her and I'm going to kill whoever hurt her."

I nodded, because his thoughts mirrored my own.

"Why now?" Rome asked. Judah shook his head not understanding the question.

"Why come out the shadows now?"

Judah looked at him surprised. "So, you haven't heard? You might want to turn your phone back on or check the Chicago headlines. I'm sure your men have been trying to contact you."

Rome frowned before he took a seat back in front of his computer, his hands flew across the keyboard before his face contorted in rage.

"Mutha F****!" He hissed snatching up his phone turning it on. It instantly began to ding with the calls and the text messages he missed.

"Thanks to your digging you've marked you and your whole family for death. My brothers were safe as long as they weren't aware of what was happening to them. It's the reason I had to die. Once I became aware, I became a danger they could not allow to live."

I walked around the table to see what Rome was looking at.

"Dammit!" There were images on his computer screen of the whole top level of his apartment building burning.

"They dropped a bomb on your place forty-five minutes ago. The papers read that it was a gas leak. Good thing nobody was hurt."

"Bullsh*t nobody was hurt. My computers were in there. Somebody gon' have to die for this!" His phone rang and he turned around to take the call.

"What the f*** happened?" He barked into the phone.

Judah continued to speak to me. "You two believed you had defeated a monster with the little stunt you pulled today. You could not be further from the truth. You may have defeated a small monster, but you've awakened a dragon. And it's not going to stop until you and everybody that knows the truth about it is dead."

"Who the f*** is they?!" Rome hissed coming back in to the conversation.

"I suspect the same man that has my little sister. Every time I get close to finding out who it is, something happens to throw me off the scent." His gaze fell on Rome. "Which is why I've come to recruit you. I've been watching you for a while. To say that I'm impressed with your technical ability is an understatement. I believe you will be a great asset to the team."

"What team?"

"I head up a small group of men who handle a wide range of things from security to search and rescue."

Rome and I both lifted an eyebrow. "Search and rescue?"

Judah chuckled. "Yep…"

"So, you CIA?" Rome asked.

"I'm what I need to be to accomplish my mission at the time."

Rome threw up his hands. "Yeah, cause that's real clear, it's not cryptic at all."

Judah chuckled. "I figured a smart guy like yourself would understand." He put his hand on my shoulder, none to gently.

"Since all your chances for running for president are shot now, you might as well come into the family business. Thanks to your little stunt, I'm going to have to pull all three of you. Who knows how long Naphtali and Levi have before they try and take them out as well? Alone, they may have a chance at succeeding. Us together, they have no chance in hell."

I agreed. If this dragon he spoke of was that big, it would take all of us together to bring it down. Alone, it stands a chance of defeating us. He must have seen the compliance in my eyes. The smile that was more like a grimace grew on his face.

"Welcome to my world, boys. The first thing we need to do is kill you and everybody you love.

****

Joseph

I could not breathe easily until I laid eyes on my wife and child to know that they were okay. Judah had not lied. We needed to leave now. On our way to the hospital, Rome hacked into the security feed of my penthouse. It had been ransacked and my computer stolen. We didn't have long before whoever that was made their way here and I needed to get Journey, Ayana, and Abigale to safety.

Judah assured me he had an excellent doctor on his team that stitched them up and got them back together when needed. He said he was one of the best in the world. That knowledge did little to stem my worry. Last I saw Journey, she was in stable condition, but not well enough to move.

And then there was our baby she carried. The doctor said he didn't know if the little one was going to make it. If only I could turn back---

My thoughts stalled as I took in the man walking down the hall towards us. I had never in my life seen anything like him. He was a big man who wore a black cowboy hat and duster. He didn't look as if he belonged in this day or time. His fathomless dark eyes took us in as he passed.

Something in the very pit of my being responded to him. For some strange reason, I felt a strong kinship to him. He must have had the same effect on Rome and Judah, because they too turned their heads to watch him as he continued out the door, the duster blowing behind him, making him appear as if he had black wings.

I didn't know what I expected when I rounded the corner into Journey's room, but it wasn't the sight that greeted me. She sat up in the bed bright eyed and glowing. As soon as she saw me she raised her arms to me.

"My King!" She cried as her big beautiful eyes pooled with tears.

As I walked to that bed, I thanked God for sparing a wretch like me.

Journey

Seeing Joseph, Rome, and the big stranger walking into my room right behind The Preacher filled my heart with happiness. His parting words were troubling. He said the next time I saw him the world will be on fire. But somehow, looking at my brother, my man, and whoever this powerful stranger was that had eyes like Joseph, I knew we were going to be okay.

Rob, my mother, and Albert woke up as the men walked in the room, Ayana still slept in my little brother's arms.

"Hey, hey, hey…Y'all made it back in one piece. Good job, boys!" Albert gushed, the relief at seeing Joseph safe clear in his eyes. My mother jumped up to hug Rome.

"I'm so glad y'all made it back. I was praying for y'all the whole time!"

My eyes never looked away from Joseph as he approached me, gently taking me into his arms. Everybody else in the room just seemed to fade to black. In this moment, it was just he and I.

"Baby, how do you feel?" He asked softly as he sat on the bed next to me.

"I feel like I was touched by an angel. Did you see him, Joseph? Did you see the angel?"

He smiled nodding his head. "She's right in front of me. How does your shoulder feel?"

I reached up and moved my gown back a bit. "I can still feel that I have an injury, but it doesn't hurt anymore."

His eyes fell to my stomach and a sad look came on his face. "And the baby?"

I took his hands and put them against my stomach. "He's fine. He's going to be a strong warrior just like his daddy."

The smile that came on his face made me fall in love with him all over again. "He?"

I nodded. "He."

"Got to go, little bro."

A deep scratchy voice came from the back of us causing the room and everybody in it to come back into focus. I peeked around Joseph to the big man that stood behind him. This had to be one of his siblings that The Preacher told me about. Although he wasn't dark like Joseph, he did favor him.

Only where Joseph's beard, mustache, and hair cut were always trimmed and lined to perfection, this stranger's not so much.

Don't get me wrong, he was handsome. Very, but in a violent kind of way. No, scratch that…Savage.

He felt like a savage. His beard and mustache covered his face, making him look like a wild man. When his cold gaze fell on me, I shivered. Without being told, I knew that he was broken. He felt like Joseph had felt the night he'd killed all those men in the Jamaican restaurant. I squeezed Jo's hand.

"Baby, this my—"

"Brother." I said cutting him off. He turned to look at me surprised.

"How did you know? I'd only just found out."

I smiled. "I told you I talked to an angel."

His brother gave him and Rome a signal as if to tell them we were out of time.

Joseph turned back to me. "Journey, do you trust me?"

Without hesitation I nodded. "With my life."

He smiled. "Life as we know it is going to change. But that's alright. Because I'll always be here for you. And I'll always keep you safe. That's my word."

I frowned as another chill came over me. These were the Preacher's exact words. "Is everything alright?"

"It will be, just as soon as we all die."

After saying those very frightening words, he scooped me up into his arms, and then he made sure Robert had Ayana and began to head toward the door. He stopped at Albert's bed.

"Let's roll, old man."

Albert nodded. "Right behind you, kid."

I looked back at what was the beginning of our family before my gaze fell on Joseph's face.

"Did you say we all had to die?"

His eyes came to mine as he carried me through the open doors. "You said you trust me, right?"

In his gaze I saw a new beginning. In this moment, he and I were leaving behind everything we've known before today and walking boldly into the unknown.

Gently I ran my fingers through his beard. "Have I told you yet that I love you?"

He shook his head. "The three words my soul longs to hear."

I leaned in and gently kissed his lips. "I love you. I love you with my whole heart and soul. And I'm not afraid to walk into the future with you."

"Together, we can handle anything." He whispered.

"You promise?"

He nodded. "I promise."

The Epilogue

Journey

"We can put you a greenhouse right here in this spot overlooking the river."

I stood with Jo taking in our new home. He'd taken a job working for his brother's security firm called, *Security in Law*. And apparently the new position came with some amenities, including a beautiful new home on his brother's five-hundred acres of land in the Canadian Mountains.

Not only did Jo get a new home, but so did Rome and Albert, who too had taken a position with Security in Law. My mother and Rob had moved in with Rome, but I didn't expect that arrangement to last. A little birdie may have let it slip that Albert was getting ready to propose to my mom.

I turned to look back at our home that was nestled deep in the tall Blue Spruce trees. The place was spectacular. It was ten times as beautiful as the cottage. Plus, when I looked out my kitchen window I had the perfect view of the mountains and the rushing river that ran alongside it. Our home was big enough for Ayana to have her own room as well as the new baby.

"What do you think? Are you happy?" Jo asked turning away from the amazing view to look at me.

Poor baby, he was so worried about me, about the way I was handling my new lot in life. I laid my head on his chest wrapping my arms around his waist.

"I don't think I've ever been so happy. It's so peaceful here. The trees and the mountains, and the river, it's all so very beautiful."

He held me close protecting me from the brisk wind that encircled us.

"They say the winters are pretty severe here in Canada."

He was fishing to see if I was lying to him about being utterly happy. I leaned back in his arms, taking in my handsome, strong warrior.

"You forget I'm from Chicago. I'm not afraid of Canada's winters."

"That's another thing that worries me. You're from Chicago, is the seclusion here going to drive you crazy?"

I looked at him as if he had gone loco. It's true, Judah's property was very secluded. He had a house here and the small group of men that worked for him had houses and families here, not to mention Rome and Albert's, but you wouldn't know it. There was so much space and forest between us that it was easy to forget we weren't the only ones here.

"Do you know how tired I got of constantly hearing police sirens and ambulances?" I shook my head. "This peace and quiet is a blessing from on High. No, baby, the seclusion is not going to drive me crazy. In fact, I welcome it with open arms."

With our hands clasped together, he and I walked back towards the picnic area and our little family. Albert stood at the grill flipping burgers. My mom brought him out some more stuff to put on the grill. He leaned over and whispered something in her ear that caused her to blush before she swatted his arm, no doubt telling him to behave.

I chuckled, she was always telling him to behave, but something told me she liked his naughtiness…

Jo and I settled down at a picnic table and he lifted a piece of fruit to my lips. I shook my head and ate it. The man was always trying to feed me. I had to keep reminding him that I was only a couple of months pregnant and that my appetite hadn't changed that much.

"Do you think Judah will come and have dinner with us?" I asked around a mouth full of cantaloupe.

Jo shook his head. "I doubt it."

Although I didn't show it, that saddened me. Judah didn't mingle much with the rest of us. In fact, he didn't interact much with anybody but his men. Joseph said it was because he wasn't used to dealing with civilians. He said his brother had been in the military most of his life and that was all he knew.

Jo reached up and smoothed out my frown that I hadn't even been aware was on my face.

"Don't worry about him, baby, he'll come around."

Rome sat down on the bench seat across the table from us and tossed Joseph the paper.

"I don't know what branch of government your brother works for. You know I've been trying to find out. Every time I ask him, his answer is more cryptic than the last."

"I'm sure it won't be long before you find out." Jo muttered as he began to look through the paper.

Rome shook his head. "The man is a ghost, he and his whole crew. My guess is CIA." He pointed to the paper Jo held in his hand.

"He got to be pretty high up there to pull something like that off."

"The flag hangs half-mast as the Hill mourns a great loss." Joseph read out loud.

"In a horrific plane crash, Senator Warren, his beautiful wife, and their only son Joseph Warren, who was due to announce his candidacy for senator of Florida, all died when their plane crashed somewhere over the Atlantic Ocean. Search crews have been out all morning looking for the bodies. Everyone on the plane is presumed dead. Along with the Warrens were Joseph's fiancée, Journey Reevers, her daughter that she shared with Mr. Warren, her mother, and two brothers. It is believed they were on their way to attend the secret wedding of the couple, who had all but announced their engagement on PMZ."

Wow! How quickly life can change. One minute you're walking down the path you thought almost for certain was for you, and in the next, you're headed in the complete opposite direction. It was official, Journey Reevers is dead.

In a way that troubled me a bit, but I knew it was something that had to happen. Before we'd left town, I'd insisted we go back to the cottage to at the very least, get the necklace Jo had bought me that went with my engagement ring.

When we got there, we couldn't even turn down the street because the fire department had blocked it off. Someone had set my cottage on fire. Jo said it was nothing for me to worry about, but I knew we were in danger. Why else would they have to fake our deaths?"

However, we were safe here. Jo no longer went by Warren, he'd decided to go by his real father's last name which is Law.

Journey Reevers was dead, I was soon to become Journey Law.

"I don't know how my brother pulled that off, but I must say I don't know how my future brother-in-law pulled this off either." Jo said flipping the page.

"A very sad day for Macon Technologies." He began to read.

I looked over his shoulder as he did. There was a big picture of several business men being led out of a building in handcuffs.

"Jeff Barnes, CEO of Macon Technologies fled a burning house, leaving his major investors to stay and clean up the mess. Records of the company's long history of embezzling and racketeering mysteriously became public, linking key players of the company's development to wrongdoings that's going to leave Macon Tech bankrupt and several people faced with jail time."

Jo's gaze rose to Rome, he nodded his head once. "I'm impressed."

Rome shrugged. "All in a day's work."

Not many people could see the sadness in my brother. Like Judah, he's been withdrawn, lost in his own thoughts, constantly on his laptop feverishly searching for her.

"How you feeling, big bro?" I quietly asked.

He exhaled as he rubbed the back of his neck. "Incomplete." His gaze rose to Jo. "I need you to look after my mother and little brother for me."

Jo nodded. "You going to try and look for Nak again?"

"I can't stop until I find her."

We all sat quiet for a while. I was kind of sad that my brother was leaving to go back in, placing himself in danger, but I'd never seen him in love before. If this woman was able to capture Rome's cynical heart, she was definitely the one for him.

"You know… something just came back to me, I don't know if this will help you or anything, but I believe Nak's mom is in a nursing home." Jo said rubbing his chin.

"She told me her mother was dead. I found a death certificate and a place of burial."

"Naw, they have a really messed up relationship. When her mother fell sick, she put her in a nursing home under an alias."

Rome stood. "Why are you just now telling me this?"

Jo chuckled. "I'd forgotten till just now."

Without saying another word, Rome walked away disappearing in the trees. I watched him go, sending up a little prayer for him and Nak. I had never met this woman, but I knew she must be one bad chick to get my brother, who is by far one of the smartest men in the world to fall so hard for her.

Jo shook his head. "I hate to admit this, but I actually feel sorry for the poor bastard."

"Why do you say that?"

"Nakhti is hell on wheels."

I opened my mouth to ask him to expound on that, but right then, Robert ran out the house with a huge smile on his face.

"Come quick! Ayana just took her first step!"

We all took off for the house.

Well…

It seems you guys are going to have to check out Rome and Nak's story for yourselves. I'm sure it's going to prove to be quite interesting.

But I'd be remiss if I left without telling yall this:

After meeting the Preacher, I looked up the word he'd called himself at first, *Qoheleth*. It is a Hebrew word that means *Gatherer*. He'd said that the next time I saw him, the world will be on fire. I don't want to go into too much detail, to do so would be me taking away from someone else's tale that I'm sure you all will read soon.

But Jo thought us having to fake our deaths and move to secluded mountains in Canada was the drastic change that was coming our way.

It was not even close…

A storm was coming, and nothing in my life prepared me for what lay ahead of us…

However, the promise Jo made me the day he took me from the hospital would prove to be true.

There was nothing he and I could not face together…

BONUS CHAPTERS!

Take a sneak peek into upcoming novel by Edwina Fort!

Falling For Rome

Chapter One

Beautiful Surprise

Nakhti

I put the car in park and checked my GPS. This couldn't be the right address. The big grey building looked as if it had been one of those old industrial warehouses before it was turned into an apartment building. Several men and boys stood outside the building at the door, some looked like they were dealing, and some looked like they were hanging out with the dealers. I raised my eyebrow at a group of young girls in short skirts and shorts that walked by laughing and posing, trying to catch the eye of one of the men.

"Oh hell no." Reaching in my bag I took out my phone and pressed one.

"What's up, Nak?" The deep masculine voice came from the other end.

"What the hell, Jo? I'm in the hood." He chuckled.

"Yeah, I know. Did I forget to mention that?" I sat back in my seat leaning my head back against the head rest. I was too damn tired for this.

"Nak?"

I exhaled. "I'm here."

"Come on darling, don't give me the silent treatment. It's not that bad. I just need you to find out what information he has about me and my family, and then erase it. I don't give a damn if you have to wipe his whole system clean. Somebody has been digging real deep and my gut is telling me it's him. We are at re-election time and we can't afford any slip ups. This guy is buried in mystery, I need to know what he knows before he knows what he knows." I rolled my eyes.

"So, how am I supposed to get in there? This place is a fortress. Can you get me the blue prints to the building?"

"Already in your mailbox." Silence came from the other end for just a moment. "I wouldn't have asked you to do this on such short notice, I know I was pulling you from another assignment and you've had no recovery time. It's just that whatever system he's working with is impenetrable from the outside. I've had the best hackers on the Agency's payroll trying to crack it. It's impossible. The only way in is through the front door." I exhaled, in no mood to put up with some ignorant thug, gangsta, wannabe playa.

"And you're sure this isn't a job that Miller or Terry could handle?"

"Neither Miller or Terry will be able to get through those doors. I need the best on this one. I told you he laid out Michaels and Baker. And get this, he was handcuffed at the time. Had I not come out the room when I did, he would have snapped Tom's neck. There's not a man around that can resist that pretty, innocent face of yours. It causes them to let down their guard and then like a black widow, you strike, which makes you perfect for this job. Just look at it this way, you get in, you get out. You'll be home, wherever that is in no time."

"So, if things get out of hand with this civilian, can I kill him?"

"You have no idea how much I want to say yes to that. But alas, he's my lady's brother and she loves him. She'll be crushed if anything happens to him and I can't stand seeing her hurt. But hey, the quicker you gather my information, the quicker you can be done with it."

I grunted eyeing the man that was approaching my car with a spray bottle and a windshield squeegee that looked as if he'd *borrowed* it from the nearest gas station. Reaching in my briefcase, I pulled out a five-dollar bill before letting my window down.

"Wash your windows for you, beautiful lady?" He asked smiling, showing off his rotting teeth. The smell of alcohol and unwashed flesh singed my nose.

"I'll give you five dollars if you *don't*." He grinned as I handed him the money.

"Generous as well as beautiful. Have a blessed day." I rolled my window back up.

"Fine, but this is my last assignment." I said into the receiver. "I'm too old for this sh*t. I'm retiring." He chuckled again.

"Get out of here, you can't retire at thirty-four. I need you to have my back. I'll feel naked without you."

Dammit Jo... he knew he had my loyalty for life. He knew that there was nothing I wouldn't do for him. The man had saved my life on more than one occasion. He and I went way back to the days of being two green eared Seaman Recruits. All the way up through becoming the only two minorities in our SEAL unit.

It wasn't easy and several times I wanted to quit, but Jo never let me. He pushed me until I became the soldier that my father never was. My father who left home because I was just a stupid girl and not the boy he wanted, had tried several times to become a SEAL, but could never make it through BUD school. Not only did I make it through, I became a decorated soldier in my own right.

When Jo left the military for the Bureau, he took me with him. Again, pushing me to be more than I thought I could. Yes, I was loyal to him, unquestionably, but I was tired and he needed to know that.

"I can and I will. I'm thirty-four, but I feel sixty-four. You remember what happened last month in Libya?"

"Yeah."

"I still hear ringing in my ear from that sh*t. I don't think I will ever get my hearing back on my right side."

"You got too close to the fireworks."

"It's just the way it played out. Anyway, I said all that to say I quit after this Jo, I'm serious. The agency already fired me, why won't you just leave me the hell alone?" He chuckled, the charming bastard.

"Because you're the best man I got in the field. I won't be able to run for office unless I know you have my back." He repeated for the second time, knowing what those words did to me. I bit down on my teeth determined to stand my ground.

"Yeah well, I'm done after this."

"Nak, on a serious note…" He said, brushing off my words.

Sh*t!

"Be careful with this one. I took this kid for granted and he surprised the hell out of me. He's smarter than you can imagine. He doesn't look it, but he is. And he's dangerous. My sources tell me he's responsible for many a stiff found floating belly up in Lake Michigan. You're on his turf, everybody within twenty city miles either way is loyal to him till the death. Keep your eyes open, and whatever you do, don't take this kid lightly."

I eyeballed the hustlers standing outside of the building and farther down on the corner. It was nothing about them that appeared spectacular, just your everyday average thugs. However, Jo was the most skilled soldier I knew, so if he told me not to let down my guard, then I won't.

"Alright, I'll be in touch." Hanging up the phone I slid it back in my briefcase.

For just a moment, I sat enjoying the silence of my rental car. I had no time to rest from my last assignment for Jo, well, for his father really. The mission like most of my missions called for me to get close to a man and then kill him.

Pablo Consuela, an Argentinian drug lord had thought to blackmail the senator with some compromising photos to try and get him to vote to pass some legislation that would make it easier for him to move his product in The Gulf. I didn't know all the details, it wasn't my job to. My job was to retrieve the photos and erase them from any hard drive they may be on, and then put old Pablo out of his misery.

A job I had done flawlessly until I got too messy making my escape and ended up with a bullet wound in my side. I shook my head, this was just another sign signaling that it was time for me to walk away from this life. Jo didn't believe me, but I was going to show him, this was my last mission. When it was over and I was paid, I was ghost. I was disappearing in a way that even *he* couldn't find me.

I was going back home.

Nobody knew where my home was because I barely knew where it was. The only thing or shall I say the only person holding me there was my mom. I put her in the nursing home ten years ago under an alias. And the only way for the nursing home to contact me was through a message service that I checked from time to time, waiting for the call saying she's dead.

But I have yet to get it, so I guess she's still alive.

Maybe she was just waiting on me. Waiting to look me in the eye one more time and blame me for being the reason daddy left. Waiting to hit me one more time for not being the boy my father wanted more than he wanted either of us. Waiting to let me know just how much she hated me before she took her last breath.

After this job, she'll get her chance if she wasn't dead. Exhaling I pushed those thoughts from my mind. Those are the kinds of thoughts that can get you killed on a mission. Those were the thoughts I was thinking when the bullet penetrated my flesh the day before yesterday.

I reached in my suitcase for a pair of eyeglasses that would complete the look I was going for and slid them on my face. Then I popped two pain pills in my mouth because my side was killing me. I hadn't even had time to get it looked at. I had to stitch it up myself, lather it with a tube of Neosporin, and slap a damn bandage over it.

Perks of the job…

When I was prepared, I stepped out the rental car and after locking it, headed toward the building.

"Daaaammmnnn!" Several of the men said as I approached, looking at me as if they had never seen a pretty woman in a two-piece fitted skirt suit carrying a briefcase.

Men…

Jo was right. For as long as I could remember, men have fallen over themselves for my face that *did* look very innocent, only to end up with their noses broken for thinking I could be taken advantage of. My face was one of the reasons the agency had hired me in the first place. They knew with my innocent looks, I would be able to slip under most people's radar.

"She look like a sexy school teacher." One of the men that was holding a red cup in his hand said. Judging by the redness of his eyes he wasn't drinking juice. I lifted my eyebrow at him checking my watch. Damn, it wasn't even ten o'clock. The smell of marijuana was also very strong in the air.

"Man, if she was my teacher, I would have stayed in school." One of the younger guys who looked to be fifteen or sixteen responded. I kept walking as if I didn't hear them. Blocking the door with both of his hands on the frame was another young man who could be no more that twenty-one or twenty- two.

He wasn't a bad looking guy. As I approached him, he passed the blunt he was smoking to another man that was much older than him sitting on the stoop. He slowly blew out the smoke as he took me in. When it was clear he wasn't going to move I stopped, but I bit down on my teeth to hold on to my temper.

Okay, so let me tell you guys why I got fired from the agency. Yes, I have an innocent face that most men consider beautiful. I look soft and approachable. Jo once described me as the girl next door. That being said…I don't have the constitution to match my looks.

I'm not friendly or soft and I could give a damn about beauty. I have a short fuse and I'm easily irritated. I may have used lethal force a time or two when pushed the wrong way. And I may have used excessive force when one of my directors thought it was alright to grab me and try to force me to kiss him one night while we were all at a bar celebrating the promotion of one of our colleagues. I was aware he was drunk, but it did little to assuage my irritation at his action.

I smashed his face into the bar, breaking it. Anyway, the agency said their hands were tied; I had too many complaints on my record to continue.

I told you guys that story to try and get you to understand what I was going through standing here in front of this civilian, allowing him to get away with his actions.

"How can I help you, sweetheart?" He asked.

"Is your name Romeo Reevers?" For a moment a look of surprise crossed his face before he shared glances with a few of the other men. Now that I had mentioned that name, none of them were smiling anymore. The air got really tense. Even the men farther down on the block had come to attention.

Jo had been right. Whoever this Romeo was, they were very loyal to him.

"Who's asking?"

"Brenda Bonita," the lie slid easily from my lips. I had studied Romeo's file on the plane ride home. What this situation called for was a case worker.

"That's all I'm at liberty to discuss with you unless your name is Romeo Reevers." I continued.

He chuckled. "You the law?"

I reached up and pushed the curly strands of hair that hung by my ear behind it, an act that made me appear soft.

"Excuse me?"

"Police." He said losing patience with me. "Are you the police?" I softened my eyes.

"Oh no! Nothing like that." He looked at me for a minute to determine if I was telling the truth. I blinked slowly, allowing my long lashes to sweep across my doe shaped eyes.

"Aight, follow me."

"Yo Rob, what you doing man?" The older guy that still held the blunt in his hand asked.

"Relax, G. She cool." I looked back at the other men and they all wore a look of astonishment that he was taking me inside the building. As I followed him through the halls that were surprisingly very clean, he kept stealing glances at me.

"You look like some kind a case worker." He said, still fishing for my identity. I smiled at him. I liked the kid.

"Something like that." I told him.

He nodded. "Jo sent you, didn't he? To keep an eye on Rome?" I chuckled surprised by how astute he was.

"Something like that."

There were several children playing in the hall outside one of the apartments on the first floor. It looked as if the building had four levels. I could hear loud rap music playing from another apartment. We walked through a door that led to some stairs.

"I hope you don't mind taking the stairs. The elevator is broken and Rome's place is all the way up on the top floor." I smiled at him, yeah, I liked this kid.

"I don't mind."

When we got to the fourth level, there was a keypad on this door that wasn't on the others. Standing directly in front of it he keyed in a four-number code.

7,9,5,6...Got it.

I noted the fact that the fourth level was not open to the rest of the building. There seemed to be very little activity on this level. In fact, once we walked out of the stairwell, the door locked automatically when it closed behind us; there seemed to be only one other door that I could see. On this door was another keypad, he quickly keyed in the code.

3,2,9,7...Got it.

My eyes widen behind my glasses as we walked through the door. It was a loft, a very spacious loft, a nice very spacious loft. For the third time in a matter of minutes, I was pleasantly surprised. The tall floor-to-ceiling windows ran along the east side of the loft, they looked to be at least twenty feet tall. They were also covered by beautiful golden drapes.

The loft itself had to run along the entire length of the building because like I said, it was roomy. One could play a game of football in its open space or what you American's call soccer. There wasn't a lot of furniture, it didn't look as if Rome invested in that.

However, I now understood why I had been assigned this mission. Along the entire length of the north wall was a state of the art computer system. Secured to the lovely rust colored brick wall had to be at least twenty flat screened monitors. Although they were turned off, one couldn't help but wonder what appeared on them when they were turned on. In front of the elaborate system was a single plush leather chair on wheels.

It was a chair for a king.

A king whose throne was in front of several very impressive computer screens.

One thing was for certain, this beauty was something you wouldn't *ever* expect to find in the heart of the ghetto. My fingers twitched in anticipation of finding out what was stored on that massive hard drive. He spared no expense for it. There were million-dollar corporations that could not afford one such as it.

My guess was the owner of that beautiful system was lying in the bed that wasn't too far from it. Rob walked to a wall and hit a button, opening the curtains that were closer to the bed just a little. However, it was enough to shine a burst of sunlight into the loft. I came to a stop in front of the bed looking down at the occupants.

The man that I would assume was Rome lay sleeping on his stomach, my eyes traveled over his muscled back to the equally muscled arm that hung out the bed. He had on a pair of black jeans and expensive gym shoes. Asleep next to him completely naked was a very voluptuous young lady. Only the lower half of her body was covered with the sheet.

Rob wore a goofy smile on his face as he too stood looking down at the two. I could tell right off this kid was a rascal. His aim was to shock me with this. I looked at him and lifted an eyebrow, poor baby, it would take more than this to shock me.

"Yo Rome, you got a guest." He said hitting the man's shoe.

"Beat it, chump." The sleeping giant grumbled turning over in the bed without opening his eyes. Rob chuckled hitting his shoe again.

"Get up, nigga."

"What I tell you about using that word?" Rome mumbled without opening his eyes. He had a very deep voice. The younger man didn't respond, instead he looked up at me with that devious grin still on his face. He nodded in a way to tell me to watch this.

Rome opened his eyes and turned to look at him, sitting up slightly. "You deaf, punk?! What I tell—" his words stalled as his light brown gaze came to rest on me.

Although I didn't show it, for the fourth time since coming to this place, I was completely taken off guard.

Rome was gorgeous.

He looked at me through a pair of amber eyes that missed nothing. He'd just woke up from a deep sleep and judging by the empty Hennessy bottles and cups, it had been a drunken sleep, yet his eyes were sharp. They took me in making me feel as if he was reading me like an open book. I shifted on my feet feeling uncomfortable with that. No one has ever looked at me that closely.

He ran his hand over his head.

"What the f*** Rob." He growled. The grin on Rob's face grew wider as he blinked his eyes innocently.

"Bruh, you got a guest." He said gesturing towards me. Now that he mentioned it, I could see the resemblances between the two. Only difference being Rome was clearly older and his eyes were a lighter shade of brown than Rob's. He pointed at his little brother in a way that told him he will deal with him later.

"Hey," he said tapping the shoulder of the sleeping girl. She came awake with a smile on her face.

"Hey, daddy," she purred. I rolled my eyes, Rob chuckled.

"Get up, you gotta bounce." He told her. And for the first time she looked and saw us. With a squeak she snatched the sheet up to cover her breasts.

"Can you give us a minute?" Rome asked me, gesturing toward the other end of the loft where a living room area was. I lifted an eyebrow at his rude tone.

"Sure," I told him before turning to walk towards the sitting area.

As I did, I casually lifted my hand and slipped the bug from my watch, positioning it just right between my fingers. I used the same hand to ease down in the brown leather chair, securing the bug at the same time.

To the left of the chair I sat in was a huge brown leather couch, or what looked like a couch, but was really a modern rendition of a couch. It screamed contemporary bachelor pad. As if to confirm that, a ridiculously big flat screen TV was mounted to the brick wall to my right. In front of it on the floor were several gaming systems. There were quite a few game controllers sprawled on the floor around them.

When I looked back towards the sleeping area, it was to see Rome's amber gaze still on me. He was now sitting at the foot of the bed with his elbows resting against his knees. If I was the blushing type, I would be doing it right now seeing that he had watched me walk this whole distance. Finally, he turned to look up at his brother.

"Why you didn't take her downstairs to ma's place? Why the hell you bring her up here?" Rob, who had watched the whole exchange with that goofy grin on his face now wore a look of fake shock.

"Ma not home."

"So?!" Rome growled up at him, his face transformed in his anger.

Rob chuckled, not fazed a bit in only a way that a little brother could. "My bad, man. I just didn't think about it."

"You play too much." His brother responded standing up grabbing his t-shirt at the same time. When he brought it over his head, his muscled arms and chest flexed impressively. He was very tall as well.

"That's your damn problem." He continued admonishing his kid brother before he turned and noticed that the girl had not moved from the bed, she was in fact playing like she had just drifted back to sleep.

"Ay... Ay, shawty, you got to bounce. Get your sh*t." He called down to her. Amazingly she woke up and stretched, letting the cover fall from her ample breasts once again. Rob grinned shaking his head.

"Rome, you gon' call me?" She asked as she unashamedly slid out the bed reaching down to retrieve her dress from the floor.

I shook my head, women like her gave our whole species a bad name. If a man had talked to me the way he'd just talked to her, the only call I would be worried about is the anonymous one to the city morgue, telling them where to find his body.

"Rob, make sure Kiesha get to her car safe—"

"Tonya!" She interrupted him, finally insulted. Rome chuckled as he scratched his head walking towards the bathroom.

"Who the f*** cares." Was his only response as he went into his bathroom shutting the door behind him.

"Okay, you can call me Kiesha, just call me...Please!"

"Come on, shawty. I'll walk you downstairs." Rob told her as she angrily slid her feet in her heels.

"It was nice meeting you, Brenda." He called to me as they headed toward the door.

"Nice meeting you too, Rob." It really was. I don't know why he chose to make my job easier, but he had. Had he not brought me up here, there was no way I would have gotten through that group at the door.

And had I by some miracle gotten through them, I would have never made it past the locked door on the steps.

Well... Not this easily anyway.

Rome took his time in the bathroom, I heard the shower start. I was not delusional to think it wasn't a test when it really was. Jo was right. This man was smart. He was trying to feel me out before talking to me. I was careful where I let my gaze roam. Although I couldn't see them, I was quite certain this whole building was wired with cameras.

Slowly, I got up and walked to the nearest window. The drapes were opened slightly, allowing a perfect view of the ghetto below. My eyes narrowed at the roof of the building across the street, there was a man standing on it leaning against the door smoking a cigarette. When he caught me looking at him, he winked.

My gaze went to the corner store at the end of the block, several men stood outside talking, but when one of them noticed me looking, he winked.

What the hell?

I looked towards the opposite corner, there was a man sitting on the porch of a building there, it looked as if he was smoking a blunt. When he noticed that I saw him, he winked.

"What are you looking for?" Rome's deep voice came from behind me causing me to nearly jump out of my heels as I whipped around, stopping myself from reaching for the piece strapped to the inside of my thigh. I looked up at him half startled and half surprised. How in the world did he walk up on me without me hearing him? He chuckled as he flopped down on his couch facing me.

He smelled good. Now dressed in a white t-shirt and a pair of blue jeans, he even looked good. I was surprised to see that I was capable of being attracted to the thug type. Who knew?

"Did I surprise you?" He asked. For a minute my mouth just hung open. Damn, can he hear my thoughts?

"Yes." I told him truthfully. He was continuing to do that.

"Sorry about that. How can I help you Ms..."

"Brenda Bonita," I said walking toward him to shake his hand. He didn't reach for my hand, instead he studied me with that unnerving gaze of his. I had to force myself not to look away.

Get a grip Nak. You are not getting ready to let this young thug unravel you. Get it together!

I took a deep breath withdrawing my hand as I eased back down in my chair.

"It's common decency to shake your guest's hand in greeting." I admonished as I lifted my briefcase laying it gently on the granite table in front of me.

"It's common decency not to lie when your host asks you your name." My eyes rose to his.

"I told you my name. Why would I lie?"

He grinned then still studying me with that sharp gaze of his. "I don't know, but I'm sure I'll find out."

I removed several papers from my briefcase. One of them being a copy of the contract he signed with Jo.

"I've been sent here from Senator Warren's office. As you know, your sister a…" I looked at the name on the paper although I knew it by heart. "Journey Reevers is romantically involved with Joseph Warren, Senator Warren's son. I've been hired to make sure the senator and his son's reputation remain on the up and up." I smiled warmly. He did not return my smile. In fact, the more I talked, the angrier he became. The little muscle in his jaw was working overtime.

"Of course you have nothing to worry about, I am a professional. Half the time you won't even know I'm here. I'm sure you are a responsible young man and would not be willing to do anything to jeopardize the senator's and future senator's office, what with all the work they do for communities like this." He sat up on the couch.

"Wait, let me get this straight. You come into my house to tell me, a grown ass man, that you're my what? Babysitter?" I smiled.

"Well, I wouldn't put it in those terms…but, yes." He narrowed his hypnotic eyes at me.

"Funny, you don't come across as a babysitter. Why do I feel as if it's a killer staring at me through your eyes?"

It took every bit of my training not to break my cover in that moment. Nobody has ever seen the real me.

Never!

I looked away, shuffling through the papers to cover my momentary lapse.

"I don't know what you're talking about, young man."

"You can kill all that young man, bullsh*t. It's not doing what you're hoping it would."

"And what is that?" I asked lifting my gaze back to his, daring him to say it. He didn't speak right away. He just let his eyes travel over my body in a way that made me feel warm all over.

"Discouraging me from imagining what those beautiful deceptive eyes of yours will look like rounded in pleasure as you come apart for me over and over again." I loudly cleared my throat. He smiled when he saw he had ruffled my feathers.

"Mr. Reevers—"

"Rome." He corrected.

"Romeo, let's go ahead and get a few things straight. I will not tolerate sexual harassment of any kind. If you sexually harass me again, I will call Joseph Warren and inform him that you've breached your contract. If you give me a hard time in anyway from this point on, I will call Mr. Warren and tell him you've breached your contract, in which point, the actions that Mr. Warren discussed with you will be taken." I looked at him giving him my no-nonsense look.

"Is that understood?"

About the Author

Author Edwina Fort is a writer who writes with a passion and purpose. She was born and raised in Chicago, but now resides in the South. Although she is new to many, this author has been writing for many years and has given her unique style of writing away freely at no cost to those who would receive. Her passion for writing came about at an early age and developed into what it is today based on her experience and life lessons. With her stories, she wants to redefine all that we've been taught to believe and shed light on our truths and potential. Writing is her calling and she wants to share that gift with you through the pages of her work. Each book will take you on a memorable journey you will find hard to forget.

www.ingramcontent.com/pod-product-compliance
Lightning Source LLC
Chambersburg PA
CBHW031144050726
47495CB00018B/517